THE BLOCKBUSTER DRUG

A NOVEL BY

GARY REED

Rev. January 18, 2017

ISBN/SKU:9780692836552
ISBN Complete:978-0-692-83655-2

Published by Top Quark Publishing Co., Union, Ky. 41091.

PRAISE FOR THE BLOCKBUSTER DRUG

Smart, suspenseful and funny as well. Entertaining and diverse characters throughout. It gives an inside look at the battle between a health insurance company and Big Pharm with lives and big money at stake. It's realistic as it mirrors so many cases about popular drugs which turned out to have negative effects. The heroes are your normal everyday workers; your friends and neighbors. You'll cheer at the end! - *AMAZON Reader*

I really enjoyed this well-written thriller. Gary Reed has a knack for weaving together a dramatic story filled with exciting action and colorful characters. ... What brings it home is that the story Reed tells is something you can imagine really affecting you or someone you know... We all rely on drugs to keep us and our loved ones healthy... for better or worse. I highly recommend this page-turner! - *AMAZON Reader*

The author, Gary Reed, successfully mixes a fictional novel about a Medical Director out to do good with a history about the often misunderstood health care industry. The plot quickly develops with a lineup of diverse characters that are constantly balancing their decisions. The short chapters keep the reader engaged as it allows Reed to continually keep the us abreast of the various subplots. Well worth the read. - *AMAZON Reader*

GARY REED

THE BLOCKBUSTER DRUG

A NOVEL BY

GARY REED

PROLOGUE

"We've got all your test results now. I am afraid the news is not what we were hoping for," the oncologist began, pausing to allow the couple sitting before him to prepare themselves. "Mr. Meinhardt, the imaging studies show that you have a large mass."

The oncologist let that sink in, before continuing.

"You have two adrenal glands – one on top of each kidney. The mass sits on top of the adrenal gland on the right side of your body. Based on its size and features, it appears to be a tumor.

"Assuming it is a tumor, then – based on your endocrine profile and your symptoms – I believe your tumor began in the outer, or cortical, layer of your adrenal gland.

"In other words," the oncologist concluded, "It looks like you may have adrenal cortical carcinoma. That is a cancer – one that is pretty rare, especially for someone your age. But one that is aggressive."

The patient and his wife looked at each other, then at the oncologist. Their expressions revealed more shock than comprehension.

"We need to operate to remove the tumor," he said to the couple. "When we do that, the pathologist can examine the tumor tissue under the microscope and tell us for certain what we're dealing with. We will also remove some lymph nodes, and maybe some other tissue, to assess if the cancer has spread."

"You cut that goddam thing out of me, you hear," Dan Meinhardt said.

"We'll get the surgery scheduled promptly. Removing the tumor will give you some symptomatic relief. If it is what I think it is, when you have recovered from the surgery, you are going to need chemotherapy with some drugs that have sometimes been effective with this cancer.

"Unfortunately," the oncologist continued, "beyond surgery, we don't have any really great protocols for treatment if this mass is what I think it is. We should hope for the best, but I need to warn you that your prognosis may not be good. I think you need to prepare yourself for the possibility the available treatment options may not be effective."

"Well, goddam," Dan Meinhardt said quietly. "So, you don't even know how to treat me?"

"A lot of research goes into breast cancer, lung cancer, and other cancers that affect the largest numbers of people. These more unusual forms of cancer don't get the same attention."

The patient's wife spoke. "What about the Cleveland Clinic? I hear they got them a bunch of smart doctors up there. If you don't have any good answers, maybe we should – you know – talk to them?"

The oncologist smiled. He knew to expect that question, or a variant of it.

"Actually, I think that's a good idea," he said. "But I think we need to find out if your health plan will cover that. The Cleveland Clinic is not in every health plan, and it can be incredibly expensive."

TUESDAY, JANUARY 26 – CINCINNATI MARKET OFFICE

With the breakup of his marriage, the sale of his medical practice, and the death of his father, for Spencer Doss the past year had been difficult. Add to that his – perhaps rash – decision to move to Cincinnati to take a position as the Regional Medical Director for a large managed care company, and the year had been a something of a disaster.

What he faced now, three weeks into his new job, Doss reminded himself, should be easier. Building a new life in a new city and mastering a new job should be positive, energizing challenges. But, as he stared out his office window at the lead-gray January sky, he was not feeling energized. In fact, he had a pervasive sense that his life had lost its direction and excitement.

He had hoped his new position would allow him to influence the health – the lives, really – of the health plan's members in some positive way. But his current position – not the one he had been promised – primarily involved reviewing requests he could not authorize. Some requests were for the health plan to pay for treatment by out-of-network providers, when the same treatment could be obtained at less cost from in-network providers. Other requests were for treatments that were unnecessary, inappropriate, or dangerous.

Sometimes, as in the case before him, the request was driven by the understandable hope that an out-of-network – and typically out-of-town – facility would be able to provide a cure when, in fact, no cure was available.

The case involved a 66-year-old male who had adrenal cortical carcinoma – a rare and usually fatal cancer. As was often the case with this cancer, it had already metastasized before it had been diagnosed. The patient wanted the health plan to agree to pay for treatment at The Cleveland Clinic – which was out-of-network. The Cleveland Clinic was top notch, but neither the patient nor his in-network oncologist suggested any reason to believe The Cleveland Clinic could offer anything that could not be obtained locally at considerably less cost – and less inconvenience to the patient and his family. Doss suspected the oncologist knew as much, but found it easier for the HMO's medical director to be the bad guy.

If the health plan's guidelines allowed for payment to a non-contracted provider, the utilization review nurses on his team could pre-authorize payment, but by law, only a licensed physician could deny payment authorization. The review nurse had found no ground on which to approve the request, and so had prepared the paperwork for him to deny it. All he had to do was fill in a brief explanation for the denial and sign the form. But before he could bring himself to do so, the review nurse, Nikki Flores Santos, interrupted.

"Dr. Doss," she asked, "do you still have that authorization request for the guy with adrenal carcinoma?"

"It's right here in front of me. I was just looking at it."

"You said that cancer's pretty rare, right?"

"Fortunately, yes. Why do you ask?"

"Because I've got another one," she said. "This one wants to go to Duke."

"Who is the oncologist?"

"Raj Patel," Santos responded. "Same as the other case. He's got a good reputation."

"Get me his phone number. Maybe I'll give him a call and see what's going on."

Doss reviewed the information on the second case. Age 69. Male. Married. No prior history of cancer. A pathologist confirmed the diagnosis two weeks ago.

Whatever problems I think I've got, Doss reflected, *these guys have it worse.*

After speaking with the oncologist and confirming his suspicion, Doss denied both requests. *Now I'm the bad guy*, he thought, knowing how he would be characterized *– a nameless corporate bureaucrat who is more worried about profits than saving lives.*

On second thought, he amended the forms to authorize the oncologist to consult with The Cleveland Clinic in the first case and Duke University Medical Center in the second. *The oncologist*, Doss told himself, *will at least be able to confirm his treatment plan is as good as there is.*

He walked to the cubicle where Santos worked and offered her the completed forms. As he did so, he couldn't shake the feeling he was overlooking something. His concern was evident on his expression.

"Don't worry, Dr. Doss," Santos told him, "you get used to it."

"I don't want to get used to it," Doss replied. "I don't want to reach a point where I don't care." Concerned that sounded harsh, he smiled and added, "But I think I could get used to you calling me 'Spencer.'"

Santos took the forms, saying nothing.

"I wonder if anyone else has seen cases of this cancer recently," Doss said, as much to himself as to the nurse. "Two cases so close together is probably just a coincidence, but if there were more, I'd have to wonder what's going on."

"Why don't you ask for a Spider?" Santos offered.

"A what?"

"I'm sorry, Dr. Doss. I mean Spencer. I forget this is all new to you. Our claims system runs lots of standard reports for various departments. But you can request a special report. For example, you can request a report that shows how many cases we've had of something, like adrenal cortical carcinoma, in the last year, or two years, or three years – whatever you want, within reason. IT calls that kind of report a 'SPDR.' The acronym stands for 'Specially Programmed Data Reports,' but everyone calls them 'Spiders.'"

Doss vaguely recalled the reports from his orientation and training sessions, and was happy to have Santos walk him through the request process. After following him back to his office, she efficiently showed him how to bring up the screen on his computer that would allow him to request a SPDR. She then guided him through the various fields on the screen.

"Remember," she stressed, "the system is not going to search patient records. It is going to search claims that have been submitted to us. When a doctor or hospital submits a claim, the claim must include a diagnosis. Actually, it is supposed to indicate the primary diagnosis and any secondary diagnoses."

Doss nodded. He understood that from the claims his own practice had submitted.

"After you tell the programmers what you want them to find, you have to tell them what you want them to show on the report. Say you want them to find how many cases of this cancer we've had over the past five years. That's fine, but you also have to tell them what you want to know about those cases." Pointing to a place near the bottom of the screen, Santos added, "You do that down there."

Doss nodded again, to show he was still following.

"Do you want to know who the members were?" Santos explained. "Do you want their claims histories? And so on. Just check the boxes for what you want."

Doss studied the screen.

"The problem is," Santos explained, "a lot of times you don't know what you want until you get the report back and you know what you're dealing with."

Ten minutes later, Doss submitted an electronic request for a special report showing how many new cases of adrenal cortical carcinoma the company had in each of the last five years. On the assumption the report would identify no more than a small handful of additional cases, he also requested reports with three-year medical claims histories for each of the cases. Finally, he asked for the pharmacy claims histories for each of the cases. He expected he would learn nothing more than what the reports looked like.

He was wrong.

THURSDAY, JANUARY 28 – IT SPIDER UNIT

A program placed the SPDR request submitted by Dr. Spencer Doss in queue and, two days later at 8:15 a.m., the program automatically assigned the request to the next available programmer in the SPDR unit. The next available programmer was Maya Naidu.

Naidu opened the request and noticed it was from a new medical director. The request was not particularly challenging, but Naidu found it interesting. She wondered why the company did not more often mine the vast amount of data in its claims system to look for trends in illnesses and to identify what drove those trends.

Naidu finished her work on the request and submitted it before going to lunch, but the claims system would not actually run the request until that evening. The claims system processed almost 100 million claims each year. To avoid slowing the system, the system ran SPDR requests in off-peak hours. She spent the afternoon processing a number of more routine requests, and left at 5:00 p.m.

At home, Naidu prepared dinner for her husband, Kanha, and her daughter, Ashika, and made sure Ashika completed her homework. Ashika was a good student, but was not as dedicated to her schoolwork as Naidu had been at her age. Ashika's passion was dancing. Not American dancing, or ballet, but traditional Hindu dance. Naidu and her husband paid for Ashika to train with a well-regarded teacher in Hyderabad, taking lessons each week by Skype. Maya Naidu thought it incongruous to study ancient Hindu dances using the most modern technology, but like any American parent with adequate means, she encouraged her daughter to pursue her passion.

Naidu braced herself for perhaps the most precious, but often most emotionally difficult part of her day. Each evening she spoke – also by Skype – with her mother, who still lived in the same house where Maya and her brother had grown up, in Hyderabad, India. Her mother's health was declining rapidly. The doctors did not expect her to make it through the year. It was heart-wrenching to see the changes from so far and not to be there to help.

Naidu had arranged with her supervisor to take time off in late April, so she could return home and see her mother again. She had chosen late April, because Ashika wanted to participate in an important dance pageant in Hyderabad then. But as her mother's health deteriorated, Naidu had become increasingly concerned her mother might not hold on that long. If her mother passed away sooner, Naidu would have to take her time off sooner, and Ashika would not be able to participate in the dance pageant.

Naidu could do nothing about those things now. Determined to put each area of her life in its own compartment, she willed herself to focus on her mother. Although the older woman had the usual complaints about her health, her spirits seemed good, and the call went well. Naidu was relieved.

With that behind her, she turned on the laptop computer she had brought home from work and tried to put her family concerns aside.

The claims system had run the reports requested by the new medical director. The first report was supposed to show how many plan members had been diagnosed with adrenal cortical carcinoma in each of the past five years. The report showed 4 cases five years ago, and 5 cases four years ago. Three years ago, there were 7 cases. Then, two years ago, the number jumped to 47 cases. Last year, there were 64 new cases. Naidu realized the medical director must be trying to figure out what was driving those increases.

Although the report looked fine, she double checked her programming to make sure she had not made any errors. She then turned to the medical claims histories – a separate report for each member. Each claims history contained one line of data for each medical service for which the health plan had received a claim during the three-year period before the first adrenal cortical carcinoma diagnosis. Naidu doubted the medical director would have requested claims histories if he had known his search would get so many hits. She decided to go a step further than the medical director requested. *After all, he was new.*

She organized the claims histories for the 127 members into a data base and compiled a summary of the cases by gender and age. There were more women than men – about three women for every two men. Most of the members were more than 60 years old. Most were on Medicare and enrolled in one of the company's Medicare Advantage plans.

She re-sorted the claims data to see what diagnoses the patients had in common before their initial diagnosis with adrenal cortical carcinoma. Many were overweight and had high cholesterol, high blood pressure, and type II diabetes – the combination doctors called "metabolic syndrome." Naidu preferred to think of the syndrome simply as what happens to people when they eat American food, especially fast food, and drink too many soft drinks.

Working efficiently, she created a separate data base for the unlucky patients' pharmacy histories and searched it for the drugs the patients shared. More patients had taken one drug – Hepaticin – than any other, although not all had taken that drug. Nonetheless, Naidu thought the new medical director would find it interesting that more of the members with this cancer had taken Hepaticin than had taken the drugs so many seniors took, like the cholesterol drug, Zocor, or the blood pressure drug, Lisinopril.

She sent both reports to her supervisor, who would do a quality-control check in the morning before releasing them to the medical director. It was nearly midnight.

FRIDAY, JANUARY 29 – CINCINNATI MARKET OFFICE

At 10:30 the next morning, Spencer Doss opened the SPDR report on the health plan's experience with adrenal cortical carcinoma. The plan, he saw, had 4 cases five years ago, 5 cases four years ago, and 7 cases three years ago. According to the medical literature, the incidence rate for adrenal cortical carcinoma was one – maybe two – cases per million per year. Given the number of members the health plan had, those numbers were about right.

In the most recent two years, however, there had been a dramatic increase in the number of cases – 47 cases two years ago and 64 cases last year. The increase was alarming.

The claims histories – three years of claims for each of the 127 members diagnosed with the cancer – were voluminous. He set those aside and looked instead at the table the programmer had put together to profile the affected patients. Many of the patients were on Medicare, which was interesting because adrenal cortical carcinoma almost never occurred in persons old enough to "age into" Medicare. It occurred mainly in children age five-and-under and in adults in their thirties.

Unsure what to make of that, he turned next to the summary the programmer compiled of the drugs taken by the adrenal cortical carcinoma patients during the three years prior to their diagnoses. According to the summary, the drug most common to the 127 patients was Hepaticin, the expensive drug introduced a few years ago as the first drug to treat fatty liver disease.

Fatty liver used to be a problem mainly in alcoholics, Doss knew, but with the obesity epidemic overtaking the country, some experts estimated that 25% of the population might have Non-Alcoholic Fatty Liver Disease or "NAFLD." Patients who had NAFLD were generally over weight, had high blood pressure, and often had diabetes or were well on the way to developing it. They also usually had high cholesterol and high triglycerides. But not adrenal cancer.

By itself, fatty liver disease usually did not have any symptoms, but it could lead to progressive inflammation and scarring and ultimately to cirrhosis of the liver. When fatty liver disease became progressive, the diagnosis changed from NAFLD to Non-Alcoholic Steatohepatitis or – since everything in healthcare has an acronym – "NASH."

After Hepatitis C, NASH was the second leading reason people ended up needing liver transplants. Even before new drugs came on the market to treat the leading form of Hepatitis C, NASH had been on track to take over as the leading cause of liver transplants – at least, until the FDA had given accelerated approval to Hepaticin.

The demand for the drug had been huge, and the drug's developer, the giant multinational Galaxy Pharmaceutical Company, had priced the product to maximize its profits. It argued that compared with the cost of a transplant, Hepaticin's price was a bargain – never mind, Doss groused to himself, that most people with fatty liver disease, even those with the progressive form of the disease, were never going to need liver transplants.

He pulled up the prescribing information – what drug companies call the drug's "label" – for Hepaticin. He saw that, strictly speaking, the Food and Drug Administration had only approved the drug for the progressive form of the disease – Non-Alcoholic Steatohepatitis, or NASH.

He saw nothing in the drug's "label" that would suggest a link between Hepaticin and adrenal carcinoma. The drug manufacturer had reported no cases of the cancer during clinical testing.

Doss looked in the company's online personnel directory for the head of the company's pharmacy operations. He jotted down the name Brett Winslow and Winslow's corporate email address. Doss sent a brief email introducing himself as a new Regional Medical Director and asked the Pharmacy Vice President if he could have someone look to see if there was anything in the medical literature suggesting a possible link between Hepaticin and adrenal cortical carcinoma.

As he was finishing that message, he got an email from someone named Maya Naidu. "Dr. Doss," the email read, "I ran your SPDR. I hope it is satisfactory. If you have any questions about the report, please let me know. If you will be needing another report for this project, you will have to be submitting a new request, but if you are satisfied with my work, please indicate in the comment section that your request is for a follow-up report and that you will be requesting that I do the work. Maya."

Doss replied, thanking Naidu and telling her that he would indeed be submitting another request and would request that it be assigned to her.

He pulled up the SPDR request screen and requested a report showing how many plan members had taken Hepaticin in the previous five years, broken down by year. He asked to have the results sorted by gender and by age. He also wanted to know how many members taking Hepaticin had developed adrenal cortical carcinoma while taking the drug and how long they had been on the drug before being diagnosed with adrenal cortical carcinoma.

That done, Doss started to reach for the phone to call his father, to discuss what he had found. Just as quickly, he realized – with sadness – he could no longer do that. He knew survivors who lost someone close often wanted to tell that person about something interesting that had just happened. He knew the urge would diminish with time. But still it reminded him of the void in his life that his father's death had created.

SATURDAY, JANUARY 30 – LAW OFFICE OF DEVIN GARNER

It was Saturday morning, and Devin Garner sat uneasily at his desk, sipping the black coffee he had just brewed. With the Medawar trial over, he had come in to begin the work of getting caught up on his other cases. But after the adrenaline rush of trial work, it was hard to focus on the humdrum matters on his desk.

The Medawar case had easily been the most important case he had ever tried. His client was a young surgeon, Rafiq Medawar, who had been charged with murdering his wife, Ann Lindsey Medawar – the socially prominent scion of one of Cincinnati's most wealthy and politically powerful Cincinnati family.

Rafiq Medawar had gone to a sleazy "No Tell" motel with a nurse. Ann Medawar had surreptitiously followed him from the UC Trauma Center, where he worked, to the motel. She had made a video of him and the nurse entering the motel. Her body was later found nearby. She had been shot to death.

The circumstances were fodder for gossip and innuendo, but the evidence against Rafiq Medawar had consisted largely of the fact that his family was Middle Eastern. From that fact, the prosecutor had mistakenly deduced that Medawar was Moslem – which in turn had led the prosecutor to conclude that the doctor had killed his wife in a rage when she confronted him with the evidence of his infidelity. From the start, the case had generated intense coverage in the local media. In view of the publicity, the prosecutor – who had designs on higher office – had been unwilling to admit his mistake, forcing the case to trial.

The trial had been all-consuming and tremendously exciting, and the win had been sweet. What's more, the media attention and the win had significantly raised his profile in the city as a criminal defense attorney.

The problem was, Garner didn't want to be a criminal defense attorney. At least, not for much longer.

He had not been a federal prosecutor – one those mandarins who make their names prosecuting white-collar crime and then move to a job with a prestigious law firm representing corporate clients. He had got his start the hard way – taking assignments from the court, handling cases the understaffed legal defender's office couldn't or didn't want to handle, and building his practice through referrals from his clients and other attorneys.

The retainer Dr. Medawar had raised from his family had been the largest fee he had received in a criminal case to date – and quite possibly the largest he would ever get in a criminal matter. But he had put a tremendous amount of time into the case. On an hourly basis, he had earned less than any of the big law firms in Cincinnati charged for a first year associate, fresh out of law school.

But it wasn't just – or even mainly – the money. Dr. Medawar was a decent, well-educated guy. And as far as Garner could tell, he had been innocent. In a criminal practice like his, a client like that was the exception.

As a solo practitioner doing criminal defense work, his clientele would consist largely of drug users and drug dealers, wife and child abusers, drunk drivers, and the like – the blue collar and no collar folks whose cases filled the criminal dockets. Most of his clients would come from broken homes and would have too little education. Even those that did not have substance abuse problems would typically have poor impulse control and other mental health problems. Nearly all would lie to him.

He did not want to spend his career – his adult life – with people like that. It deadened the soul.

He desperately wanted to break into product liability litigation – especially cases involving defective drugs. That work was intellectually challenging, and it was where a lawyer like himself could make a really nice income – if he was good. And lucky. Best of all, that work involved championing the rights of injured people, and that appealed to him.

The Medawar trial had burnished his reputation as a criminal lawyer. But in doing so, he wondered, had it limited the cases that clients would seek him out for and that other attorneys would refer to him?

Garner sighed.

He couldn't afford to think about such things, he told himself. *Even if he landed a solid case against a drug company, where would he get the money and other resources needed to prosecute a case like that?*

He opened on the file on his desk, forcing himself to concentrate.

TUESDAY, FEBRUARY 2 – HEALTH PLAN CAFETERIA

As Doss approached the company cafeteria, he saw Eileen Wang waiting for him just outside the cafeteria entrance. He wasn't surprised she was on time. Wang was the company's in-house attorney assigned to the Cincinnati office. She had participated in a meeting he attended the previous week, and he had been impressed by her quiet intelligence and her affable, but professional approach to things. He had asked if he could discuss something with her, to get her advice. She in turn had asked if they could do that over lunch, as her schedule was jammed with meetings.

As he approached, he got a better chance to see his new colleague than he had during the earlier meeting, when everyone had been seated around the usual conference table. She wore a nice suit that conveyed the same professionalism he recalled, but which did not hide the fact that she was a very attractive woman – mid-thirties, petite, pretty. Her facial features were characteristically Chinese, and she spoke with the slightest accent – not so much an accent really, as the fact that she occasionally formed sentences in ways that might be grammatically correct, but sounded awkward to the ear of a native English speaker.

"Dr. Doss?"

"Please call me Spencer. Thanks for agreeing to let me bother you during lunch."

"No bother at all, Spencer."

After they made their selections and found a table in a corner, Doss decided it best to avoid small talk and go directly to why he had asked to speak with her. He briefly described seeing two cases of a rare cancer in one day. He recounted that he had requested an SPDR to see if he was simply dealing with a coincidence or if the health plan was seeing more cases than it should be seeing.

"I requested the report because something didn't feel right," Doss explained. "But to be honest, I did it mainly to learn how to request an SPDR. I didn't really think I'd find anything interesting."

The attorney listened attentively.

"But what I found concerns me," Doss continued. "A lot."

Doss pulled a single piece of paper from the folder he had brought with him and slid the paper across the table so Wang could see it.

"It's just a bar graph. It shows how many cases of this cancer the company has seen in the last five years. Given how many members we have, five-to-ten new cases a year are about what you would expect, and that's what you see five, four and three years ago."

Doss pointed to the last two columns on the chart.

"Then, the numbers jump over the moon. In the last two years, we've had 111 new cases."

Wang looked up from the chart and stared at Doss. Certain now that he had her attention, he plunged ahead with his explanation.

"This cancer mainly occurs in kids age 5-and-under and in people in their 30's – people in our age group. Someone in the Spider unit did an analysis for me of the ages of the patients with this cancer. In the last two years, we've had about a dozen new cases in those age groups – again, about what you'd expect. But that means we've had almost a hundred cases outside the expected age ranges, mainly in older patients. That's insane!"

Wang nodded, indicating she was following.

"I also requested the pharmacy histories for the patients with this cancer. A lot of these patients – not 100% of them, but an awful lot of them – were taking Hepaticin."

"Hepaticin?"

"It's a relatively new drug, introduced about four years ago, to treat fatty liver disease. It's the latest blockbuster drug."

"You think there's a connection between this drug and this cancer?"

"Maybe I've just read too many action novels where the hero says, 'I don't believe in coincidences,' but yes, that's what my gut tells me."

"How can I help?"

"Well, I'm not sure what to do next," Doss explained. "I was hoping you might have a suggestion."

Wang asked, "What were you thinking?"

"I was thinking we should report our cases to the FDA. I know a treating physician can do that, not that they do, but can a health plan medical director do that?"

"You can do that without violating the privacy law, if that's what you mean. But I'm not sure if the FDA will accept reports from anyone other than a treating physician. I've never had that question come up. I don't think it's ever occurred to anyone around here to report this kind of thing."

"Am I out of my lane?'

Wang smiled. "No, it's just that people get so busy doing whatever they do, they never think about anything else. Or they have the thought, but decide they would rather leave by five o'clock. I'd say you're being proactive, responsible. That's a good thing."

"Thanks."

"I'll look into that and let you know."

The attorney took a bite of salad. After she swallowed, she asked, "Have you thought about writing something up? Getting this published?"

"I don't think I have enough information. Medical journals want statistical analyses. What I've got is not much more than anecdotal."

"The great thing about a health plan like this is – we've got lots of resources. We just don't always know what we've got or how to use them. Why don't you talk to one of our actuaries, and see if they can help with the statistics?"

"I'm new here." Doss replied. "I don't know anyone. Are you thinking of someone in particular?"

Wang picked up her smart phone. "Here, I'll send you a name. Ingrid Berg. She is the lead actuary for our Medicare business. She's incredibly smart, but she's also really nice. She cares."

"I'm glad I thought to ask you for help."

"Asking for help is actually not a bad way to get to meet people around here," Wang said. "As long as you don't make a pest of yourself."

"Uh, oh! Am I making a pest of myself?" Doss asked.

"No, but if you want to make friends, you need to do more than talk shop. Tell me something about yourself.

And not about where you went to school. Something personal. Like why did you take the job here?"

"Okay," Doss said. He took a moment to form his thoughts. "Last year," he began, "my wife divorced me. She said I was spending so much time trying to build my practice, I didn't pay enough attention to her, to our marriage. She was right. The irony is, I sold my practice to pay off the divorce settlement and what remained of my medical school loans. While all that was going on, my father died. This opening came along, and I thought it would give me chance to make a fresh start."

"New job, new town, a whole new life?"

"Pretty much."

"You must have been a difficult person in that past life of yours," Wang said, smiling, "to be reincarnated as the medical director of an HMO."

"I'm more concerned," Doss responded, playing along with the joke, "about my next life. What do you think is in store for someone who spends this life as the medical director of an HMO?"

"You sell your practice to a hospital?"

"Yeah. As you know, hospitals are gobbling up primary care practices. They want to lock in the patient referrals."

"Didn't they want you to stay with your practice?"

"They did, but I wanted to make a fresh start."

"But this was a big jump. There must have been something that pushed you this way."

"I think it had to do with my father's death. He was a practicing physician much of his career, but after he completed his residency, he did a two-year stint at the CDC –

the Centers for Disease Control. He also spent an important part of his career teaching medicine. He was always interested in public health – actually, in what we now call 'population health.' Treating individual patients is at the core of the practice of medicine, but he felt it's also important to think about how to prevent people from getting sick in the first place, or how to manage a population of patients who have some illness. Why are people getting sick and what can we do to help them? What can we do to keep them from getting ill in the first place?"

"We talk about that around here a lot," Wang said. "But we don't do nearly enough."

"My mother died when I was in junior high. I got close to my Dad, and when I started showing interest in science, he began giving me books about scientists doing science. He was always on the lookout for books about doctors or epidemiologists tracking disease outbreaks – Ebola, that sort of thing. The sort of thing they do at the CDC. Eventually, I got hooked."

"Why didn't you pursue that instead of going into private practice?

"By the time I finished my residency, I had a lot of bills from medical school, and no savings. I had gotten married, and my wife wanted me to start earning some money. You don't make much money in the Public Health Service or Doctors without Borders.

"The opening here was a position that would focus on population health. After I was hired, but before I started, that position was eliminated, and a position as Regional Medical Director came open."

"Maybe your luck will turn around," Wang said, standing. "Listen, it's been really nice talking with you, and I hate to be rude, but I have to run to a meeting."

"Not so quick!" Doss objected. "You didn't tell me anything about yourself."

"I went to the University of Colorado undergrad, and the University of Michigan for my law degree."

Doss shook his head. "Something personal."

Wang smiled and said, "I'm single."

As he watched Eileen Wang walk away, Doss hoped his luck was indeed about to change.

WEDNESDAY, FEBRUARY 3 – GALAXY HEADQUARTERS, LONDON

Sir Alec Bright, the CEO of the giant British drug company, Galaxy Pharmaceuticals, handled with his usual ease his opening remarks at management's regular quarterly meeting with stock analysts. "As you can see from the report the company released this morning," he summed up, "our strategy is working. Revenues from our existing products, especially Hepaticin, were strong in the fourth quarter, and we have some very promising products in our pipeline."

Sir Alec, as the press called him, turned the podium over to the company's Chief Financial Officer, who did the usual run down of the company's performance during the past quarter and full year as compared with results of the previous year. His remarks made frequent reference to earnings per diluted share, EBTDA, CAGR and other financial esoterica.

Next, the company's Chief of Clinical Science discussed upcoming patent expirations and new drugs in development – in the "pipeline" – including promising drugs in ongoing Phase 3 clinical trials and others that would soon enter Phase 1 or 2 trials.

Sir Alec retook the podium and opened the floor to questions. As usual, many of the questions seemed to serve no purpose other than to allow the analyst to say to clients, "Well, as Sir Alec told me this morning ...."   A few of the analysts, however, asked questions Sir Alec deemed spot on.

"Sir," one analyst shouted, "you don't seem to be making much progress in the Far East, China in particular. Are you concerned about that?"

"Some of those countries are very challenging to do business in. But as our people know very well, I rather agree with your assessment, and we are going to focus on expanding our business in East Asia – and in China in particular – this year, and I suspect for the next several years."

"Is it true," another demanded, "that you are close to wrapping up the investigation by the authorities in the United States? Seems like that's been on the books a long time now, wouldn't you say?"

"I'm not going to comment on any negotiations that may or may not be happening, but I do want to stress, as you've heard me say before, we consider that a legacy problem. The issues that are the subject of that investigation took place before I came on board. We have a whole new team in senior management positions, and I have made it very clear that I expect people in this company to act only in the most ethical way. I am not – the company is not – going to tolerate any of the things the authorities there are concerned about."

Hands shot up, and Sir Alec ignored them. "I just want to add, for the record, that I am not conceding that any of our people did any of the things they are accused of." Sir Alec gave the audience a big smile. "I have to say that, you know, just to keep the lawyers happy, and all that. But I want to reiterate. This company is not going to tolerate that sort of thing."

"They all say that," the analyst muttered to no one particular. "But the proof's in the pudding, isn't it?"

THURSDAY, FEBRUARY 4 – MINISTRY OF PUBLIC SECURITY

The next day's financial press in Beijing devoted a brief story to the giant drug company's quarterly report under the heading, "Galaxy Targets China Market." The media accounts did not escape the notice of Guo Shengkun, the Minister of Public Security for the People's Republic of China.

In the United States, every city and town has its own police force, as does each county and state. The result is a patchwork quilt of police squads – some large and well trained, others small and poorly trained. The U.S. approach – based on historical practice and a deep-seated concern about placing too much power in any one entity – decentralizes authority. But in doing so, it gives rise to frequent jurisdictional squabbles and to the need for "joint" task forces to deal with regional problems. It also leads to many crimes and criminals falling between the cracks.

China and many other countries have a single national police force, with offices in each state or province and in each municipality, from the largest cities to the smallest hamlets. In China, the Ministry of Public Security controls the national police force. Located in Beijing, the Ministry oversees the work of the Public Security Bureaus in each province. As the Minister of Public Security, Guo Shengkun was in effect the country's top cop.

Guo, however, had an unusual background for someone in that role: Before his appointment, he was a businessman with no prior experience with law enforcement or police work. He had a Ph.D. in business administration, and until recently, his career had been in aluminum manufacturing. In fact, until his appointment as Minister of

Public Security, the capstone of his career had come when he left his long-time employer, a state-owned aluminum manufacturing company, and founded a giant new aluminum manufacturing company, where he served as CEO. His selection in November, 2012, to head the country's police force – and thus to carry out the anti-corruption campaign of newly appointed President Xi – had been a big surprise.

But given his background, it was not surprising that Guo was an avid reader of the business news. And so it was that he noticed the report concerning Galaxy Pharmaceutical. Guo forwarded the story to the chief of the Public Security Bureau in Shanghai, where Galaxy China had offices. Guo noted the passage referring to an ongoing investigation in the United States.

"Am I to believe," he demanded of his subordinate, "that this company misbehaves in the USA, but not in our country?"

FRIDAY, FEBRUARY 5 – IT SPIDER UNIT

Generating the new reports requested by Dr. Doss proved challenging, but Maya Naidu preferred that to the humdrum of more routine projects that did not challenge her programing skills.

The first report Dr. Doss wanted was one that showed how many plan members had taken Hepaticin, broken down by year. That was the easy part. She could pull that directly from the pharmacy system. Capturing and sorting the gender and age of those members was not particularly hard either, but it was not as simple as it sounded, because she had to get age and gender information from the enrollment system – a completely separate system.

Naidu, however, had a minor problem with the request. The medical director only provided the name of the drug – Hepaticin. She could not search on a drug by its name. She needed the "NDC" numbers for the drug. Every drug was identified by its National Drug Classification or NDC number. Each form of the drug – capsule, tablet, liquid – got its own number. Extended release versions got their own numbers too, or at least special, distinguishing digits in the NDC. So did each dose – e.g., 0.25 mg, 0.50 mg, and so on. Drug companies also assigned separate numbers to drugs manufactured by another company and repackaged by the drug company.

Given that, Naidu was not surprised when Willow Halfmoon, the woman in Pharmacy tasked with providing NDCs, responded to her inquiry with 14 NDCs for Hepaticin. Naidu made sure her program included all 14 NDCs. She checked to make sure she had captured each number exactly right. Then she double checked.

It was considerably more difficult to create a search that would find which of the Hepaticin-takers had developed adrenal cortical carcinoma *after* they had begun to take the drug. She had to pull the Hepaticin data from the pharmacy claims system, the diagnoses from the separate medical claims system, and then combine the data. But that wasn't the hard part. The SPDR system readily lent itself to Boolean requests for "A" and "B" – a member who (A) who had taken a certain drug and (B) had such-and-such a diagnosis. But it was trickier to get the system to do temporal searches – "A" *before* "B".

When she had that solved, she tweaked her program to generate a report that would show the date of the first pharmacy claim for Hepaticin and the date of the first claim with the adrenal cortical carcinoma diagnosis. From there, it took only a few additional commands to have the program calculate the number of months between the member's first claim for a Hepaticin prescription and the first diagnosis.

That evening, after completing her domestic chores and chatting with her mother, Naidu pulled up the results of her searches, anxious to see if her programming had captured what the new medical director wanted.

The first report appeared fine. The main report showed large, year-by-year increases in the number of members taking Hepaticin, beginning four years ago. The tab showing how many of those members had developed the cancer appeared to be in order as well.

Naidu pulled up the second report. It had run beautifully. The first column showed the member number. The second and third columns showed the member's first and last names. The fourth column showed the date of the first pharmacy claim for Hepaticin. The fifth column showed the date of the first claim with an adrenal cortical carcinoma diagnosis. And the final column showed the number of months between the two dates. *The new medical director would never know tricky it had been to get that right!*

Naidu ran her cursor down the final column. The numbers varied some from row-to-row, but seemed to cluster around 12 months. With a few additional commands, Naidu was able to able to tweak the report to show the average and the most common number of months between the first prescription and the adrenal cortical carcinoma diagnosis – in the patients who developed that condition. The average time was 11.8 months. The most common was 12 months.

Although she did not believe in reincarnation, she told herself she must have been a good person in her past life that her programming performed right on the first attempt and she would not be spending tomorrow trying to fix it.

Naidu hit the "submit" commands for the reports, sending them to her boss for his review in the morning, knowing he would not find any flaw in her programming.

Naidu felt sorry, however, for people who had this cancer and wondered what the new medical director intended to do with the information.

FRIDAY, FEBRUARY 5 – CHEMOTHERAPY, CINCINNATI

Dan Meinhardt was one of those men whose years in school had been short and years in low-wage jobs long. He paid little attention to politics, never studied the financial pages, and for years had refused even to listen to the evening news. He belonged to the same Catholic parish where his parents had gone to Mass. As with many men in his circumstances, he believed it was important for a man to work and best to defer to the wife on domestic matters. Like many such men, he was not much for reading.

While the chemo drip slowly worked its way into his body, he sized up the man in the next chair – a tall, thin, aristocratic man, with skin that hung loosely from his arms, and well-groomed silver hair. Meinhardt figured the man to be some sort of business executive, probably very successful.

"Mind if I interrupt?" he asked the man. "I'm Dan Meinhardt, by the way. I understand our wives have been talking. Actually, knowing Norma, she's done most of the talking."

"Sam Carson," the second man replied, lowering *The Wall Street Journal* he had been reading. "Nice to meet you, but wish it were under different circumstances."

"Yeah, me too, goddam it. My wife says you've got the same goddam thing I have."

"Adrenal cancer?"

"Yeah. Here's what I been meaning to ask you. You take a drug for fatty liver? I mean before you got this goddam cancer?"

"Hepaticin? Yes, I did," the businessman responded. "Why?"

"Well, you see, my goddam regular doctor, Dr. Goldbach, he says I've got fatty liver, and I have to take this goddam drug, Hepaticin, and next thing you know, I got this goddam cancer. I see this cancer doctor here, and he says I never had a fatty liver to begin with. I know I didn't go to medical school, but if you ask me, there's something goddam wrong here."

"You think Hepaticin has something to do with your cancer?" the businessman asked, trying to make sense of the other man's rant.

"Well, I don't know that it did, and I don't know that it didn't. My wife, she says lots of people take that drug, and they don't have any problems, it might all be in my goddam head. But I think something's just not goddam right."

"I don't know what to tell you. Maybe you should listen to your wife."

"Been listening to her for forty goddam years. Good woman, really, but she'll talk your goddam arm off. Anyways, what did your doctor tell you? Does he think you have a goddam fatty liver?"

"Never came up, actually."

"Well, you ask him and let me know what he says. Something ain't right, that's for sure."

"I'll do that, but listen, I see Dr. Goldbach too, and he seems like a pretty smart guy. He's very experienced. He's board-certified, has great credentials. He's been around a long time. You might want to give him the benefit of the doubt."

"Maybe. Maybe. Nice talking with you now."

The businessman pulled his newspaper up, thinking it might shield him from further conversation. But when his session ended, he asked the nurse to check with Dr. Patel. "I want to know if Dr. Patel believes I have fatty liver. Not what my history says. I want to know what he thinks."

"If you have a few minutes, I can check your chart and see."

"Thank you," the businessman replied. "You're very kind."

THE BLOCKBUSTER DRUG

MONDAY, FEBRUARY 8 – HEALTH PLAN, CINCINNATI

Eileen Wang checked the website maintained by the Food & Drug Administration – "FDA" to lawyers and nearly everyone else. She quickly located a link to the FDA's MedWatch service, which allows healthcare professionals and consumers to report "adverse events" – suspected side effects of FDA-regulated drugs, medical devices, and cosmetics. She downloaded the reporting form for healthcare professionals and scanned the instructions to see if they restricted reporting to treating physicians. Finding no restrictions on who could report an adverse event, she attached the form to an email to Spencer Doss.

"Spencer," she wrote, "it looks like you can report what you found, but you may want to have your staff fill out forms for each of the members with this condition and send the forms to their treating physicians as well. If you ask the physicians to sign the form and send it in, maybe some of them will. The FDA may take reports from treating physicians more seriously, and in any event, the more reports, the more likely the FDA will actually be interested. Nice meeting you. Please keep me posted on this."

An hour later, Doss opened the email from Eileen Wang. He downloaded the form to his own computer, and then created a new email to the utilization review nurses on his team. He attached the MedWatch form and the SPDR report listing the patients who had developed adrenal cortical carcinoma while taking Hepaticin. He asked the nurses to divide up the list and fill out a form for each patient, for the patient's physician to sign. He also asked that they create a duplicate form for his signature. He hit the "send" key.

Moments later, Santos and two other nurses asked if he had a list of the physicians he wanted them to send the forms to, and whether he meant the prescribing physician or the oncologist.

"I'll get the names and addresses!" he emailed back.

Doss pulled up the SPDR screen once more and requested the names and addresses of the physicians who had prescribed Hepaticin for the adrenal cortical carcinoma patients. He requested Maya Naidu handle this request as a follow up to her earlier SPDR.

After submitting the request, he sent Naidu a brief email explaining he needed the names and addresses so he could contact the doctors for the patients identified in her earlier report, which he attached – both for her convenience and so there would be no confusion as to which patients. He explained that, if feasible, he wanted that information for the *prescribing* physicians – the physicians who had prescribed Hepaticin.

That evening, after a quick dinner, Doss ignored the exercise bike in the corner of his studio apartment, the spy novel he had begun on Saturday, and the television. Instead, he put his company laptop on the kitchen table and logged on to the company website. After entering his password twice, he pulled up his adrenal cortical carcinoma file.

He created an outline and began preparing the letter he would submit to the FDA with the adverse event reports. He drew up each of the medical and pharmacy claims histories one-by-one and began working his way through them, making notes on a legal pad as he did. It was after 11:00 p.m. when he completed a draft letter to the FDA and logged off.

TUESDAY MORNING, FEBRUARY 9 — EMAIL EXCHANGE

The next morning, while finishing breakfast, before heading into the office, Spencer Doss logged onto the office network remotely. After a quick check of his email, he typed a brief message to Brett Winslow, the pharmacy VP, and to Eileen Wang, indicating he had drafted a letter to the FDA describing the surprising number of adrenal cortical carcinoma cases the health plan was seeing in patients taking Hepaticin. He attached the draft letter. As an afterthought, he decided to copy Robert Wiseman, M.D., the company's Chief Medical Officer. Wiseman was his boss and the physician who had convinced him to take the job with the health plan.

Doss had no way of knowing this, but Brett Winslow generally dealt with routine email only during a thirty-minute period set aside for that purpose first thing each morning. The email Doss sent arrived in Winslow's email in-box during that thirty-minute window. It got a prompt – and icy – response.

Winslow's reply email began with an apology for not getting back to Doss sooner. Winslow explained he had just received from his staff the research Doss had requested. Their research showed nothing in the medical literature linking Hepaticin to adrenal cortical carcinoma. For emphasis, the email added: "Repeat: Nothing."

"Thank you for letting me see your letter to the FDA and giving me an opportunity to comment," Winslow's reply continued. "I need to ask that you NOT send your letter at this time. The minute the FDA gets your letter, it will send it to the drug manufacturer – Galaxy – for comment.

Hepaticin is a blockbuster drug for them. They are not going to be pleased. We are about to go into our annual negotiations with Galaxy. We will be negotiating for rebates across all the drugs they make. If Galaxy gets upset, it could refuse to pay us rebates, or it could cut back on what they are willing to pay us. That would put our pharmacy plans at a serious disadvantage."

Doss studied the email, trying to unpackage what it meant. He was aware health plans negotiated deals with drug companies. The health plan would agree to include the pharmaceutical company's drug on its formulary, or agree to put it in a tier that required a smaller payment from the member, and in return, the drug company would pay rebates, tied to how much of the product the health plan's members purchased. The rebates in effect lowered the cost of providing prescription drug coverage, and thus lowered the rates the HMO or insurer had to charge in premium. Lower rates attracted more members, and more members meant more leverage with drug companies. But he was as unfamiliar with the actual negotiations as any consumer.

Winslow's request, Doss decided, was precisely what he feared when he first thought about taking a position with a health plan – that he would be asked to put the health plan's bottom line above patients. He had not expected the moment to come so soon. He hit "Reply All," and fired back: "Brett: We're seeing new cases of this cancer occur in 4 or 5 new patients each month, nearly all them in patients taking this drug. For most of them, it is going to be a death sentence. How long do you want me hold up? I'm not used to weighing the company's bottom line against patient lives."

A reply was not long in coming.

"Spencer, I'm looking at your data, and they are not as clear as you think. All I'm proposing is that you hold up a few weeks until we get past these negotiations, and that you not blindside Galaxy. We do an awful lot of business with them, and I'd like you to discuss what you think you're seeing with them before you drop a bombshell like this. You haven't been around here long enough to know this, but Galaxy pays us a lot of money each year. About $50 million last year. I think we owe them a heads up. Besides, they may have answers that will put your mind at ease. You've got to remember, once you send something like this to the FDA, you can't take it back."

Before Doss could respond, an email from Robert Wiseman, the Chief Medical Officer, hit his in-box. "I want both of you, in my office, 9:30 a.m. I don't want to see another email on this before then."

The Cincinnati market office occupied three floors in one of three buildings in an office complex just off the expressway in mid-town Cincinnati. Corporate headquarters occupied a much larger building in the same complex. It was just a short walk between the buildings.

TUESDAY AFTERNOON, FEBRUARY 9 – IT SPIDER UNIT

Maya Naidu was amazed the new medical director wanted to take her to lunch to thank her for the work she had done. She had probably prepared over a thousand reports, and no one had ever done that before. Often, she did not even get a "thank you" email. She decided to work on his latest request next, out of turn, hoping she would have it finished before she met him for lunch – or at least be able to discuss with him any problems she might run into.

She was able to pull the names of the prescribing physicians from the database she had already created. She "bumped" that list against a table containing the current office addresses for the physicians in the health plan's network.

The report ran nicely, listing each patient who had taken Hepaticin and developed the cancer, with the name and address of the prescribing physician below the patient's name. As she skimmed the report, she realized certain doctors' names appeared two and even three times. It occurred to her that some of the physicians might have prescribed the drug more often because they were gastroenterologists, not primary care doctors. She tweaked the program and ran it again to show the physician's specialty next to his or her name.

On a quick glance, it looked like the primary care doctors had far more adrenal cortical carcinoma patients than the gastros. *Well, Dr. Doss could decide if that was important.*

Naidu submitted the report for the usual quality control review.

WEDNESDAY, FEBRUARY 10 – C-SUITE, HEADQUARTERS

Doss met Brett Winslow, the company's Vice President of Pharmacy, only moments before the two were invited into the C-Suite office of the company's Chief Medical Officer. Winslow was a slim, 50-something man, intense, but cordial. Doss was sure the other man was taking his measure as well.

After only the briefest of greetings, Robert Wiseman – who remained standing behind his desk – got directly to the point. "I don't ever want to see another email exchange like I read this morning. Pick up the phone. Or have a meeting. But these email wars – and they go on around here all the time – kill us. These emails last damn near forever."

Turning to Doss, and lowering his voice, Wiseman continued. "What if some prick lawyer sues us, claiming we should have done something about this drug sooner? Once he gets his hands on that email you sent, it's going to be Exhibit No. 1. He's going to enlarge it and put it on a poster board. By the time he's done, the judge and jury are going to know it by heart."

"Yours is almost as bad," he said to Winslow. "And you should know better."

Wiseman sat down. He let his message sink before continuing.

"Here's what's going to happen," he said finally. "Spencer, you're going to hold up sending your letter to the FDA for a couple weeks until Brett's people get to have their sit down with the people from Galaxy."

Turning to Winslow, he said, "Brett, you're going to arrange for Spencer to talk with someone at Galaxy. One of their safety people, not the people you're negotiating with. We've got to keep these issues separate."

He looked at Doss, then at Winslow.

"Are we clear?" he asked. "Anybody not understand?"

Both men shook their heads.

"Brett, I'm sure you have things to do. I need to speak with Spencer a moment."

After Winslow excused himself, Wiseman spoke in a more relaxed tone. "I don't want you to get the wrong impression. I think it's terrific you are pursuing this. A lot of people in our business just keep their heads down, do their nine-to-five, and go home. You've done some really good work here. I am *not* telling you to drop this. Understand?"

Doss nodded.

"But you've got to learn how to make allies. Take Brett. He does a great job with our pharmacy operations. Our Medicare prescription drug plans are doing better than anyone expected. He built our mail order pharmacy from scratch, and it's now one of the largest in the country. So, give him some credit. Don't assume everyone else has their head up their ass."

Unsure that saying anything would help, Doss simply nodded.

"In the movies, in suspense novels, in comic books, one guy swoops in and fixes everything. Jack Devin, Jack Reacher, Superman, whoever. In a corporation – and in my experience, in real life – that doesn't happen. When somebody like you goes the extra mile, it can make a real difference. But only if he can get other people to work with him.”

Doss nodded again.

“Again, good work making this association. Have you thought about writing this up for publication? I find that just writing things up that way helps me think things through. Helps me make sure I’m not missing something.”

“Maybe,” Doss said. “Not sure. I’ve made arrangements to meet Ingrid Berg. I thought her people might be able to help me with the statistics. That might tip on the scales on whether I’ve got something publishable.”

“Ingrid is tops. She’s wicked smart. You’ll like her.”

Doss hesitated, then decided to stick his neck out. “I almost forgot. The patients who took Hepaticin and got this cancer. I was also going to send letters to the docs who prescribed Hepaticin and ask them to report the possible association to the FDA, to MedWatch. Any concern with my going ahead and doing that?”

“No, go ahead. As long as it comes from their physicians, and not us, that’s fine. Let the FDA figure this out. It’s their job.”

WEDNESDAY, FEBRUARY 10 – ACTUARIAL UNIT

When Doss arrived at her office, Ingrid Berg greeted him pleasantly. Doss had used the time since his dressing down to go the cafeteria in the headquarters building for coffee. When he saw the cafeteria was now selling Starbucks coffee, he decided to buy two cups and offered one to Berg.

Doss guessed Berg to be fifty-something. She was dressed conservatively, had mostly gray hair, wore wire-rimmed glasses. She had an engaging smile, and when she spoke, she did so quietly and deliberately. *One of those introverts*, Doss guessed, *who are so smart, and driven, they succeed in the business world despite themselves.*

Berg thanked Doss for the coffee and asked, "What's up?"

Doss explained he had encountered back-to-back cases of adrenal cortical carcinoma.

"That's a pretty rare cancer?"

"That's right," Doss agreed, impressed with her knowledge. "I assumed it was just a coincidence, but when I checked, what I found was that five, four, even three years ago, we have only four or five or so cases of this cancer a year – about what you would expect given the number of members we have. But since then, the number of cases has really jumped. Altogether, we've had 127 cases in the last five years, 64 of them last year. And weirdly, many of them are seniors. I checked to see what drugs these people were taking, and quite a few – not all of them, but a lot of them – were taking Hepaticin."

"That's the drug for fatty liver?"

"Right. Bob Wiseman thinks I should write it up. But that means I need some help with statistics. I was hoping you, or maybe someone on your team, could help."

"We're actuaries, not epidemiologists. Testing for statistical significance is a whole different specialty. Let's assume that the people who take this drug are getting this cancer more than other people. Or, just certain people with fatty liver are getting it. You're going to want to know if the difference in the rate at which these people are getting this cancer is statistically significant."

"I have someone on my team who can help you with that. Her name is Tam Nguyen Phan. In fact, I'm pretty sure Tammy will jump at the chance to work on this. But determining statistical significance can be tricky. There are different ways to do that, and the people who are really good at this know which approach is best."

Doss noticed Berg had not touched her coffee. He wondered if she even drank coffee.

"I don't want to discourage you," Berg continued. "I just want you to know our limitations."

Doss assured her he would be happy with whatever help her person could provide.

"I'll ask Tammy if she can take a stab at statistical significance. But if you want to publish, you're going to have to find someone with experience working with statistical significance. Someone with a Ph.D. Maybe you can get help from a medical school. Just promise me you won't try to publish with just whatever Tammy can provide."

Doss agreed.

"Spencer, I hope I'm not sounding negative. I think it's great you're doing this. We've got mountains of data, and we could be doing a lot of good with our data, but we're not. The drug companies hire us occasionally to mine our data to see how long patients take a drug, or something safe like that, but no one is systematically mining our data to see which drugs work, which don't, and which are making people sick in ways no one expected. Health plans don't see any money in doing that, and the drug companies are not going to pay us to do that."

Doss absorbed what she said. "I'm a doctor," he responded. "I want to help people. That's a given. But putting that aside, it costs the company a lot of money to treat people for cancer, for other drug side effects."

"You're preaching to the choir," Berg said. "Send me what you have, and I'll talk with Tammy."

WEDNESDAY NOON, FEBRUARY 10 – INDIAN RESTAURANT

Maya Naidu drove Dr. Doss to an Indian restaurant in Clifton, not far from the University of Cincinnati, and, as they made their way through the usual Indian-restaurant lunch buffet, answered his questions about the various dishes.

When they returned to their table, Naidu made sure to mention she had completed the new report he requested. "You should have it in your email."

"I've got it, and I've already forwarded it to my team, so they can get the letters out," Doss said. "I saw your email on my cell phone, so I didn't try to read the attachment, but it's just the names and addresses, right?"

"Well, I was adding the specialty, you know, whether they are primary care doctors or stomach doctors. I was doing that because some of the doctors had more than one patient on the list. I am thinking, they must prescribe an awful lot of this drug if they have more than one patient developing this cancer. Am I not right?"

"You are absolutely right."

Doss pointed to what he was eating. "Tell me again what this is," he asked. "It's good."

"Chicken Tikka Masala. I knew you would you like it. It's just chicken and rice with a tomato sauce. It's to Indian food what spaghetti is to Italian food – something everyone likes."

"Maya, how long have you been in this country, if I may ask?"

"Almost sixteen years now. I am a citizen and everything."

Doss touched the center of his forehead with his finger. "You're married?"

"Yes," Naidu acknowledged, understanding that Dr. Doss was referring to her bindi, the small red dot on her forehead. Wearing a bindi did not necessarily mean a woman was married, but she saw no reason to correct Dr. Doss. "My husband is from India, too. We have one daughter."

"That must have been a big decision to leave your country to come the United States."

"I have an arranged marriage," Naidu volunteered. Naidu knew this shocked and fascinated Americans. Naidu could tell that she had surprised Dr. Doss.

"It was completely an arranged marriage, but you must understand a girl does not have to marry any boy her family selects. In fact, I did not like the first boy they wanted me to marry, and I told my parents I would not be marrying him. They were very disappointed, because his family was wealthy, but they respected my decision.

"Kanha, my husband, was the second boy they arranged for me to marry. His parents brought him to our house, and his parents and mine talked. Eventually, Kanha and I were allowed to go for a walk and talk. Just for about fifteen minutes.

"When we were out of hearing distance from our parents, he told me that he had to tell me something. He said he was afraid it would make me be rejecting him, but he wanted me to know before I am making my decision. He told me that when he finished school, he hoped to go to America.

"I asked if he was definitely going to do that, or if this was just something he was thinking about – that maybe he would be doing, or maybe he would be changing his mind.

"He said he was definitely going to America, most definitely, and that I should not be marrying him if I were not willing to go with him to America. That's when I decided I would be marrying him."

"You had been wanting to come here?"

"I had never given it any thought. It had never occurred to me as something I could be doing. But I liked the fact that he had enough respect for my feelings that he wanted to tell me before we got married."

"You had to make a big decision, at a young age."

"Well," Naidu said with a sly smile, "it helped that Kanha was really good looking – sexy. And smart and funny. And of course, many of my friends knew someone who went to America, or who was thinking about it, or had just returned.

"We got married about a month later," Naidu continued with her story, "and then I did not see him again for a year. We wrote to each other sometimes. He was finishing his university in New Delhi, and I was finishing my university in Hyderabad. He was studying electrical engineering, and I was studying information systems – programming, basically. When we graduated, we lived in his parents' house for a few months until we got jobs in the United States, and we were able to be coming here."

Not sure what questions might be appropriate, Doss asked, "Where are you from originally? What part of India?"

"Hyderabad. It is in the South of India. This food," Naidu said, pointing to their plates, "is from the northern part of India. We have many different foods in South India."

"You speak Hindi?"

"Some, but my first language is Telugu. My family speaks Telugu. People in Hyderabad speak a number of different languages, but most people speak Telugu or Urdu, so I had to learn both."

'Telugu?" Doss asked, mispronouncing the name of the language.

"Telugu," Naidu repeated, pronouncing it correctly. "It's the third or fourth most common language in India."

"Where did you learn to speak English?"

"In school. Many people in India – and in Hyderabad, of course – speak English."

"Your life is an amazing story," Doss said. "How old is your daughter? Does she speak Telugu or Hindi at all?"

"Ashika is fourteen. She speaks Telugu, and some Urdu. Many kids whose parents come here from India, they do not want to be having anything to do with India. They only know this country. But Ashika tries to be staying connected to our family and our culture. She is studying traditional Hindu dance. She wants to participate in a festival in Hyderabad in a few months."

"It must be hard," Doss mused, "to study traditional Hindu dance in this country."

"Not as hard as you might think. Just like a lot of American girls will be doing ballet or gymnastics when they are young, a lot of girls from Indian families will be doing traditional Hindu dance. If you come downtown here on India Day, during the summer, always they are having a show where the girls can perform. Of course, by the time they are teenagers, most are dropping out or wanting to be doing Bollywood dance. But Ashika is not like that. She is really dedicated. She has a tutor in India. She takes lessons by Skype."

"She studies ancient Hindu dance with a tutor in India by Skype?"

Naidu saw Dr. Doss loved the irony of that. "Yes, but I am not sure she will be making it to the festival."

Naidu's mood had visibly changed. "My mother is old and frail and ill, Dr. Doss. We don't expect her to live very much longer. I have made arrangements so I can go home and visit my mother before – while I still can."

Doss said nothing, letting the woman tell her story at her own pace.

"I am scheduling my time off so Ashika can go with me and dance in the festival. But I am afraid my mother's health may be making it necessary for me to go sooner. We cannot be affording two trips back to India in one year, even if I could get that much time off, which is impossible."

"I am so sorry, Maya. That must be hard."

"It is hard, but I am a very practical person, Dr. Doss. I will just have to see what happens."

"When did you last get to see your mother?"

"Last year, but we talk every night. Well, it is night here, but it is first thing in the morning in Hyderabad. When it is Monday night here, it is Tuesday morning there. Very confusing, but it is being so much better than when people who came to this country could only be corresponding by letter, or maybe not at all."

"Well, I hope everything works out," was all Doss could say.

SATURDAY, FEBRUARY 13 – GARNER LAW OFFICE, CINCINNATI

Dan Meinhardt and his wife Norma sat across the desk from the young lawyer. The law office was in Cincinnati's less fashionable west side, not far from the lower Price Hill neighborhood where he and Norma lived. The lawyer was the hotshot who got that doctor – the one who shot his wife – off scot free. Norma had seen him on the news and had made the appointment.

"Here's the thing," Dan Meinhardt told the attorney. "I took this goddam drug my doctor prescribed, and now I got this goddam cancer nobody ever heard of, and the cancer doctor says it's probably gonna kill me."

"So, you want me to help you with your will?" the young attorney, Devin Garner, asked.

"What do I need a goddam will for? I ain't got no goddam money. Do I look like I'm rich?"

"So, how can I help you, Mr. Meinhardt?"

"I want to know if I can sue the goddam drug company, or the goddam doctor who told me to take that goddam drug."

"What drug are we talking about?"

"Hepaticin. For fatty liver."

Norma Meinhardt reached into her purse, which she clutched on her lap, and produced the pill bottle and handed it to the attorney.

The attorney wrote "Hepaticin" on his legal pad.

"Who prescribed it?"

"Sylvan Goldbach. He's my doctor, see. And he says I've got a goddam fatty liver. And he tells me I have to take this."

"How long ago was that?"

"I don't know. Maybe two years ago, maybe a little more. Why don't you go ask goddam Walgreens? They should know. Paid them enough."

"And now you have cancer?" Garner asked.

"Yes, goddam it."

"You said it's a kind of cancer no one's ever heard of?"

"Well, I never heard of it. Goddam cancer doctor knew about it, of course. He's the one who told me I had it."

"And what's his name?" Devin asked, trying not to lose patience.

"Patel. Ain't that right, Norma?"

"Raj Patel," Mrs. Meinhardt added. "He's over by U.C."

Devin jotted on his legal pad, "Oncologist – Raj Patel – University of Cincinnati."

"Mr. Meinhardt, do you recall what Dr. Patel called this cancer? Did he have a name for it?"

"Yes, goddam it!" Dan Meinhardt exclaimed. "That's what I'm been trying to tell you. It's called adrenal cancer. Something like that."

Norma Meinhardt pulled a 3 x 5 index card from her purse and passed it to the young attorney. She had written the name of the cancer on it in block letters.

"And you think this drug," Garner looked at his notes, "Hepaticin, caused this cancer?"

"I think you should sue the goddam company that made it. I see those ads on television all the time. If you took this goddam drug, and now you got this goddam condition, you may be entitled to compensation."

"Mr. Meinhardt, you can only recover damages if the drug caused you to get sick. In other words, if we sued the drug company, we would have to be able to prove that Hepaticin caused you to develop this cancer."

"Well, goddam!"

"So," Garner asked again, "what makes you think that this drug caused you to develop this cancer?"

"All I know is, I never had cancer. Nobody in my family ever did. And then I took this goddam drug, and the next thing I know, I got this cancer nobody ever heard of."

"Mr. Meinhardt, I'm not saying you don't have a case, but the drug company has an army of lawyers. They have really good lawyers. They will argue that just because you took this drug and then you got cancer, doesn't prove the drug caused you to get cancer. In other words, they will argue that just because one thing happens and then something else happens, doesn't prove the first thing caused the second."

"Can you explain that," Meinhardt instructed the attorney, "so my wife here can follow you?"

Garner smiled despite himself.

"Here's how the drug company lawyers always put it. They'll say, 'After a spring rain, the farmer heard frogs croaking down by the lake. That's when the farmer knew it had rained frogs.'"

"So, you don't want to take my case because the goddam drug company is going to tell a story about some goddam farmer and his goddam frogs?"

"I didn't say I won't represent you," Garner responded, choosing his words carefully. "I'm just saying we're going to have to do some investigation first, and find out if you have a case."

"What about the doctor?" Norma Meinhardt asked. "He told Dan he had fatty liver and that's why he had to take this drug. And then, when Dan got sick, and they ran all those tests, the biopsy and all that, the cancer doctor, Dr. Patel, says Dan never had fatty liver to begin with."

Garner knew clients frequently believed they could sue doctors and hospitals for making a misdiagnosis or some other error, even though the mistake caused no damages. If the doctor misdiagnosed fatty liver, the patient couldn't recover damages unless the misdiagnosis actually caused some harm.

"That could be important," Garner said, trying to be encouraging without committing to anything.

"Well, you see," Norma Meinhardt continued, "that same thing happened to this other man. Dr. Goldbach said he had fatty liver too and prescribed this drug, and he didn't have fatty liver either."

"What other man?"

"Sam Carson. He is in chemo with Dan," Norma Meinhardt explained. "He ended up with this cancer too. That's where we met him."

Suddenly, the case began to seem interesting.

"Like I said," Dan Meinhardt added, with his usual emphasis, "There's something goddam wrong here."

"Here's what I'm going to do," Garner said. "I'm going to print off some forms that I need you to sign, saying I can get copies of your medical records and talk to your doctors. I'm also going to ask you to sign a form that says you are hiring me to represent you. If I decide there's no case, you won't owe me anything. If I decide to pursue this, then I will get paid a percentage of anything I recover, plus my expenses. If I don't recover anything, you don't owe me anything."

Garner printed off the forms and handed them to Dan and Norma Meinhardt to sign.

"I'll look into this, and then we can decide where we go from there."

SATURDAY, FEBRUARY 13 – CINCINNATI MARKET OFFICE

It was Saturday morning, but given Brett Winslow's reaction, Spencer Doss decided to come into the office and take a harder look at whether there was a link between Hepaticin and cancer.

Doss logged onto Medline and searched for articles that discussed adrenal cortical carcinoma *and* Hepaticin, but got no hits. He searched for articles on the incidence of adrenal cortical carcinoma and found nothing to indicate a recent uptick in cases.

The articles he did find were mainly technical and narrow in focus, but generally contained brief overviews of the cancer. As he had recalled, adrenal cortical carcinoma chiefly occurred in two age groups – in children 5 or younger and in adults from about age 30 to age 40.

In children, the condition was genetic. Researchers had found an association between the disease in these young victims and a mutation in the tumor suppressor gene P53. It occurred about 0.3 times per million lives per year – about three new cases for every ten million people. Those, however, were not the cancers associated in his data with Hepaticin use.

For adults in their thirties, no one seemed to have a good explanation why the disease struck when it did, or why it affected women somewhat more often than men. Adrenal cortex carcinomas *were* known to occur sometimes in people with certain genetic disorders. But those disorders were exceedingly rare, and – like the cases in children – they were generally linked to mutations in specific tumor suppressor genes. Those rare genetic conditions clearly did not explain the upsurge in late-in-life cancers the health plan was seeing.

Studies, of course, linked many types of cancer to risk factors such as smoking, a high-fat diet, or a sedentary lifestyle. Many studies also linked various cancers to exposure to specific cancer-causing substances in the workplace or the environment. But Doss was not able to find any studies reporting an association between any of those factors and a person's risk of developing adrenal cancer – although some researchers suggested smoking *might* be a risk factor for adrenal cancers.

Doss gave up on medical research and turned to the medical claims histories Maya Naidu had delivered in response to his first SPDR request. As he scanned through the medical histories, he saw that most of the cancer patients had NASH diagnoses. That would explain why they were taking Hepaticin, he thought, but not why they got adrenal cancer.

He had promised himself he would spend at least part of the afternoon exploring the city. So, just before 1:30 p.m., he gave up, logged off his computer, and left the office. In connection with work, he had made visits to each of the city's hospitals, with tours arranged by the hospital's business people. On his own, on weekends, he had been to the Union Terminal building, the massive Art Deco building that once was a major train station, but which had long since been converted into a museum center. He had also visited the former home of William Howard Taft in downtown Cincinnati, and the Krohn Conservatory in nearby Eden Park. This afternoon, he planned to visit the National Underground Railroad Freedom Center in Cincinnati's

Riverfront area. *Visiting the Underground Railway center was a must*, he thought, *but not likely to cheer me up.* In fact, sight-seeing alone seldom improved his mood.

He suspected that his down mood – at the moment, at least – came at least in part from the fact that the next day was Valentine's Day. Many people would be celebrating that evening rather than on Sunday. He would not be one of them.

TUESDAY, FEBRUARY 16 – PHARMACY DEPARTMENT

Brett Winslow had caught an earlier-than-usual flight back from Chicago, where he had met with the staff of the company's mail order pharmacy. He now found himself with the rare and pleasant problem of being in his office with unscheduled time on his hands. He decided to use the time to call to his contact at Galaxy to confirm the scheduled time for negotiation of the new rebate contract.

While he had his counterpart from the drug company on the line, he broached the subject of arranging for one of Galaxy's safety people to discuss Dr. Doss's concerns about a possible association between Hepaticin and adrenal cancer. Winslow stressed that conversation had to be entirely separate from the rebate negotiations. His contact promised to get back to him promptly.

Winslow checked the health plan's stock price. It was up a little. He then opened his email to make sure there were no messages that could not wait until morning.

One email header contained the always ominous label, "PERSONAL AND CONFIDENTIAL." Winslow opened the email to see what it was about. In a brief message, the sender introduced herself as the vice president of an I.T. security firm. She apologized for the out-of-the-blue email, but said that in her work for a major corporate client, she had come across a posting that criticized him personally and contained information his company might regard as confidential. She explained that the details, including the URL of the website, were in the attachment. She wished him well and included her name, title, address and phone number.

Winslow immediately thought of Spencer Doss. Alarmed that Doss may have posted a rant about Hepaticin, or about the health plan's response to his concerns, Winslow clicked on the attachment. As he did, Winslow thought: *If Doss is behind this, his career as medical director is going to be the shortest on record.*

In fact, the attachment was a routine anti-HMO screed, accusing HMOs of putting profits before people, and so on. It singled out the health plan where he worked in particular, claiming the health plan put AIDS and HIV drugs in a tier that required patients to pay 50% of the cost of the expensive drugs. It alleged the company did that to discourage people with AIDS or HIV from enrolling, and urged people to write the company and demand that the Pharmacy VP, Brett Winslow, be fired.

"Same old crap!" Winslow muttered to himself, as he deleted the email.

But by then, the attachment had planted instructions deep in his computer's code.

WEDNESDAY, FEBRUARY 18 – HEALTH PLAN CAFETERIA

Spencer Doss made his way through the cafeteria line and began to look for an open table when he saw Eileen Wang and asked if he could join her. No sooner had he taken his seat, when Brett Winslow – who appeared to be on his way out of the cafeteria – approached.

"Galaxy wants to send their top U.S. safety guy out here next week, while my team is meeting with their business people in Newark," Winslow announced. "Their guy is going to call you, probably this afternoon. Can you meet with him next week?"

"No problem," Doss replied. "I'll work something out with him. Should I send him a summary or something in advance, so he's prepared?"

"No, they specifically said for you not to do that." Winslow turned to Wang. "He wants to bring a couple people with him. One of them will be an in-house attorney, so Eileen, you should sit in."

"Happy to," Wang said. "Thanks for the heads up."

Turning back to Doss, Winslow added. "Just remember, my team will be negotiating tens of millions of dollars in rebates with Galaxy. Make whatever points you feel you need to, but try not to piss them off." With that, Winslow turned and walked briskly toward the exit.

Doss looked at Wang and smiled. "I guess I didn't make a good first impression with him."

"That reminds me," Wang said. "You have to be careful what you say in email. Email hangs around forever, and it's the first thing opposing counsel ask for when they sue us."

"Bob Wiseman already gave me the lecture, but thanks." Doss bit into his sandwich.

"You know why they don't want you to send them anything?" Wang asked.

"Not a clue. You'd think they would want to be prepared. I would."

"They don't want anything in their files," Wang explained. "If it turns out you're right, they don't want evidence in their files they knew about this and didn't do anything."

"Is that why they are bringing an attorney?"

"Probably," Wang said. "The attorney can take notes and write up a summary, and if they get into litigation later, they can claim they don't have to produce the lawyer's work product, because he prepared his notes in anticipation of litigation."

"Sometimes I feel like I'm playing a high-stakes game, but don't know the rules."

"You'll get the hang of it. Did you send the Med-Watch forms to the treating doctors?"

"Yeah, they're in the mail," Doss said. "Considering how rare this condition is, an odd thing turned up when we got the list of prescribing doctors to send the forms to. Some of these guys had more than one patient with this cancer."

"They must have prescribed a lot of it," Wang said thoughtfully. "Either that, or you're missing something."

"That's what I'm thinking, too."

THURSDAY, FEBRUARY 18 – ACTURIAL DEPARTMENT

Tam Nguyen Phan – "Tammy" to her friends, but never to her family – had a master's degree in biostatistics and had wanted to pursue a Ph.D., but her family and friends had talked her out it. *If men thought she were too smart*, they had told her, *they wouldn't want to date or marry you.* Phan was inpatient with that. She wasn't sure she believed it, and in any event, she didn't want to date or marry someone obviously less intelligent than herself.

In the rational part of herself, she reasoned that a Ph.D. would not be a problem. But her subconscious whispered that men who were nice, good-looking, with decent jobs, and who were willing to date a woman with a Ph.D., didn't grow on trees. Frequent questions from her mother about when she was going to get married and settle down didn't help.

But money had been a problem too. After getting her master's degree in biostatistics, she had taken the position in the HMO's actuarial unit to replenish her funds. The job was a good one and paid reasonably well, but she was bored by it and had begun to think again about pursuing a Ph.D.

And so, she was pleasantly surprised when her boss, Ingrid Berg, mentioned to her that one of the company's regional medical directors had noticed what seemed to be a connection between a new drug and a rare cancer. The medical director was hoping someone could help him determine if the association between Hepaticin and this cancer was statistically significant.

Phan saw the assignment as an opportunity.

After discussing the project with Berg and reading some articles about Hepaticin online, she arranged to meet with Dr. Doss to be sure she understood the project.

Doss ran through what he had found and the data Maya Naidu had pulled for him.

"You want to know if this is statistically significant," Phan summarized.

Doss agreed.

"Are you accounting for any risk factors besides this drug?" Phan asked.

"We don't have any known risk factors," Doss replied, "except genetic, and those account for the cases in kids under five."

"Do you want to get this published?" Phan asked.

"At some point, maybe, but at this juncture I'm just trying to figure out if there's something here to worry about. I look at the numbers, and I think there is something seriously out of whack, but maybe I'm missing something. I don't want to send up an alarm if this is just coincidence."

"I really want to work with you on this. Just looking at your numbers, I think you're onto something. But if you want to publish, you should get somebody with a Ph.D. in biostatistics, who does this kind of analysis for a living, to work with us."

"Let's jump off that bridge," Doss agreed, "if and when we reach it."

"One more thing," Phan said. "Do you understand the limitations on your data?

"You mean," Doss asked, "that I've only got 127 cases, and not all of them took Hepaticin."

"Well, yes, of course," Phan said, moving to one of the whiteboards that lined the conference room's walls, "but that's not what I meant." She drew a long line horizontally across the board, and wrote "Jan. 1" at the left end and "Dec. 31" at the other end.

"Most of our members stay with us for years, but not all of them do. In Medicare, which is what I'm familiar with, most members join effective January 1, which makes analysis easy. Others enroll during the year. Some die, move out of the area, or decide they don't like us and go to a different plan."

Phan drew several lines parallel to the horizontal line, each starting and ending at a different point – representing the periods during which hypothetical individual members were enrolled.

"You have no way of knowing," she continued, "but some of your cases may have taken Hepaticin before they enrolled with us."

She drew a stick figure next to one of the parallel lines. "Assume this guy took Hepaticin for two years, and then joined our plan on January 1," she said.

"On January 5, his oncologist gets back from spending the holidays skiing in Vail and gives him the bad news. The office visit generates a claim. The oncologist's back office staff puts the cancer diagnosis on the claim form, and submits it to us. In our data, that case is not associated with Hepaticin, because we never saw a claim for Hepaticin. He's a false negative."

Phan drew another stick figure, and put long hair and a skirt on this figure. "This lady is 80 years old. She's been on our Medicare Advantage plan for years. She eats too much and doesn't get any exercise. She is obese and develops Type 2 diabetes and fatty liver. She's been on Hepaticin for a year-and-a-half.

"Open enrollment period comes around, and her daughter persuades her to switch to a cheaper plan. In January, her doctor gets back from a week in the Caribbean and tells her she has this cancer. She's now with some other health plan. We never see a claim with a cancer diagnosis, so she's another false negative. She shows up in your data as someone who took the drug and never got this cancer."

"These things don't cancel out. Some of your didn't-take-the-drug members may have taken it, but you don't know that. And some of your took-the-drug-but-didn't-get-sick members may have actually gotten sick, but you don't know that either."

Phan slid back into her chair. "If you had better data, you might have something that is statistically significant. Or, not."

"I am going to meet with the drug company's people next week," Doss confided.

"I'm not sure I can get you anything that quick. We expect CMS to announce the preliminary rate for Medicare Advantage plans for next year, and I'll be tied up – along with everyone else – figuring out how that impacts our plans."

"Okay, then I'll brief you on what the Galaxy people have to say, and we'll go from there."

FRIDAY, FEBRUARY 19 – CINCINNATI MARKET OFFICE

Doss prepared a new request for an SPDR – this one capturing prescriber information for *all* Hepaticin scripts, not just for the patients who developed adrenal cortical carcinoma. He asked that the report show the top fifty prescribers by total scripts and by the number of unique patients getting the drug, for each year since the drug launched.

After hitting the "send" key, he called Maya Naidu and told her another request was on its way. He asked if she could hang onto the data underlying the report, because he was going to ask someone to analyze the data further. Naidu assured him that would not be a problem.

"How is your mother doing?" Doss asked.

"She seems to be doing okay, Dr. Doss, but she looks so much older than she did even a few months ago. It is very sad."

"And your daughter's dancing?"

"Ashika is very excited. Her teacher thinks she will be doing very well if she can perform at the festival. That is her dream, Dr. Doss, but I don't know if my mother will live that long."

SATURDAY, FEBRUARY 20 – CINCINNATI MARKET OFFICE

On Saturday, Doss worked out for an hour at a nearby gym before heading into the office. He downed a bottle of water when he got out of the shower and another on the short drive from the gym to the office. It was bitterly cold – the coldest day of the year. Old snow stood in spots where it had been pushed into piles earlier in the week. Gusts of strong wind, hinting of new snow to come, only made things worse.

As soon as Doss stepped out of his car into the cold, he immediately felt an urgent need to empty his bladder. He rode the elevator impatiently to the 7th floor, used his pass card to open the door to the floor, and without bothering to open his own office, dropped his laptop, jacket and gloves at his administrative assistant's cubicle. He walked quickly back through the door and into the lobby, where the restrooms were.

Minutes later, feeling more comfortable, he attempted to re-enter the locked portion of the floor, but could not find his pass card in any of his pockets.

When he left his things inside, he realized, he had left the pass card in his jacket pocket. Frustrated, he used his cell phone to call building security, and explained his problem. The guard promised to be right up.

Three minutes later, the usual Saturday security guard stepped off the elevator. The guard, who by now was accustomed to seeing Dr. Doss in the office on Saturday mornings, greeted the medical director politely. "Good morning, Dr. Doss. How are you?"

"Frustrated," Doss replied. Doss noticed – not for the first time – that the security guard, who appeared to be in his mid-thirties, was exceptionally thin, almost emaciated. "How are *you*?" Doss asked. "You look like you could afford to pick up some weight."

"Not on my salary," the guard shrugged.

Doss knew some studies seemed to show that individuals who adhered to a very low caloric diet seemed to live longer. But Doss was skeptical and thought this young man was too thin. He also knew from past conversations the young man wasn't very bright.

"What's the problem?" the guard asked.

Although Doss had just explained the problem on the phone minutes earlier, he ran through the situation again.

When he finished, the guard looked at him apologetically. "Dr. Doss," he replied, "I'm not supposed to let anybody in that doesn't have their card."

Doss stared at the security guard in disbelief. He noticed the man's name on the name plate on his uniform – Sean Higgins.

"Sean," Doss said, "my card is inside. So is my jacket, and my car keys are in my jacket. I can't just turn around and go home, because my jacket and car keys are inside."

The guard appeared to think the situation through for several moments. "Well, under the circumstances," the young man concluded, "I think my boss would let me make an exception."

"Thank you," Doss replied.

"But Dr. Doss, I'm going to need to see some identification."

The request was idiotic, Doss thought. *He knows who I am!* But he decided not to argue. He kept his driver's license in his wallet, and he kept his wallet in his hip pocket. So, at least he had his wallet and driver's license. He removed the driver's license from his wallet and handed it to the guard.

"You wait here, Dr. Doss, and I'll see if I can find your jacket."

A few minutes later, the security guard re-emerged from the office with the leather bomber jacket Doss wore.

"Dr. Doss, I need to have you remove your card and your keys from your jacket."

Doss did as instructed and handed them to the guard, who used the card to open the door to the floor. Doss followed the security guard inside and watched as he used the keys to open the door to the office with the name "Spencer Doss, M.D." on it.

"Looks like everything is in order," the guard said, handing Doss his driver's license, pass card, keys and jacket.

As the guard left, Doss noticed that the guard had given him not only his own pass card and keys, but had accidently handed him the master key to all of the office doors in the building.

"Hey, Sean," Doss called to the security guard.

When the guard turned around, Doss held up the guard's keys.

"Oh my God!" the security guard exclaimed. "Oh my God, thank you! If I lost my keys," he said, "my boss would fire me. Oh my God, thank you."

"I'm sorry," Doss said, "but I am going to need to see some identification."

The security guard looked at him uncomprehendingly.

Doss decided not to push his luck and surrendered the master key to the overly thin, but not overly bright, young man.

Doss tried to settle in and get some work done, but he quickly realized he no longer felt like working. On impulse, he rang the number for Eileen Wang. He knew she too sometimes worked on Saturday mornings, but given the weather, he fully expected her voicemail.

"Spencer, what's up?"

Doss was caught off guard for a second both by the fact that she answered and by the whole caller-identification thing.

"I came in this morning to work," he explained, "but my heart isn't in it. I'm thinking about going exploring. What should I go see?"

"There are a lot of things to see in Cincinnati, especially the zoo. It's really nice. It's supposed to be one of the top zoos in the country. But given the weather, you might want to try the art museum. It's in Eden Park, so it's really close."

"Is it nice?"

"Yeah. For a regional art museum, it's pretty good. It's not the Chicago Art Institute or on the same caliber as some of the museums in New York, but it's worth seeing."

"Interested in being my guide?"

Wang surprised him again, by agreeing.

"I'll meet you in the lobby," she said, "in about fifteen minutes."

SATURDAY, FEBRUARY 20 – CINCINNATI ART MUSEUM

As Spencer Doss and Eileen Wang walked through the art museum, looking at the artwork and getting to know one another better, Doss was focused more on his companion than the artwork. But – perhaps because of his discussions with Maya Naidu about her daughter's dancing – he was intrigued by a small statute on the main floor. The museum highlighted it as being among its most iconic works.

The statute – of a four-armed god – was obviously Hindu. According to the plaque, the statute depicted Lord Shiva, in the form of Nataraja, the Lord of Dance, performing the cosmic dance of Tāndava. The dancer had what looked like a chubby infant – like a cupid, but ugly – under one of his feet. Doss used his smart phone to snap a picture of the statute and another of the information plaque.

He and Wang decided to have lunch in the art museum's small restaurant. While waiting for their orders to arrive, Doss used his smart phone to research the Hindu statute.

He quickly learned that what, in the statute, appeared to have been an infant was actually the dwarf Apasmāra, who represented ignorance in Hindu mythology. According to a brief description in Wiki, Apasmāra could not be killed, because if Apasmāra could be killed, people could attain knowledge without effort, dedication and hard work. This would lead to the devaluing of knowledge in all forms.

To subdue Apasmāra, Lord Shiva adopted the form of Nataraja – the Lord of Dance – and performed the cosmic dance of Tāndava. During this dance, Nataraja suppresses Apasmāra by crushing him with his right foot. As Apasmāra is one of the few demons destined to immortality, Shiva forever remains in his Nataraja form suppressing Apasmāra for all eternity.

Doss thought that image was fascinating. "It's not that different from the way we think about education and about science and medicine,' he commented to Wang. "It requires constant effort to learn – to overcome our ignorance."

Wang smiled, rolled her eyes, and said she preferred the impressionists. "Besides," she added, "I prefer the Western notion that we're making progress against ignorance. That we're not just running – or dancing – in place."

TUESDAY, FEBRUARY 23 – GARNER LAW OFFICE

Over the past two weeks, Devin Garner had carefully collected the medical records for Dan Meinhardt, advancing from his own funds the exorbitant fees the doctors' offices charged for making copies. By the time the records arrived, Garner had read enough about Hepaticin, fatty liver disease, and adrenal carcinoma on the internet to feel confident he could follow the records.

Specifically, he knew he was looking not just for references to fatty liver disease, but also for references to "Non-Alcoholic Steatohepatitis" or "NASH"– which is what Hepaticin was supposed to treat. He had also figured out – and confirmed with his personal physician – that he should also be looking for references to "Non-Alcoholic Fatty Liver Disease" or "NAFLD" – the more common, but not progressive form of the disease. Of course, if he took the case, he would need to have a physician or nurse review the medical records as well.

Beginning late in the afternoon, after he had completed his court appearances for the day, Garner worked his way through his copy of the medical records of the primary care physician, Sylvan Goldbach, M.D. He found the entry where the physician had first diagnosed fatty liver and had prescribed Hepaticin. Garner found a log of prescription medications and confirmed the physician had prescribed Hepaticin and had authorized a number of refills. That all seemed to be as he expected, but he could not locate any record of an x-ray, CAT scan, MRI or lab test supporting the fatty liver diagnosis – let alone a liver biopsy or anything else that would confirm a NASH diagnosis.

He noted the date on which Dr. Goldbach made the referral to the oncologist, wrote "statute of limitations?" on a yellow Post-It note, and stuck it next to the date, as a reminder to mark his tickler system. If there was a case here, he didn't want to blow it by missing the deadline to file suit.

Garner turned next to the records of Raj Patel, M.D., the oncologist. Those records turned out to be more difficult to follow, because much of the terminology was unfamiliar. Garner scoured the reports of several x-rays and a CAT scan, none of which mentioned fatty liver, "NAFLD" or "NASH." He did find an entry that said, "Discontinue Hepaticin," but without any explanation or elaboration.

Uncertain what to do next, Garner did a Google Scholar search – looking for any source that mentioned *both* "Hepaticin" *and* "adrenal cortical carcinoma" – but found nothing.

He had already read the official product literature – what drug companies called the product's "label" although it was several pages long. He knew it contained no reference to any association with cancer or with adrenal cortical carcinoma specifically, but he re-read it anyway.

The product literature reminded him that the drug was made by Galaxy Pharmaceutical Company, a British company. Galaxy was one of the largest drug companies in the world, but Garner did not know much else about it. He Googled "Galaxy" and "lawsuit or allegations or verdict." The search pulled up quite a few hits, mostly ads by law firms specializing in drug product liability litigation, bragging of litigation and settlements with the giant drug company. He saw nothing that mentioned Hepaticin or adrenal cortical carcinoma.

He logged onto the EDGAR database, which provides access to the reports that publicly traded companies must file with the Securities and Exchange Commission or "SEC." He located the most recent annual report filed by Galaxy, checked for the usual footnote for "Litigation and other contingencies," and skipped to that page. The form had a lengthy disclosure of an investigation by the U.S. Department of Justice into "off label" marketing by the company and alleged kickbacks paid to physicians to prescribe certain drugs, but the investigation appeared to be old, and it did not involve Hepaticin. The filing also described in vague terms the status of product liability litigation involving a number of the company's other drugs, but again nothing relating to Hepaticin.

He checked each of the company's filings since its annual filing. He again saw nothing pertaining to Hepaticin, except reports on sales volume, revenues, and the like. One report mentioned termination of a supplier in India, but nothing of any interest.

Garner called his wife and let her know he would be late.

He logged onto Westlaw, the starting point for legal research for most lawyers. He searched for court decisions involving Hepaticin, but aside from the usual patent litigation, found nothing.

He switched to PACER, the public access system for federal court dockets, and conducted the broadest search he could think of for cases involving Galaxy as a defendant and the drug Hepaticin. Aside from patent litigation and the occasional mention in disability cases that the petitioner was taking Hepaticin along with various other drugs, his search turned up nothing. He searched for cases that used the words "malpractice" and "Hepaticin" in the same opinion. Again, nothing.

This may be the cleanest drug on record, he thought. He put the tentative statute of limitations date in his tickler system, logged off, and shut down his computer.

He wrote himself a reminder to make an appointment to see the oncologist, then turned out the office lights, and locked the door as he left.

WEDNESDAY, FEBRUARY 24 – GALAXY MEETING

Spencer Doss showed the team from Galaxy Pharmaceuticals Company to a conference room, where Eileen Wang was waiting. Doss had exchanged names and hasty handshakes with his guests in the lobby, but he wasn't sure he would remember names. So, as the Galaxy contingent took seats around the conference room table, he asked everyone to introduce themselves again – *to be sure Wang got their names in her notes*. Doss began by re-introducing himself as a Regional Medical Director for the health plan. Eileen Wang introduced herself as well.

Boris Bardin, Senior Vice President for Post-Market Surveillance, led the Galaxy USA team. He was a large, intimidating man who quite naturally made people think of a Russian bear.

Bardin was accompanied by Nancy Allerton, a Senior Associate General Counsel for Galaxy's US operations. She was petite, wore an expensive-looking suit, and without saying much gave the impression of being very intelligent.

The third and final member of the delegation was Hyun Ho, a statistician who reported up the chain to Bardin. He was a short, chubby, twenty-something, who wore a checked shirt and a black-and-white tie. Actually, the tie was black, but decorated with a series of equations in white, of the sort one might find on a physicist or mathematician's blackboard. His business card indicated he had a Ph.D.

Ho knew his fellow countrymen invariably had trouble figuring out how to pronounce his Korean first name, "Hyuan." As he often did during introductions, he interjected, "Please call me 'John.' Everyone does."

Doss connected his laptop to a jack built into the conference table, enabling him to display the PowerPoint presentation in his computer on the screen in the conference room. He had not used PowerPoint before, but Wang had insisted he learn how to use it. *Except when exchanging emails*, she told him, *people in corporate America communicated with each other through PowerPoint decks*. In a world in which people defended their ground by projecting "death by PowerPoint," she joked, he could not afford to be an unarmed combatant.

Using the PowerPoint slides, he walked the Galaxy team through the data. He began with a simple bar graph, with three columns rising perpendicular to the x axis. "The columns on this chart," Doss explained, "show the number of new cases of adrenal cortical carcinoma we had five, four and three years ago. As you can see, we had 4 cases five years ago, 5 cases four years ago, and 7 cases three years ago."

Doss noticed "John" Ho was typing at a furious rate. Doss figured Ho for an intense video game player.

"According to the literature, adrenal cortical carcinoma is pretty rare – one or two cases per million lives, per year," Doss continued. "As you can see, five, four and three years ago, given our membership, the number of cases was about what you expect."

Doss clicked to a new slide, which added a bar showing 47 cases two years ago. "And then all of sudden," Doss commented, "two years ago, we're off the chart in terms of expected incidence."

As he spoke, Ho typed the new number into his own laptop.

"And this is last year," Doss added, showing a bar with 64 cases. "For this condition, that's an epidemic."

"Adrenal cortical carcinoma generally appears in two age groups," Doss told the Galaxy contingent, although he imagined they had done their research on this cancer, and knew what he was about to say. "It hits kids age 5 and under. Those cases are genetic. And it hits adults from about age 30 to about age 40. Thirty-somethings, basically. No one seems to know why."

"Here is a new version of the bar graph," Doss said as he clicked forward. "The blue areas in the columns represent the cases in kids 5-and-under. The green areas represent cases in adults 30-to-40 years old at diagnosis. And the grey areas represent cases outside those two age groups."

Doss smiled and added, "I picked grey, because most of the cases in our members, outside the expected age groups, occur in people 65 and older. And as you can see, we have a lot of this cancer outside the expected age bands. Basically, you don't expect to see this cancer in seniors, but all of a sudden, we're seeing an awful lot of this cancer in seniors. We are trying to understand why."

Doss clicked to his next slide, which added a line to the bar graph showing how much the health plan spent year-by-year on Hepaticin. "As you can see," he explained, "this increase in cases occurred after Hepaticin was introduced, and during a period when our members' use of Hepaticin was also increasing pretty dramatically."

Doss moved to a new series of slides showing the monthly number of ACC cases and the prescription volume for Hepaticin.

Bardin sat impassive, but "John" Ho squirmed in his seat. He looked as if he could barely contain the impulse to jump in. Doss knew what Ho wanted to argue: *The mere fact that the number of cases of adrenal cortical carcinoma had increased over the last two years, while Hepaticin sales were also increasing, was not enough to prove the drug caused the increase in the number of cases.*

Doss clicked to a new slide. "On this slide," Doss narrated, "the bars are color coded to show the relative portion of the new cases that took Hepaticin, and the portion that – so far as we know – did not take Hepaticin. The cases occurring in members who took Hepaticin are shown in red, and the cases occurring in members who did not take Hepaticin are shown in black." The bars on the graph were mainly red.

Doss paused to allow "John" Ho to catch up.

"As you can see," he continued, "the number of adrenal cortical carcinoma cases who were not on the drug – shown in black – increased only marginally, in line with increases in our non-Medicare enrollment. Basically, those are the cases in kids and in the 30-somethings. The number of cases among members on the drug – shown in red – increased dramatically."

"That," Doss explained, "is why we wanted to share this with you."

"Last slide," Doss promised. "This slide," he said, "shows the average and the modal or most frequent time in months from the first prescription for Hepaticin to onset of adrenal cortical carcinoma among Hepaticin users who had developed adrenal cortical carcinoma. The average time was 11.8 months, and the most common time was 12 months."

Doss indicated that completed his presentation.

Bardin looked at his colleagues and asked if they had any questions before he responded.

"Dr. Doss," Ho began, "have you analyzed your data for other risk factors?"

"No, I have not," Doss conceded. "I am not aware of any established risk factors for this cancer except *maybe* smoking. Are you?"

Ho shrugged his shoulders, as if to say, *"Your problem. Not mine."*

"Unless we get a claim from someone for smoking cessation aids," Doss said after the awkward standoff, "we don't know if our members smoke. I couldn't adjust for that. But we have no reason to believe huge numbers of our members suddenly began smoking about the time Hepaticin came on the market."

"Are you claiming," Ho asked, "that there is a statistically significant relationship between taking Hepaticin and development of this carcinoma?"

"I'm not a statistician," Doss replied. "I have not done a statistical analysis, but I think any physician seeing these numbers would be concerned."

Ho checked his laptop and shot another question at Doss. "We show you guys paying a lot more for Hepaticin than you do. Do you know why that is?"

"We pay for a lot of Hepaticin through our stand-alone Medicare Part D – Medicare prescription drug plans," Doss replied. "We don't provide medical coverage for those members, and therefore we don't know how many – if any – of those people developed adrenal cortical carcinoma. I didn't think it made sense to include what we paid for those members."

Ho signaled he had no more questions.

Bardin looked hard at Doss. "Dr. Doss, where are you going with this?"

"No decision has been made. The company wanted to wait until we shared this information with you before we made any decisions."

Bardin said nothing. The silence continued for several long moments.

"Speaking just for myself," Doss said finally, "I don't see how we get around sharing this with the FDA. They are in a better position than we are to determine if what we are seeing is occurring elsewhere, and if a warning is appropriate. I think we owe that to our members and to the public."

Bardin said nothing.

"Even if we weren't concerned about people getting sick and dying," Doss continued, "we would have to be concerned about litigation. If Hepaticin is responsible for this increase in adrenal cortical carcinoma, it's going to come out eventually. When that happens, there is going to be a lot of litigation, and we don't want plaintiff lawyers suing us, accusing us of sitting on this information."

"Plaintiff lawyers are a bunch of fucking whores," Bardin exploded, his face turning red. "They will sue anyone they think they can shake down."

Bardin rose from his seat, walked a few feet away, and poured a cup of coffee. When he returned to his place at the table, he sat the coffee down, but remained standing. "Thank you for sharing your concerns with us," he said finally, "but your data are completely unlike our experience. We did not encounter this cancer in our clinical trials, here or abroad. We have not encountered this in any of our post-marketing surveillance."

Bardin picked up his coffee cup, took a sip, and sat the cup back down. "Dr. Doss," he continued, staring directly at Spencer Doss. "Can you explain *how* this drug might cause someone to develop adrenal cortical carcinoma? Or, why most of your plan members who take this drug do not develop it?"

"No," Doss conceded, "but that would be true of most cancers."

"I did not think so," Bardin replied. "Certainly, I can think of no possible mechanism, and I have been doing this for a long time now."

Bardin picked up the coffee cup, but apparently lost interest in it, and sat the cup down. "These people – the ones with this cancer – are older," Bardin continued. "They have fatty liver and probably many other problems. Most of them are probably taking several other drugs. If you look at all of their conditions and all of the drugs they are taking, you are guaranteed to find an association – maybe more than one. Any competent statistician will tell you that."

Bardin asked Doss to reverse his PowerPoint to the slide showing Hepaticin sales and the monthly number of ACC cases. "If you look closely at your data," Bardin lectured Doss, "you will see that the introduction of our drug occurred almost two years before you began to see any uptick in cases of this cancer. Given the number of your members who were taking our drug, and given what you think the incidence is of patients who develop this cancer after taking our drug, you should have seen an uptick sooner – if Hepaticin really did cause this cancer.”

“Look at your own chart, Dr. Doss.” Bardin demanded. “It shows this. Our product was on the market, and your members – in large numbers – were taking it, for almost two years before you see any increase in the number of cases of this cancer.”

Bardin picked up his coffee cup, and once again put it back down without drinking from it. “Do not speak to me about latency periods, and such. You cannot say affected members develop this terrible cancer after 12 months, on average, and then say you did not get an uptick for two years because it takes that long for these patients to develop this cancer.”

“It is true,” Bardin said, lowering his voice, “that our sales and your payments for our drug have increased over the last two years, and so – apparently – has the number of cases of this condition you have been seeing. But that proves nothing, my friend.”

Bardin’s face twisted into a smirk. “My taxes have also increased in each of the last two years, but my tax situation did not cause these people to get sick. My weight and my blood pressure have gone up too, in each of these last two years, as my doctor will tell you. But my weight did not cause these people to get ill. My blood pressure did not cause these people to get ill.”

Doss smiled and said, “I take your point, but these people did not get to share your bonuses, and they did not get to dine with you in first class restaurants in Newark and London. But they did take your drug.”

Bardin snorted and turned to his younger colleague. "John, Dr. Doss says my analogies do not hold water. Can you shed any light on this situation?"

Ho had been tapping away at his laptop at a frantic pace. He looked up and smiled. "I have done a statistical analysis," he responded. "Something interesting is going on here, but based on the figures you have given us, there is no statistically significant relationship between Hepaticin use and these cancers."

He glanced at his computer screen. "You haven't given me enough data to do a dose-response analysis, but if you could show a dose-response relationship, you would have told us about it. And as Boris pointed out, the uptick in these cancers does not correspond with the timing of the entry of our product on the market, even assuming your twelve-month-to-onset figure."

Bardin thanked Ho, and turned to Doss. "It is easy to say, 'What's the harm of warning people that there may be an association?' I think you know the answer to that.

"First, some people who need this drug will refuse to take it. Without Hepaticin, many of those people are going to need liver transplants. That is not good for them, and it is not good for your company's bottom line.

"Second, if we warn people of every conceivable risk that might possibly exist, and most of them turn out to be unwarranted, no one will pay any attention to our warnings. Too many people ignore them as it is, and then turn around and sue us."

Having delivered the message he apparently come to deliver, Bardin allowed himself to drink some of his coffee.

"Are you saying," Doss asked, "that you haven't gotten *any* reports of patients developing adrenal cortical carcinoma while taking Hepaticin?" His question sounded more defensive than he had hoped it would.

"None – aside from those you asked your doctors to submit to us."

Bardin glared at Doss. He was apparently accustomed to others bending to his will.

Doss said nothing.

"Unless you have something more than you have shown us today," Bardin pronounced, "the FDA will not act on this. I think this upsurge in this cancer is concerning, and I hope you figure out what is causing it. But I am convinced that if you look at your data again a year from now, it will be clear that this upsurge was not related to this drug. I think you will find that this cancer cluster is just one of those anomalies that occur. The number of cases will go down just as mysteriously as it went up, and no one will be able to say why.

"This happens, as you know," Bardin continued, only a little less animated. "But people get all excited. They want to have a reason why. They see excess cancers of one sort or another, and they blame it on the water, or the power lines, or a waste dump. These things rarely turn out to be what people think."

Bardin paused before continuing, as if to signal a change in topic.

"My friend, I see that you are a good doctor, one who cares about patients and who is interested in population health. That is the latest buzz word, no? Population health? And you have all this wonderful data to mine. My company would like to collaborate with you on any number of projects. I think we could do good work together. And, of course, we would pay your company very well for you to mine your data for us. We have set aside three million dollars US for such research this year. Our people are discussing this with Winslow in Newark this week."

Bardin stared hard at Doss.

"But, obviously, we cannot ask you, or your employer, to do such work for us if you are publishing articles or going on a crusade claiming our drug causes people to get this rare cancer. All of the fucking plaintiff lawyers will say, 'you must respect Dr. Doss, because you pay him, you pay the HMO where he works, to do this work for you.'"

"Dr. Doss, you will think about this and talk to your management, and not do anything rash. As you know, Hepaticin is a very important product for us, and it is helping a great many people. If you were to damage its reputation, and hurt sales, well, we have lawyers too – very good ones."

Bardin let that threat hang in the air.

"You will show us out now."

WEDNESDAY, FEBRUARY 24 – EMAIL EXCHANGE

On his return to his office, after showing the Galaxy contingent out, Doss had an email from Brett Winslow, the Pharmacy VP, asking how the meeting with the Galaxy safety people went.

Doss hit "reply." He attached the "Hepaticin-Adrenal Cortical Carcinoma" PowerPoint he had used, and responded: "I ran through our data, using the PowerPoint I'm attaching. When I was done, they told me I was full of crap. They threatened to sue us if we disclose what we have found. And then, they said how much they liked me. They said Galaxy would like to pay us several million dollars for us to mine our data for them, as long as we don't disclose our data linking Hepaticin to adrenal cortical carcinoma."

Moments later, Winslow replied. "They are talking with us here in Newark about data mining. They have some very interesting projects they want to pay us to do. They haven't said anything to us about suppressing our data. They just said they can't pay us to mine data for them if they are fighting us in public, saying we don't understand our own data. Their position makes sense. We would do the same thing."

Doss responded, "We both know they want to pay us to cover this up."

"We're still in Newark, but we're going to wrap up here tomorrow. Just don't do anything until I get back, and we can talk this through."

Doss closed Winslow's email and saw he had an email from IT Security. The email – machine-generated and apparently prompted by his "full of crap" remark –

scolded him for using profanity in company email, and warned that another violation could result "in disciplinary action, up to and including termination."

Doss looked at the computer in disbelief. After a moment, he said "Fuck you" to the computer screen, closed the email, shut down his computer, and told his administrative assistant he was headed to the gym.

FRIDAY, FEBRUARY 26 – ONCOLOGIST'S OFFICE

Just five years out of law school, Devin Garner always felt insecure when meeting with his clients' physicians. The fact that Raj Patel, M.D., the oncologist treating Dan Meinhardt, was cerebral, intense, impatient, and fifteen years older didn't help. Polite, but to the point, the physician briefly ran through the diagnosis, his treatment plan, and the prognosis, which was not good.

"I gather this is a somewhat unusual or rare cancer?" Garner asked.

"Yes, but not unheard of. It occurs once or twice in a million persons, per year."

"But aren't those cases mainly in much younger patients?"

"That's true. It is unusual to see this cancer in someone Mr. Meinhardt's age. But not impossible. In any event, that doesn't prove Hepaticin causes this cancer."

"Mr. Meinhardt tells me you have another patient with this condition."

"Two others, but one – a woman – died. Three altogether."

"Had they all taken Hepaticin?" Garner asked, putting on the table the question he most wanted answered.

"You told my secretary you were going to ask that. I checked. The answer to your question is 'Yes.'   I agree that's very interesting. But it doesn't prove causation. It could just be a coincidence. Hepaticin is a relatively new drug. Galaxy is promoting it heavily. You've probably seen the ads on television. It's being heavily prescribed. It could just be people with fatty liver are more prone to this. Look, it could be something else. Or, just a coincidence."

"That reminds me," Garner responded. "Did Mr. Meinhardt have fatty liver disease?"

"No." The physician glanced at his watch. "That's in my notes."

"Actually, your notes just say 'discontinue Hepaticin.'"

"Oh, sorry."

"What about the other two patients?"

"Off the record?"

"Sure."

"They didn't have fatty liver disease either. Some people are overprescribing this drug. That happens sometimes with a new drug."

"One last thing," the young attorney promised, "and then I'm done. If you were in my shoes and you wanted to know if there is a connection between Hepaticin and this cancer, what would you do? Where would you start?"

"Have you reviewed the medical literature?"

"I didn't find anything, but that's not my area of expertise. I'm going to need to hire someone to do that, but I hate to spend the money without more to go on."

"Then, I'm not sure," the physician responded, clearly out of patience. "Did you check MedWatch?"

"MedWatch?" Garner asked, scribbling the name in his notes.

"It's a site maintained by the FDA. It's where hospitals and physicians report adverse events related to drugs. Consumers, too, I think."

TUESDAY, MARCH 1, C-SUITE, HEADQUARTERS

It was Tuesday morning, and Spencer Doss was meeting again with his boss, Robert Wiseman, M.D., and with the Pharmacy VP, Brett Winslow. With his usual enthusiasm, Winslow began with the news that his team's negotiations the previous week with Galaxy Pharmaceuticals had gone very well, but told Wiseman there had been an unexpected development.

"Galaxy wants to contract with us to mine our claims data," Winslow explained. "Our company has done some one-off projects for various pharma companies before, but what Galaxy proposes is more than just a one-off project. Galaxy has several very interesting – very substantive – projects. If those work out, it anticipates a steady flow of work."

"How much work are we talking about?" Wiseman asked.

"Galaxy proposed a budget of $3 million for the balance of this year, if we're interested."

"That would enable us to set up a dedicated unit," Wiseman mused. "It could spend – I don't know – 40%, maybe 50% of its time doing research for us, and the rest of its time doing research for Galaxy and whatever other customers we could attract."

"That's what I was thinking," Winslow concurred. "Senior Management will have to approve our taking this on. The legal department will have to work out the details of the contract. I imagine the Privacy Office will have to sign off on the specific projects."

"This is something I've wanted the company to do for a long time," Wiseman said. "I don't expect any problem getting the Senior Team to sign off on it." Wiseman tapped the end of his pen on his desktop, staring at Winslow. "So, what's the catch? Nothing is this easy."

"Galaxy insists on the ability to terminate the contract on very short or no notice," Winslow replied. "They are concerned that we" – at this, Winslow glanced at Doss – "will go public with concerns that Hepaticin may be linked with cancer. If that happens, they want the right to terminate the contract."

"They want the contract to say that?" Wiseman's voice and facial expression conveyed his incredulity.

"No, they just want the contract to say they can tear up the contract at any time," Winslow explained. "But they made it clear that's why."

Wiseman again tapped his pen on his desktop again, thinking. He looked at Doss and asked, "Spence, where are we on this? I want to do this deal with Galaxy if we can, and I think you might be interested in heading the unit that handles this work, but we're not going to take money from Galaxy to buy our silence."

"That's a job I would love to have," Doss replied. "But our data suggest a strong connection between Hepaticin and adrenal cortical carcinoma. I met last week with the team from Galaxy, and they insisted I just had an anomaly – an unexplained cancer cluster that would fade away over time.

"They pointed out we didn't start having cases as soon as we should have if Hepaticin was responsible, and I don't have a good answer for that. They brought along a statistician, a young guy, and he claimed that we did not have a statistically significant association. They claimed we had nothing the FDA would act on, but that we could damage the product's reputation and cause some people who should be taking Hepaticin not to take it.

"And then, they said they want to work with us on other projects, provided I don't go public with my data."

"What do you think about the association?" Wiseman probed. "Is it real?   I want to know where your head is on this."

"Any doctor looking at the data I have would be concerned," Doss said. "Basically, you don't see this cancer in the older population. You see it in kids age 5 and younger. Those cases are genetic. And you see it again, for reasons no one can explain, in adults from about age 30 to about 40. We've got about the right number of cases, given our membership, in those age groups. And then, beginning two years ago, we start seeing cases in people over 60, mainly Medicare members, and most of them were taking Hepaticin."

"Did you review this with Ingrid?" Wiseman asked.

"She's having one of her people look at it, and she suggested I have Andy Berkowitz in MRA look at it too. She says he's a whiz with statistics. I'm meeting with him soon."

"Let me know what they say," Wiseman concluded. "Meanwhile, I want you to go back over everything. Make sure you're not overlooking something. And then we will have to make a hard decision."

Turning to Winslow, Wiseman added, "Good work. Thanks for bringing this to us. Push ahead on getting the data mining contract done."

"Shouldn't we," Winslow pushed back gently, "figure out if we're going to attack their biggest revenue producer before we put time and money into lawyers haggling over that contract?"

"No," Wiseman said. "Let's keep our options open. If we decide to take this to the FDA, Galaxy may find it harder to cancel the contract than it thinks. They would look like a bunch of schmucks if they cancel a research contract with us because we blew the whistle on a product that causes cancer."

SATURDAY, MARCH 5 – GARNER LAW OFFICE

Devin Garner considered his time in the office on Saturday mornings some of his most productive, and he usually looked forward to it. Except for the occasional client meeting, he seldom had any interruptions, and so he could think at length about any case that needed attention. But this Saturday morning, he had only reluctantly come to the office. He had just settled the two largest personal injury cases of his career – serious auto accidents, in which his clients had been badly injured. When the settlement checks cleared, he would have more money in his law firm account than he had ever had. He felt he deserved the weekend off.

But he needed to decide whether he wanted to take on litigation against a giant pharmaceutical company, claiming its blockbuster drug caused a rare cancer. To litigate that kind of case, he would need to invest a lot of money on expert witnesses, discovery, travel, court reporters, and all the other expenses of big ticket litigation. If he succeeded, it could lead to other highly profitable product liability cases and make his career. But if he took a case like that through trial and lost, he would be broke – worse, in debt up to his eyeballs.

Garner logged onto his computer, checked his email, and seeing nothing of interest, opened Google and searched for the FDA's MedWatch site – the site Dr. Patel had suggested. Google produced a link to the MedWatch site as its first offering. He clicked to it and moved around the site, getting his bearings.

He clicked on the tab for drugs and entered the name of a drug he knew had generated a lot of litigation –

Actos, which treated type 2 diabetes, but unexpectedly led to bladder cancer in quite a few patients. Patients filed something like 3,000 lawsuits against the drug maker. MedWatch produced links to the drug's label, to FDA committee hearings, and to various safety actions taken by the FDA.

The site explained how consumers and health professionals could submit reports of adverse events they suspected were caused by the drug, but it revealed nothing about the nature or substance of any reports that had been submitted – even the number of adverse event reports for the drug. Instead, the site contained a section in which the FDA boasted about how wonderfully transparent it was.

Garner went back to the site's search engine and entered "Hepaticin." The site immediately produced similar information for Hepaticin, but – given that the drug had a less troubled a history – it produced only a few links, and nothing of interest. Once again, the site did not disclose whether the FDA had received any reports of adverse events.

He logged off the MedWatch site and logged onto Google Scholar, where he searched again for medical journal articles that referred *both* to Hepaticin by its brand name or its chemical name *and* adrenal cortical carcinoma. He had tried this several times before and had found nothing. Once again, he came up with nothing. He broadened his search, looking for articles that mentioned *both* the drug *and* cancer. *Nothing.* Articles that mentioned *both* Hepaticin *and* tumors? *Nothing.* Hepaticin *and* oncogenic? *Nothing.*

Garner looked for articles dealing only with adrenal cortical carcinoma. He selected several articles discussing the nature or incidence of the cancer and printed them to study later.

He logged off Google and logged onto MedlinePlus, the medical research site offered by the National Library of Medicine. He repeated his searches, and once again found nothing of interest.

He decided it had been a mistake to come into the office. He deserved the day off. But as he was shutting down his computer and preparing to leave, his phone rang.

"Mr. Garner," the caller began. "My name is Sam Carson. I'm in chemotherapy with a client of yours, Dan Meinhardt. I took Hepaticin, and I have the same cancer he does."

"Dan mentioned you," Garner replied.

"I was wondering if we could meet. Perhaps you could join me for lunch at my club one day next week?

TUESDAY, MARCH 8 – LAW DEPARTMENT

Eileen Wang carefully sat her first coffee of the morning down on her desk. She proficiently logged on to her computer, entered her password, and then entered it again to log onto the company's network. When the computer was ready, she opened her email. Several email headers greeted her immediately, heralding the latest drug company settlement with the Department of Justice. Galaxy Pharmaceutical Company had settled criminal and civil charges of off-label marketing, hiding safety problems, and false claims for a record-shattering $5 billion.

Wang regularly listened to National Public Radio during her morning commute. From the broadcast, she had already caught the gist of the settlement, but she could now dig into the details important to lawyers.

But first, she couldn't resist reading the several news articles in her in-box, most of which compared the settlement with other drug company settlements over the last decade or so. Most of those settlements, she knew, stemmed from drug companies selling drugs "off label" – in other words, to treat conditions for which they had not been approved by the FDA. Most of those settlements also involved allegations that the drug companies paid thinly disguised kickbacks to doctors and buried evidence of unexpected side effects.

The litany was long. And for her, at least, familiar, because she tracked these investigations for the health plan, looking for opportunities to recover some of the money these schemes cost the company. The effort had been frustrating, because while the federal courts were quick to act on complaints from the federal government, most federal judges were extremely reluctant to allow health plans and others to sue drug companies for off-label marketing and other offenses.

The government had negotiated several settlements for hundreds of millions of dollars, but in 2009, Eli Lilly paid a whopping $1.4 billion for promoting Zyprexa for off-label uses and for not properly divulging side effects. That settlement was dwarfed later in 2009, when Pfizer entered a record-breaking settlement of $2.3 billion for marketing fraud related to Bextra, Lyrica, and other drugs.

Pfizer did not hold the record for long. In 2012, GlaxoSmithKline agreed to pay an even larger $3 billion settlement to wrap up Justice Department probes into kickbacks to doctors, off-label marketing of the antidepressant drug Paxil, and understating the safety risks of Avandia – the diabetes drug that caused heart attacks and strokes.

Actually, 2012 had been a banner year for the government. In addition to the record-setting GlaxoSmithKline settlement, Abbott Laboratories paid $1.5 billion to settle charges it had aggressively promoted the seizure drug Depakote for off-label use in elderly dementia patients.

In 2013, Johnson & Johnson settled for $2 billion after it got caught marketing its antipsychotic drugs Risperdal and a couple of other drugs off-label. Although not as eye-popping as Glaxo's $3 billion settlement, it was still a settlement for *billions* of dollars.

The articles uniformly gushed that the increasing size of the settlements indicated the Department of Justice was losing patience with the drug companies and coming down harder to force them to eliminate off-label marketing and kickbacks. The articles generally suggested that

J&J's $2 billion settlement and Glaxo's $3 billion settlement would force drug companies to change their errant ways.

That was just nonsense, Wang thought impatiently. *We'll know these settlements are forcing drug companies to change the way they do business when the drug companies cut the size of their sales staffs and remove money from their budgets for physician payments.*

Besides, she thought, *if DOJ really wanted to end to systemic violations, it would bring criminal charges against some of the business people involved. But that wasn't going to happen, because the drug companies owned too many Congressmen and senators, and those politicians had the power to slash DOJ budgets and hold up confirmation hearings for senior DOJ appointees. In any event, DOJ loved these big settlements and the headlines they generated.*

Wang turned her attention from the accounts of the older settlements to the documents released by the Department of Justice in connection with Galaxy's even larger, $5 billion settlement. She started with the Department's press release and the criminal information to which a Galaxy subsidiary had pled guilty, before studying the civil settlement. Altogether, the documents included the usual charges – off-label marketing, hiding safety problems, and false claims.

But in their public statements, Justice Department officials stressed it was particularly concerned by the extensive payments Galaxy had made to physicians in the form of speaking fees, retreats that featured more golf than seminars, and other gifts and payments. Justice Department officials went out of their way to disclose that its investigation had uncovered numerous internal emails and reports to the company's senior managers that not only detailed the extent of those payments, but stressed that the company was getting a "good return on its investment" in terms of the prescriptions these physicians and their colleagues wrote.

Wang forwarded a couple of the articles to Spencer Doss, calling his attention to the allegations of kickbacks to physicians. "This doesn't have anything to do with whether Hepaticin causes cancer, but it reminded me of your concern that some physicians might be prescribing an awful lot of Hepaticin. Of course, Galaxy's CEO says this is all in the past, and that Galaxy is now all about ethics."

***

Eileen Wang was not the only one that morning to pay particular attention to the splashy news of the Galaxy settlement.

At corporate headquarters, the Pharmacy VP, Brett Winslow, read the news stories and shook his head in amazement at the size of the settlement.

In his small law office in a blue-collar neighborhood on the west side of Cincinnati, Devin Garner nearly spilt his own coffee when he saw the settlement amount.

In Beijing, the Minister of the Public Security was also impressed by the size of the fine. "This company wants to increase its presence in our country," he reminded his subordinate in Shanghai, where Galaxy's Chinese subsidiary had its headquarters. "Are you on top of this?" he demanded.

TUESDAY, MARCH 8 – LAW DEPARTMENT

For Eileen Wang, the balance of her day slipped away through a series of meetings, phone calls and emails. *A week from now*, she thought, *she would not be able to remember what had kept her busy. She would have little to show for her efforts, except what appeared in her paycheck. Well, a paycheck was better than no paycheck. But life,* she thought, *should be about more than a paycheck.*

Ignoring several things more urgent but less interesting and important, she pulled up the reports generated by the programmer in the Spider unit and carefully studied the data.

Wang recognized the name of one of the doctors who was a top prescriber of Hepaticin – Sylvan Goldbach, M.D. Wang had met him once at a social function. He was old – approaching seventy, if not already past that benchmark – and bitter. She had heard he had been married several times and guessed he was still working to replenish savings depleted by divorce settlements. When he learned where Wang worked, he complained bitterly that HMOs treated physicians worse than Walmart treated its workers. Wang had wanted to suggest he might be happier if he got a job at Walmart, but had bit her tongue and excused herself to mingle elsewhere.

Wang forwarded the list of the top Hepaticin prescribers to the vice president of Network Contracting – the department whose people contracted with hospitals, physicians and all the other providers who agreed to accept lower payment rates in return for the higher patient volume that came with being in the company's networks. She captioned her email "Fraud Investigation" and typed "Attorney-Client Privilege, Attorney Work Product" across the top of the text field. In normal text, she asked if the physicians identified in the reports were network providers, and if so, if they were paid fee-for-service, percentage-of-premium, or some other way. If they were paid percentage-of-premium, she would need their contracts.

Then Wang had an interesting idea. She recalled that the Affordable Care Act – Obamacare – required drug companies to report payments to physicians – the idea being that opening the payments to public scrutiny might discourage drug companies from making and physicians from accepting the payments. When the government first made the "open payments" reports available to the public, The New York Times, The Wall Street Journal, and a few other media outlets ran stories on the many millions of dollars the drug companies had paid physicians in the initial months of reporting. The American Medical Association and some of the doctors who had gotten the most money complained bitterly the reports were misleading and unfair. But since then, the reporting had largely faded into the background.

Wang did some Google searches, which turned up scores of articles about the payments, but most appeared to be nothing more than re-writes of The New York Times and The Wall Street Journal reports. The Times had worked with a nonprofit organization called Pro Publica to analyze the payment data. On the Pro Publica site, she found a link to the government site that made the payment data available to the public. It took her some time to get familiar with how the government site was organized and how to search it, but with a little experimentation, she figured out how to run searches by physician.

She ran searches on each of the physicians who were on the list of top prescribers of Hepaticin. Not surprisingly, each of the top prescribers had received generous payments from the drug company. It took the better part of an hour, but she was able to download the list of Galaxy's payments to each physician. She used the data to compile a simple table of the payments each of the top prescribers had received from Galaxy by physician, by year.

As she studied the reports, she noticed that almost three years ago, Galaxy paid Dr. Goldbach to attend Galaxy's Hepaticin seminar at the Hotel Del Coronado on Coronado Island, near San Diego. *Nice*, Wang thought, *very nice.* The next year, Galaxy footed the bill for a seminar at The Broadmoor in Colorado Springs – again in late May. Last year, it had been The Cloister on Sea Island, Georgia. As expensive as those trips had been, the amounts were small compared with the total payments Galaxy had made to some of the physicians.

But perhaps because she was overdue for a vacation, Wang found herself intrigued by the lavish seminars at the famous – and famously expensive – resorts. She went through the payments to each of the other outliers and found most had gone to at least one of the lavish seminars. She added columns to her spreadsheet and marked whether the physician had gone to the San Diego, Colorado Springs or Sea Island seminars. Six of the physicians, including Dr. Goldbach, had gone to all three seminars.

Wang pulled up Maya Naidu's report showing which physicians had prescribed large amounts of Hepaticin and how much each had prescribed. Beyond the summary report, Naidu had included additional tabs that contained the raw data her report summarized. The additional sheets listed each Hepaticin prescription the physician had written, the date, how much the pharmacy had billed the health plan, and how much the health plan had paid.

Wang found the tab for Dr. Goldbach, and painstakingly added monthly totals to Naidu's Excel spreadsheet. Goldbach had been prescribing a fair amount of Hepaticin before he attended the first seminar, which may have been why he was invited in the first place. The amounts jumped considerably in the months after the seminar, and then soared. She repeated the exercise for each of the other physicians who had attended all three seminars, and the pattern repeated itself.

It was well past when she usually left the office – by now, she would usually have had dinner. But she was not about to leave. She turned to the lengthy report Naidu had created showing which physicians had diagnosed Non-Alcoholic Fatty Liver and Non-Alcoholic Steatohepatitis Disease – "NAFLD" and "NASH" – most often. Digging into the supporting data, Wang located each of the six physicians who had attended all three Galaxy-sponsored seminars. She repeated her month-by-month analysis. What she found was in some ways even more disturbing than the prescription data.

Each of the physicians had diagnosed a reasonable number of patients with NAFLD or NASH before attending the first seminar, but suddenly began diagnosing NASH much more often after the first seminar. And then – as with the Hepaticin prescriptions – they began diagnosing NASH even more frequently as the months went by. Evidently, when no one objected, they had become bolder.

She called Doss, but got his voice mail. Given the hour, that was no surprise. She left him a brief message, saying she was going to send him a spreadsheet she had put together. She asked him to call her in the morning so she could explain it. "I think you're going to find it pretty interesting."

WEDNESDAY, MARCH 9 – LUNCH WITH WANG

Following his usual morning office rituals, Spencer Doss turned on his computer, and while it was loading, checked his voice mails. He had an intriguing voice mail from Eileen Wang, left late the previous evening, telling him to check the email she was about to send him.

He scanned through the emails that had arrived since he left work the previous day and clicked on hers. The message said simply, "Attachment per my VM." He opened the attached spreadsheet, skimmed it, and dialed her number.

Wang explained what she had done and what the spreadsheet showed.

Doss listened intently, reading the spreadsheet as she explained it. "What this means," he concluded, "is that I owe you lunch. Can I buy you lunch today?"

"Just doing my job," Wang replied. "They pay me to work here too, you know."

"I know, but this took a lot of extra effort. You didn't have to do this. Besides, I've got to learn some place to get lunch besides the cafeteria."

"You don't like the cafeteria?" Wang asked. "I think it's pretty good for a company cafeteria."

"It's fine," Doss conceded. "I just don't want to eat there every day. Is there someplace else nearby where we can grab lunch?"

"Have you been to Skyline?"

"Skyline?"

"Skyline Chili," Wang explained. "If you're going to live in Cincinnati, you're going to have to learn about Skyline."

Just after noon, Doss met Wang in the lobby. On the short drive to the restaurant, Wang explained Skyline was a Cincinnati-based chain of fast food restaurants that feature Greek-style chili. "If you've been to a Greek restaurant and had spaghetti with meat sauce, then you'll recognize the taste."

Doss admitted he had never been to a Greek restaurant.

"As I understand it, Skyline was started by a Greek immigrant guy shortly after World War II. It apparently began as just another greasy spoon, but it caught on. It's only fast food, but it's addictive. People in Cincinnati love it. There are Skylines all over the city. It's as much as a part of Cincinnati as Fountain Square. But it's confusing for people from out of town, because when we think of chili, we think of Tex-Mex chili."

At the restaurant, Wang explained the main dish was spaghetti topped with chili and shredded cheddar cheese. "They call that a three-way. You can have it with beans or diced onions. That's a four way. Or, you can have it with beans *and* onions – a five way."

Doss spotted the pictures and prices for three-, four- and five-ways on the menu.

"You don't have to have that. They also serve Coneys and some other things."

"Coneys?"

"I guess that comes from Coney Island," Wang said. "It's a small hot dog on a bun, topped with mustard, chili, shredded cheese, and onions. You can ask them to leave off what you don't want."

A waitress appeared and placed two small bowls of Oyster crackers on the table, along with napkins and forks, and took their soft drink orders.

Doss asked Wang what she made of the information she had sent him.

"Not sure, to tell you the truth," Wang conceded. "Maybe Galaxy just convinced them Hepaticin is really great, and everybody should be taking it. We should just put it in the water."

"Is that what you think happened?"

"No, I think it has to do with MRA. My hunch is …"

"Help!" Doss interjected, before she could continue. "I'm struggling with all the acronyms around here. What's 'MRA'?"

"Medicare Risk Adjustment. This is really important, and they don't explain any of this to you guys – to our medical directors. I'm going to give you the two-minute version, and then I'll send you some articles with more background."

The waitress placed their drinks on the table and took their orders. Wang ordered a three-way. Doss decided to follow her lead, but asked for a Coney as well. "If I'm going to live here," he explained.

While waiting for their orders to arrive – which took only a couple minutes – Wang continued her explanation. "In our Medicare Advantage plans," she said, "CMS adjusts what it pays us based on the health status of the enrollee."

Doss knew "CMS" referred to the Centers for Medicare and Medicaid Services, the agency that ran Medicare

– and that had famously botched the rollout of Obamacare.

Wang hesitated, then corrected herself. "Actually, it's more complicated than that. The law requires CMS to adjust what it pays Medicare Advantage plans to take into account a number of demographic factors – age, gender, and so on. CMS also has to make geographic adjustments, because medical expense varies so much around country. The idea is to pay approximately what Original Medicare would spend for an average member with the same demographic profile, who lives in the same part of the country.

"It used to be," Wang continued, "health plans all tried to sign up the healthiest people. PacifiCare used to be famous for signing up Medicare beneficiaries at gyms. Congress responded by changing the law, and now CMS has to try to account for health status."

"The idea makes sense," Doss offered, to show he was following, "but that can't be easy to do."

"They came up with a bunch of categories, groups of similar medical conditions. They call them Hierarchical Health Conditions or HHC's. They pay us extra if the enrollee has any of those conditions. If someone has diabetes, they pay us so many dollars a month more for that individual, and if someone else has leukemia, they pay us a different amount a month for that person. It might be $100 a month for one condition, maybe $600 for something else."

"That doesn't sound like very much."

"It adds up when you've got a couple million Medicare enrollees, and you multiply the monthly add-on by twelve months. Remember," Wang stressed, "the great majority of our revenue comes from Medicare. We're talking hundreds of millions of dollars each year in Medicare Risk Adjustment payments."

Doss was suitably impressed. "That's a lot of money."

"But the government has come up with all kinds of rules to make sure no one cheats. I guess you have to expect a bunch of arbitrary rules when you leave it up to bureaucrats to manage something like this.

"The gist is, doctors and hospitals are supposed to put the appropriate diagnoses on their claims forms. We take the information from their claims to determine what conditions their patients have. For the most part, providers are still paid on a fee-for-service basis. A doctor gets paid $150 or whatever for an average office visit, no matter what the diagnosis is. It's the same payment if the person has the flu or diabetes or – or fatty liver."

"That's how Medicare paid my practice," Doss acknowledged.

"The doctor and his billing clerk have no incentive to make sure all of the appropriate diagnoses are captured on the claim form. It's all the same to them if the claim form says 'flu' or if it also lists morbid obesity, diabetes, high cholesterol, high blood pressure, and fatty liver. So, we have a small army of people who check medical records to make sure we're capturing all of the diagnoses that 'risk adjust' – that result in our getting paid more."

"And that's what the MRA unit does?"

"Yes. But checking medical records is expensive. They have a unit that does all sorts of statistical analyses to determine which patients' and which doctors' records are most likely to be worth reviewing."

"My Dad used to say, 'You learn something new every day,'" Doss said smiling. "I guess I can home now."

Wang chuckled. "Not if you want to find out what my theory is."

"That's right, you had a hunch what these guys were doing had to do with MRA."

"Pretty clearly, something happened at that first seminar to get these guys to start prescribing this drug out the whazoo in their Medicare Advantage patients.

"My hunch," Wang continued, "is some of these doctors got to talking – over lunch or something – and one of them came up with the bright idea that if they diagnosed their overweight Medicare Advantage patients with fatty liver disease, the MRA payment would be more. And if they were prescribing Hepaticin, we would see they weren't just diagnosing fatty liver, they were treating it. That way, we wouldn't catch them, or at least, we wouldn't be able to prove they were just making a lot of these diagnoses up out of thin air."

Doss thought about what Wang was suggesting. "So, these guys are diagnosing fatty liver to get paid more, and prescribing Hepaticin to cover their tracks, but unfortunately for their patients, Hepaticin triggers a rare cancer in some small percentage of patients."

"Seriously, you should talk with Andy Berkowitz in MRA. He's very clever, and he does a lot of statistical work. He's one of those extremely high energy people, who are really smart, but are just always going in a thousand directions, bouncing off the walls. But if you can get him to focus on what we're looking at, he may be very helpful."

"It might be helpful if the two of us could meet with him."

"I'd love to, but I've got to go down to Florida. We identified a doctor down there who was inflating his MRA scores with phony diagnoses. We turned him in to the U.S. Attorney, and the feds are prosecuting him. I'm going down to sit in on part of the trial. I want to see how it plays out, and we need someone handy in case the attorneys trying the case for government need help with something."

The waitress returned with their food. After serving their dishes, she asked Doss if he wanted a bib.

He tasted his food and rated it, "Not bad!"

"It grows on you," Wang cautioned.

Doss decided to ask Wang something he had wanted to ask since he first met her. "You speak English very well, but you have a slight accent. Did your parents come here from China?"

"Yes," Wang said, "before I was born. My parents spoke Chinese at home, and so did many of their friends. I learned English from a tutor and in school, and by the time I was nine or ten, I was translating for them when we went to the store or they had to go to the doctor – the stereotypical immigrant story." She took a bite of her lunch, swallowed, and added, "They speak English now, but it was harder for them to learn than for me. Kids pick up language easy."

"Do you speak Chinese?"

"Yes, I can speak some Mandarin, but I have trouble reading it. They've simplified the calligraphy some, but it is very hard to get proficient. It's basically all memorization. You can't sound it out like English."

"So why are you working for an HMO? There must be a lot of big law firms and corporations that would love to hire a University of Michigan Law School graduate who speaks Mandarin Chinese.”

"Some days I ask myself that question. But to do that, I would need to be better at reading calligraphy. Besides, I'm really American. I worked in a law firm the usual three years as an associate. Then, I saw this opening, and it sounded interesting. I knew there's a lot of money in healthcare, and I thought it would be a good opportunity.”

"Nobody told you HMOs are cheapskates?”

"Not before I took the job.” Grinning, she added, "But some doctors have mentioned that to me since.”

As they were leaving, Doss noticed the restaurant had a stack of tee shirts and sweatshirts on sale, with the Skyline Chili logo and the slogan, "Nothing says love like a 3 way.”

"Don't go there,” Wang laughed. "Don't even think about buying one of those.”

THURSDAY, MARCH 10 – BERKOWITZ MEETING

Andy Berkowitz, a lanky thirty-something, entered the small conference room in a hurry – apologizing to Doss for being late, while continuing to check his smart phone for messages. When he had taken a seat and put away his smart phone, he smiled broadly and signaled he was ready.

Doss handed Berkowitz the PowerPoint deck concerning what he still believed was an excess in cases of adrenal cortical carcinoma in plan members taking Hepaticin. "I don't know if this has anything to do with Medicare Risk Adjustment," Doss began, "but Eileen Wang suggested I touch base with you and see if you have any thoughts or suggestions, or can help me. Eileen and – and, well, pretty much everyone – says you're wicked smart, and a whiz with statistics."

"Thanks," Berkowitz scoffed, while flipping rapidly through the PowerPoint deck, "but if I'm so smart, how come all those people make more than I do?"

It was an old joke, but Doss smiled anyway. He walked Berkowitz through what he had done, the number of cases of adrenal cortical carcinoma the plan had seen in each of the previous five years, and the number of those that had taken Hepaticin.

"I asked the prescribing physicians." Doss continued, "to report their cases to the FDA, to MedWatch. To do that, I got a list of the prescribers and their addresses, along with the names of their patients who took Hepaticin and developed this cancer. It turns out some of the prescribers had two or three patients."

Berkowitz raised his eyebrows in an exaggerated gesture. "You're thinking – given how unusual this cancer is, even among people who are taking this drug – these guys must be prescribing an awful lot of this stuff."

"Exactly. In fact, I had the Spider unit pull the data for every Hepaticin claim we've gotten. The report ranked the prescribers by how much they prescribed. The guy who prescribed Hepaticin for the first two cases I saw – he was in the top 50 prescribers of this drug in our whole network three years running. So were some of other guys who had two or more patients with this cancer."

"You're wondering why they are prescribing so much more of this drug than other doctors."

"Exactly."

Berkowitz tapped his fingers on the table top. "How much do you know about what we do in MRA?"

"Not much, actually," Doss replied. "Eileen gave me a two-minute overview and sent me some articles. But I was hoping we could talk about what you do."

Berkowitz jumped up and went to the inevitable conference room white board. "You understand that we look for HCC's – for conditions that we get paid more for?"

Doss remembered the idea of HCC's less from Wang's high level explanation than from the articles she had sent him. An "HCC" was a "Hierarchical Health Condition" – the bureaucratic name for the couple hundred categories of diagnoses for which the Centers for Medicare and Medicaid Services, or CMS, would pay the Medicare Advantage plan more.

"Yeah," Doss said. "Eileen said that's where you come in. She explained that doctors and their billing people don't have much incentive to make sure they submit all of the conditions the patient may have, because they get paid by procedure – by office visit, or whatever. You figure out which medical records are most likely to give us diagnoses that weren't on the claims – diagnoses that will result in our being paid more."

"That used to be all we did," Berkowitz agreed. "Well, that and look for records that were likely to have wrong information – diagnoses the patient didn't actually have – so we weren't submitting junk to the government.

"But now we've got a lot of doctors who are paid percentage-of-premium, and we discovered that we had to think about the possibility some providers might be gaming the system."

"Percentage of premium?"

"We've got primary care physicians who see a lot of our Medicare members. Some of them only see our Medicare members. If they're willing, we pay them a percentage of what we get from Medicare. This is just for primary care practices. We still pay the claims, but they are financially responsible for all of the medical expenses for their patients, including specialists and hospitals, subject to a cap. We settle with them after the end of the year, and either we owe them money, or they owe us. It forces them to think about how to keep their patients well, instead of about how many ways they can run up charges."

"Basically, a form of capitation," Doss said.

"Yes," Berkowitz agreed, "but by paying them all the same percentage of what we get from Medicare, there is less haggling over what we should pay them, plus we give them an incentive to make sure they include all the diagnoses that 'risk adjust' – that pay us more."

"Good thing, right?"

"Up to a point. But South Florida, where we have a lot of this, isn't the Midwest. Eventually, we figured out that some of these practices were committing fraud. When we audited the medical records, our MRA staff started noticing there was nothing in the medical record indicating the patient had some of the conditions we were seeing on the encounters."

"Encounters?" Doss asked.

"Sorry. When practices are paid fee-for-service, they submit claims. The patient comes in for an office visit, the doctor charts the visit, notes the diagnoses on the chart, and the back office sends us a claim. When practices are capitated, or paid percentage of premium, they send in all the same information, but they aren't asking to be paid for the office visit, so we call it an 'encounter.'"

By this point, Berkowitz had drawn a diagram on the conference room white board with little drawings representing an office visit, a medical record, a claim form, and a box labelled "Health Plan" – each connected by arrows, with a final arrow extending from the health plan box to another labeled "CMS" – the universal acronym for the Centers for Medicare and Medicaid Services.

"We figured out that we had to start auditing charts to make sure it didn't occur to somebody to have their back- office billing clerks add some diagnosis codes to their encounters simply to gin up more revenue."

"The concern being," Doss summarized, "they would submit diagnoses that the patients don't actually have, and we would pass the phony diagnoses along to the government, and the government would pay us extra. We would get money we were not entitled to."

"Right! The government gets ticked off when they find out that's happened – usually because we catch one of these guys, but sometimes, because someone files a whistleblower lawsuit before we discover the problem. Eileen can tell you all about that.

"It's frustrating," Berkowitz complained, "because when we discover a problem like this, right away, people assume we encouraged the doctor, or should have caught him. In any event, we have deep pockets, so we're somehow to blame."

"I've seen some of articles about that," Doss said, "but they weren't very clear about what was actually going on."

"The news media never get this right," Berkowitz agreed. "In any event, we started spot checking to make sure that the diagnoses were charted in the medical record."

"Problem solved?"

"For about five minutes. Then, we realized some of the bad guys were still a step ahead of us. The smarter bad guys would actually put these conditions in the patient's chart, so we couldn't prove they were only using these diagnoses just to gin up more revenue."

His disbelief obvious, Doss asked, "You're saying a patient comes in for an office visit, and the doctor writes in the chart that the patient has diabetes, or cancer, or something – just makes it up?"

"It's usually not something that obvious. Maybe the patient has diabetes, but the doctor puts 'diabetes with peripheral neuropathy' in the chart. That pays more than uncomplicated diabetes. Maybe the patient has depression, which doesn't pay, and the doctor charts manic depression, which does. But yeah, there were a tiny handful of doctors who were just making stuff up."

"But if you go in and check the patient's medical record," Doss restated what he understood Berkowitz to be saying, "it's in the chart. It's documented."

"Exactly!"

"I don't see how the government expects you to catch that."

"That's where our heads were too," Berkowitz agreed, "until we did a deep dive. We started with some doctors we were pretty sure were cooking the books – usually because someone in the practice tipped us off.

"To demonstrate that the practice was creating diagnoses, or exaggerating them, we did a statistical analysis to show to what extent these guys were outliers in terms of what other primary care doctors around the state were diagnosing. These guys diagnosed some of these conditions so often they were more than two standard deviations from the norm."

"You were concerned," Doss asked, "if they were such extreme outliers, the government would say we should have known?"

"Right, although at the time, the government was not looking at that. We were light years ahead of the government on this."

"Interesting."

"Stay with me," Berkowitz said. "I'm almost at the point I need to make."

Doss motioned for Berkowitz to continue.

"Then it occurred to us to flip the analysis. Instead of waiting until we had a whistleblower, we started looking for extreme outliers."

Doss shook his head in amazement. "I had no idea any of this was going on."

"If a physician was an extreme outlier, we suspected fraud, but we still didn't have any proof," Berkowitz proceeded with his story. "So, we started looking to see if the doctor was actually treating these patients for whatever he's diagnosing. Suppose he has more manic depressives than any other doctor in the state. We had to start looking to see if he was treating more than a handful of those patients for manic depression. Was he prescribing lithium or another drug? Was he sending them for psychiatric consults? Or was he ignoring the diagnosis because he knew the diagnosis was bogus?"

"Is that a real example?" Doss asked.

"One hundred percent! Ask Eileen."

"I will."

"Here's where I'm going with this. Since then, we've developed a program based on a series of algorithms to identify what we call 'suspicious outliers.' Let me see if we have any doctors whose pattern of diagnosing fatty liver is suspicious. I'll also see if I can identify physicians are suspicious outliers in terms of their pattern of prescribing this drug. We've never looked at that before."

"Isn't that just going to give me the same names I've already identified?" Doss asked.

"If we were just looking for statistical outliers, yes. But our analysis looks for a combination of things. We do look for statistical outliers – doctors who are diagnosing a condition more than other doctors in the same specialty.

But we also look to see if the physician, for no apparent reason, all of sudden begins diagnosing more of a condition that risk adjusts. Or multiple conditions that risk adjust. We've got some other triggers. Plus, we've got safeguards built in to make sure we're not focusing on something there's an obvious explanation for. So, we're really not looking simply for statistical outliers. We're looking for what we call 'suspicious outliers.' The government really likes what we're doing."

"I thought I read," Doss replied, "the government investigated the company, or maybe still is, for how it handles MRA."

"You have to talk to Eileen about that, but as I understand it, there's an advocacy group in D.C. that wants government health care for everyone. So, every time we or another Medicare plan catch a doctor cheating and report him, this organization issues a press release saying the new incident is further proof that Medicare Advantage plans are ripping off the government.

"And whenever it issues a new press release, Senator Grassley issues his own statement, repeating what the advocacy group said as if it were his idea. I don't think they really understand how MRA works, or even want to. But Senator Grassley chairs the Judiciary Committee. With him pressuring DOJ, it didn't have any choice but to conduct an investigation.

"Besides, you know how it is. The government is always trying to extort a big settlement from drug companies, health insurers, and the other usual suspects. They like the headlines, and it justifies their budgets."

FRIDAY, MARCH 11 – PHARMACY DEPART-MENT

Brett Winslow's morning began with an unpleasant surprise. A brief story on an inside page of The Wall Street Journal reported that two large private equity firms had liquidated their holdings in Galaxy Pharmaceutical Company and were now shorting the company's stock. According to the newspaper account, the firms were acting on rumors the Galaxy's blockbuster fatty liver drug, Hepaticin, had been linked to multiple cases of a rare cancer, some fatal. A spokesman for Galaxy adamantly denied the rumors, blaming them on the short sellers.

The story, Winslow surmised, had been leaked by the private equity firms themselves. He knew that when a speculator "shorted" a company's stock, it was selling shares it didn't own for delivery at a later date, hoping to purchase the shares before the delivery date – to complete the sale – at a lower price. The speculator made money only if the stock's price dropped – as Galaxy's stock would if word got out that its most successful product was causing an often-fatal cancer.

But it wasn't enough that the price of the stock would *eventually* fall. The speculator had to deliver the shares by a specific date. Therefore, the speculator made money only if the stock's price dropped *before* the speculator had to go into the market and purchase the shares it had sold.

The Wall Street guys, Winslow figured, had somehow learned about the link between Hepaticin and cancer, and shorted Galaxy's stock, hoping to make a profit when word of the link got out. When their short sales were about to expire and word had not gotten out, they stood to lose their investment. So, they had leaked the bad news themselves – thus, guaranteeing Galaxy's stock would drop in time for them to cash in.

Anybody used to reading the financial press would figure out that much in a New York minute, Winslow thought. But what he wanted to know was: *How did the private equity firms find out about this link, or possible link, between Hepaticin and this cancer? Was Doss right – were other people seeing it too? Or, had Doss leaked it? One thing was clear,* Winslow was certain, *the Galaxy people would be infuriated.*

Winslow checked his email. As he expected, he had an email from his counterpart at Galaxy requesting – emphatically – that Winslow call him immediately.

Winslow braced himself and placed the call.

His counterpart at Galaxy delivered a message, which Winslow assumed had been carefully scripted by the company's lawyers and management: First, Galaxy would proceed with the rebate agreement it had signed, but it was putting the data mining agreement, which the lawyers were still haggling over, on hold. Secondly, Galaxy expected the health plan to conduct a thorough investigation to determine who tipped off these private equity firms to speculation about a *possible* link between Hepaticin and cancer. Finally, Galaxy wanted to know: *Would the health plan be willing to issue a statement that it had indeed investigated whether such a link existed, but had found no evidence supporting such a link?*

Winslow's counterpart claimed that people "very high up" in Galaxy wanted to sue, and he was trying to talk them out of it, but he wasn't sure how long he could hold them off. If Winslow wanted to have any chance of avoiding litigation, he needed to get back to him quickly with what the health plan was willing to do.

Winslow recognized that threat as a negotiating ploy, designed to get his attention, but he dutifully conveyed the message in a series of phone calls: first to the company's General Counsel; next, to the head of Communications; and finally, to Robert Wiseman, the Chief Medical Officer. Winslow made it clear that he hoped, at a bare minimum, that he would be able to tell Galaxy the health plan would conduct a thorough investigation. Better still, he hoped he could tell Galaxy that Doss had been suspended pending the outcome of the investigation.

Eileen Wang also saw the story. She alerted Spencer Doss about it only moments before Doss got the inevitable call from his boss.

"Did you share your concerns about Hepaticin," Wiseman demanded, "with anyone outside our company?"

"Only with the team from Galaxy."

"Are you certain?" Wiseman insisted. "You didn't mention this to a girlfriend? To your broker, your lawyer, your brother-in-law? To somebody in a bar?"

"No, no one," Doss insisted. "But if I could figure out that this cancer was occurring in people taking this drug, we have to assume someone else could have figured that out as well. Besides, for all we know, someone inside Galaxy could have leaked this."

"I don't want to know who else *could* have leaked it. I just need to know that *you* didn't."

"You have my word on it," Doss repeated, but refused to stop. "Bob, think about it. It could have been one of the prescribing physicians, or one of the oncologists.

We've got an oncologist here in Cincinnati who has treated three people who took Hepaticin and developed this cancer. I'm sure there are other possibilities. All I know is, it didn't come from me."

While that conversation was going on, Eileen Wang was having a tense conversation with her own boss, the company's General Counsel.

"Yes, I've met Doss," Wang told the company's top lawyer. "He's spoken with me several times about his concerns about the number of people who have contracted this cancer while taking this drug."

"Did he leak this?"

"I don't think so. He was really concerned this drug was making people sick. But he's a doctor, not a finance guy. If he was going to share this, he would have shared it with the FDA. Or, he would have written it up and sent it to a medical journal. I don't see him giving – or selling – this information to someone on Wall Street."

"Who else knew about his concerns?"

"He briefed Brett Winslow and Bob Wiseman. They had him brief a team from Galaxy. I sat in on that. He's asked Ingrid Berg for help from one of her people – for statistical analysis. I think she's got one of her people looking at the data. I suggested he speak to Andy Berkowitz – the statistics whiz in MRA. And like I said, he has been talking to me at each step."

"Have IT do an investigation. Line up an outside law firm to conduct an independent investigation, but let's not have them do anything substantial until we see where this is going. They probably can't do much anyway until we get the email."

"Will do."

"And keep me posted. I want to know right away if you find anything."

Wang hung up and made her next call to Liz Kolinsky, the head of the small team in IT that handled forensic IT investigations. She and Kolinsky had worked together on a number of previous investigations.

Wang explained the problem and requested Kolinsky and her team pull emails from everyone who knew of the concerns Doss had expressed about Hepaticin.

"We need to find out who all knew about this," Wang explained, "and if any of them leaked this outside the company."

"I know the drill," Kolinsky assured her. "Do you have the names of the people you already know Doss discussed this with? It will speed things up."

"I will email you a list of everyone I know of. And Liz, my name is going to be on that list."

"Oh good, we'll get to read your email."

"You are looking for communications with the outside, so you need to check phone records too, if that's possible."

"On it."

SATURDAY, MARCH 12 – PUBLIC SECURITY BUREAU

Alerted by his staff to The Wall Street Journal article, Qian Jie, the head of the Public Security Bureau in Shanghai, arrived at his office very early Saturday morning. His first order of business was to let his boss, Guo Shengkun, know that, *yes, he was aware of this disturbing new allegation about Galaxy's leading product*. He assured his testy superior he would incorporate this new development into his growing investigation.

His next order of business was to summon his own lead investigators, demanding they make a priority of finding out what they could about this newest allegation. He rattled off the obvious questions: *Had the hospitals in the Shanghai district seen this cancer in patients taking this drug? Did the low-level Galaxy employees they had been squeezing for information know anything about this? Was there anything about this in the email traffic between the managers of Galaxy China and their bosses in London?*

With that, he dismissed the rest of his team, but asked his chief deputy to remain.

"It is time," he instructed his deputy, "to execute the plan we have been discussing."

SATURDAY, MARCH 12 – MRA UNIT

When in the office on weekends, Andy Berkowitz was able to do something he could not do during the week: He could shut his office door and turn up the volume on the Bose player that sat on the corner of his credenza and play the hard rock music he found helpful to concentrating.

This morning, he was glad of that luxury. This new project energized him. It was something a little different, and it was challenging. But it was more than that. This was not about making money for his employer. It was about trying to find out if some doctors were diagnosing conditions they knew their patients didn't have, just to line their own pockets. And not just that, but – *to cover their tracks, these pricks prescribed this drug to treat a non-existent illness. And then, fuck-all, the drug causes their unsuspecting patients to get cancer.*

Well, maybe it did.

Thinking about it made him mad. He couldn't sit still. He got up and paced back and forth until he had worked out exactly how he was going to approach the problem.

He decided to tackle the diagnosis issue first, because he already had a tool for that. Well, not a tool in the conventional sense, but a program he and his team had built and de-bugged. He was used to working with it.

The program was designed to detect providers who were suspiciously diagnosing conditions that risk adjusted – meaning Medicare paid more for those conditions. Non-Alcoholic Fatty Liver Disease, or NAFLD, did not "risk adjust." So, he would ignore NAFLD and focus instead on

Non-Alcoholic Steatohepatitis, or NASH, which did risk adjust.

He looked up Non-Alcoholic Steatohepatitis in the International Classification of Diseases Manual, 9th Edition or ICD-9, which assigned a number to every conceivable medical condition. Physicians – actually, their billing clerks – used these numbers to indicate the diagnosis on their claim and encounter forms. Numbers removed the ambiguity that would arise if doctors used text descriptions of conditions, and thus made it possible for health plans to use computers to process claims. Without that, the whole system would not function.

The government had set a deadline of October 1, 2015 for the whole health care system to switch to the next generation of classification, the tenth edition or ICD-10. The new system was more detailed and used alpha-numeric designations. Some providers, however, had switched to ICD-10 early, so they would have time to work out any problems before the deadline. He looked up the number for Non-Alcoholic Steatohepatitis in the new system as well.

He then opened his "suspicious provider" program, plugged in 571.8, the ICD-9 number for Non-Alcoholic Steatohepatitis, and K75.8, the ICD-10 alpha-numeric. He directed the program to search claims with those diagnoses submitted by physicians. The program would run over night. He would have the results on Monday, or if the system got bogged down, later in the week.

That completed, Berkowitz dashed down the hall to the snack area and got a Diet Pepsi and a bag of pretzels. On the way back, juggling the can of soda, bag of pretzels, and his cell phone, he checked for messages. There was only one that wasn't spam. It was from his girlfriend wanting to know if he was going to work all day. He didn't know.

Back in his office, he cranked up the volume on the CD player and turned to the more challenging part of the project – looking for physicians who were "suspicious prescribers" in terms of how often they prescribed Hepaticin.

He pulled up the data base someone in the SPDR unit had assembled. It had every prescription for Hepaticin for which the health plan had received a claim. He studied how the data base was structured, then brought up his outlier program and modified it to search for a drug instead of a diagnosis. He made a number of additional modifications to eliminate certain of the algorithms that made sense only in the context of medical diagnoses and to add some new ones that he thought might make sense in the context of prescriptions.

That approach was not entirely satisfactory, as he had not tested the new algorithms against larger data sets, nor had he – in a single sitting – been able to create the sophisticated algorithms he and his team could construct with experimentation and more time. But if this trial worked, he would put doing that on his team's ever-growing "do someday when we're not so busy" list.

Just as he couldn't search for the name of a medical condition, but instead had to look for its ICD-9 or ICD-10 number, he could not search for a drug by name. He looked up the National Drug Classification or NDC numbers for Hepaticin and entered the list into his program.

Berkowitz ordered the program to run. Given that he did not need to search the whole prescription drug claims system, but only the data base the programmer in the SPDR unit had created off line, he could run the search right away. He didn't need to wait for the claims system to run it overnight.

He did an air drum roll, and that quick he had ... *gibberish*.

He reviewed his programming and found the error. He checked the programming again, and found another.

He tried the program once more, and this time, it generated a well-behaved report that listed, by year, the physicians the program's algorithms identified as suspicious prescribers.

The "suspicious prescribers" and their order on the reports varied a bit from year-to-year, but for the most part, the same names occurred each year. He knew he was onto something.

But for the moment, he had to wait until the system had time to run the suspicious provider reports for physicians who were – at least according to the program's algorithms – suspicious in terms of the frequency and pattern with which they diagnosed NASH. He was convinced the same physicians' names would populate those reports, but he had to wait for the reports to run to know for certain.

MONDAY, MARCH 14 – MRA UNIT

On Monday morning, Berkowitz had a dental appointment and after that, he had a lengthy meeting for which he was almost late. From there, he went straight to the cafeteria to have lunch, as usual, with several members of his own team.

When he finally arrived at his office, the NASH reports were in his email in-box. These were the reports that listed the physicians who were, in his terms, "suspicious" in the frequency and pattern with which they diagnosed NASH. To oversimplify somewhat, they were "suspicious" if they had suddenly started diagnosing NASH far more than other physicians in their specialty in their state.

The reports identified suspicious outliers in three states – Florida, Texas, and Ohio. Those states, perhaps not coincidentally, were the states in which the heath plan, and Medicare Advantage plans generally, had the most primary care physicians under percentage-of-premium contracts. Each of the three states, moreover, had several suspicious outliers.

He checked and was not surprised to see that, for the most part, the suspicious outliers – the physicians who triggered his program because of the pattern of their NASH diagnoses – were also "suspicious prescribers" of Hepaticin. *Now, he was more certain than ever he was on to something.*

Berkowitz forwarded a copy of the "suspicious providers" report to the woman who served as director for the small army of nurses and certified coders who audited medical records for compliance with the Medicare Risk Adjustment rules. He asked her to have her troops pull those physicians' medical records and do the usual MRA audits, but to give special attention to NASH diagnoses.

"Please," he instructed her, "don't just look to see if the doctor put NASH in the chart. For this one, we need to have your people look to see if there is anything in the chart that prompted the NASH diagnosis or that would support or contraindicate the diagnosis. This is a fraud investigation, so we don't want to tip off these doctors. Legal is hot to trot and insists that you make this a priority. You know how it is with Legal. Everything is ASAP. Be a sport."

He re-read the email and then added a PS: "Not sure if you've audited these fine physicians in the past, but have someone take a peek and see if you already have medical records for any of their patients from last year or two years ago. Luv to be able to give our legal eagles some nourishment while they wait for your full report."

The Law Department had not in fact requested any such thing, but Berkowitz knew that people responded quicker if the request came from Legal. Once the medical records arrived, if they contained nothing useful, no one would remember his request; and if they turned up evidence of fraud – *well, then the lawyers would take credit.*

Berkowitz opened another email and sent the two sets of reports – the Hepaticin suspicious prescriber reports from Saturday and the new NASH "suspicious providers" reports – to Dr. Doss. Since he had claimed the Law Department was involved, he decided to copy Eileen Wang as well. He explained what the reports showed and made the usual request that they let him know if they had any questions.

"I am going to be very interested," he told Wang in a separate email, "to learn what you do with these analyses, and if they lead to anything."

MONDAY, MARCH 14 – DATA CENTER

As in many large companies, the health plan's email system automatically routed a copy of every email the health plan's employees sent or received to a collection of servers in the health plan's secure Data Center. Liz Kolinsky liked to say she probably had a copy of every email sent to anybody in the health plan *before* they did.

She now directed one of the forensic IT specialists on her team to pull the emails sent to or received by any of the people on the list she had gotten from Eileen Wang in the Law Department. She instructed him to check to see if they had forwarded or shared the information about the potential association with anyone else, inside the company or outside.

She directed another member of her team to pull phone logs, which would show the phone numbers of everyone the people on the list had called. Except for callers who blocked caller identification, the logs would also identify the phone numbers from which they had received calls. Once they had those lists, they would run them through a program that would identify who owned the numbers – unless the call was from a throw-away cell phone. If one of the employees on this list had spoken to someone with a throw-away cell phone during this period – *well, that would narrow the investigation in a hurry.*

Kolinsky sent a message to the IT service staff to collect the hard drives from the company-owned computers of each person on the list. The IT staff would pull the hard drives, make a copy for the employee, and send her the original. Sometimes, she had to have that done without the employee knowing about it, but there was no point in keeping this investigation secret.

Once she had them, Kolinsky would put the hard drives in a vault in case it became necessary to subject them to forensic examination for telltale deletions. For the same reason, she also directed the local IT staff to replace the company-supplied cell phone of each person on the list, and to bring her the originals.

Kolinsky called Eileen Wang to update her on the steps she had initiated. While she had Wang on the phone, she asked Wang to walk her through how the private equity firms would make money by shorting the drug company's stock.

Wang explained that the private equity firms had somehow learned the drug was linked to this cancer. Then they placed what amounted to a big bet that the drug company's stock would fall when news of the problem surfaced. When word didn't get out on its own, Wang said, the private equity firms probably helped things along by leaking the story to The Wall Street Journal.

"Wouldn't the feds be all over something like that?" Kolinsky asked.

"We will probably get a subpoena from the SEC – the Securities Exchange Commission. It's possible the FBI or DOJ will get involved. But it will probably be impossible for them to prove how these firms learned about the problem. I'll be surprised if they can build a case."

"I've got very mixed feelings about this," Kolinsky confessed. "You know I had breast cancer two years ago. Mastectomy, chemo, radiation, the whole deal."

"I remember that."

"If this drug is causing people to get cancer," Kolinsky said, "I don't think anybody should be sitting on that information. I've had cancer, and I feel pretty strongly about that."

"Understandably," Wang said.

"But if somebody got this information – and I don't care how they got it – if they held onto it so they could make a bunch of money in the stock market," Kolinsky said. "Well, I think they are lower than dirt."

TUESDAY, MARCH 15 – PRIVATE CLUB, CIN-CINNATI

Devin Garner had never been to any of the exclusive, members-and-guests-only private clubs where the elite of the Cincinnati business community lunched and conducted business. Sam Carson, who lunched in those private clubs often before retiring as a senior vice president from one of Cincinnati's largest banks, had chosen a club in which he was a member for lunch. Garner was excited to be invited into this enclave, where the city's elite went to see friends and do business – and to be seen.

"Devin, I'm going to be candid with you," Carson began, after the waiter delivered their orders. "I've called some of the law firms I'm familiar with – the big firms that represent the bank. They all represent Galaxy, or regularly represent other drug companies. They all told me they had conflicts and could not represent me."

Garner was not surprised.

"They also told me," Carson continued, "that they didn't think I have a case."

The older man, who was showing the effects of chemotherapy, was not touching his food, but took a sip of water.

"They gave me the names of some of the leading plaintiff lawyers who do this work. They told me that if I was going to pursue this, I should hire one of them, because they could afford to bankroll a case like this. They assured me those guys would drum up a lot of publicity, run ads, and sign up so many cases Galaxy couldn't possibly try all the cases and would have to settle. The merits of the case wouldn't matter."

Carson picked up his fork and put it back down.

"They also told me those guys were a bunch of sociopaths, and not to trust them."

Garner noticed the older man's hand tremble slightly.

"As a businessman, I wanted to be successful, and I think I was. But I also wanted to be the kind of person who could look himself in the mirror in the morning. I don't pretend to be a saint, but I have always tried to be someone respectable, someone people could trust. I am not going to throw that all away to chase a lawsuit. Not at this point in my life. I don't need the money."

The waiter returned, refilled the older man's water glass and inquired if either man needed anything.

When the waiter left, the older man picked up the thread of the conversation again. "So, Devin," he asked. "How has your research come along? Do you think Hepaticin causes this cancer?"

Garner thought hard before he answered.

"That's two questions," Garner said. "I'll answer the second question first. Yes, I believe Hepaticin causes this cancer."

Garner hesitated, before adding, "But can I prove that today? No. I would need to hire expert witnesses. And not just hire them. I would need to pay them to do some research. And at this point, to build a winning case, I'd probably also need a lucky break."

"So, do you plan to hire these experts?" the older man asked.

"That would cost a lot of money, at least a hundred grand, probably more, and I've been hesitant to invest that kind of money without more to go on. To raise the money for a suit like this, I'd probably have to give a piece of the suit to one the big-name plaintiff's lawyers. Without more than I have now, I'm not sure I could interest any of them."

"Which reminds me," the older man said. "Did you see the story in The Wall Street Journal this morning?"

"Which story?" Garner parried the question. He did not read The Wall Street Journal. He couldn't afford to. But glancing around, he wondered if he was the only one in the club's dining room that day who didn't.

The older man had clipped the article. He pulled the clipping from the inside pocket of his navy Brooks Brothers sport coat.

Garner skimmed the story about the short sellers acting on rumors Hepaticin had been linked to a rare cancer. He looked across the table at the older man and smiled. "It looks like someone else thinks Hepaticin causes this cancer."

"This story in The Wall Street Journal," the older man asked. "Does that change things? Did this article put the blood in the water that attracts the big sharks?"

"Maybe," Garner agreed. "The big-name guys will certainly take a look at this. But they're not going to jump in if they think it's just the usual short-seller scare tactic."

"What will Galaxy do?"

"It will deny there is any connection. It will hire a big law firm to manage any litigation. It will hire other law firms around the country wherever cases are filed. At first, it will refuse to settle. Drug companies always do. Instead, it will pick a case it thinks it can win and force it to trial, to send a message to the plaintiff bar."

"A case they can win," the older man repeated. "In other words, they will look for a case not brought by one of these big-name lawyers. If they had their way, they would try their first case against a small firm or solo practitioner," he asked, "someone without a lot of financial resources?"

Garner nodded.

"Ideally, they would like to go up against a young lawyer, someone like you?"

"Yes," Garner admitted, aware that his candor was likely losing him a client.

"And I assume they would not want that first trial to be in some place with a reputation for big verdicts. They would not want that first trial to be in Miami, or New Orleans, or Los Angeles?"

Garner nodded. The banker had obviously done his homework.

"They would want some jurisdiction where the juries are conservative. They would prefer some place like – well, like Cincinnati – as opposed to West Virginia?"

Garner nodded again.

"What usually happens when they try that first case?"

"Sometimes the drug companies win. Sometimes it backfires, because – unlike their blue-chip lawyers – the plaintiff's lawyer is someone who actually tries cases, someone who can connect with the jury."

"Someone who actually believes in his case?" the older man stated, as much as asked.

"Exactly."

"What impact does it have if the drug company wins the first trial?"

"Actually, I don't think it much matters whether they win or lose the first case, or even the first couple cases. If the drug company wins, the big-name plaintiff lawyers shrug it off. Those guys have huge egos. They just say, 'Well, you didn't try your case against me.'"

"And if the drug company loses?"

"Truthfully, I don't think that matters much either. Like I said, the drug companies frequently have trouble with the first few cases, but they learn and adjust, and they get better each time. The only time the first trial matters is if the plaintiff rings the bell really big. If he gets a big punitive damages award, the drug company may well get skittish and start looking for the exits."

"Is it expensive for a drug company to try one of these cases?" the older man asked.

"*Very* expensive. I've heard it is not unusual for a drug company to spend well over a million dollars on that first case." Garner was pretty sure the older man already knew the answer.

"If everybody knows the outcome of the first case rarely matters, why do the drug companies insist on spending so much money trying these test cases?"

"My view?" Garner asked. "It's because those big law firms tell the drug company's management, 'You have to stand up to the plaintiff lawyers and not be bullied. You can't show any weakness. You have to demonstrate you are willing to try cases.' Management doesn't want to look weak and agrees. I don't know if the big law firms really believe it when they tell their clients they have to try some of these cases, but you can bet it makes the big law firms a lot of money. A ton of money."

"Devin," the older man said, speaking softly. "I expected to have a nice retirement. Play golf. Spend time with my grandchildren. Travel. I did not expect to spend my retirement, what little of it I am likely to have, tied to a chemotherapy bottle. As you can see, I've lost my hair. I've lost weight. When I look in the mirror, I don't even recognize myself. At first, I was in denial. Now, I'm angry."

Garner listened.

"I want to sue. But like I said, I need to be able to look myself in the mirror. I don't want to be associated with some sociopath, even if he is a big gun. And, as a banker, frankly, I also don't like the idea of paying one of – one of *those* people – forty or fifty percent of whatever damages or settlement I might get."

Oh my God, Garner thought, *he wants to hire me*!

"So, here's what I would like to propose. What if I were willing to advance the out-of-pocket costs of preparing the case for trial? Let's say, I advance a hundred thousand up front, and more if necessary, let's say up to two hundred fifty thousand. And in return, you cut your fee to twenty percent?"

Garner thought hard for a moment. This is was an extraordinary offer. It would get him in the game. He was willing to accept twenty, but figured he needed to negotiate some to hold the older man's confidence. He countered with, "Twenty-five percent."

The older man nodded assent and asked. "Would you have a better case if you can sue on behalf of two or more clients in the same case?"

"Yes. The drug company is in a much better position when it's up against just one person, especially in a cancer case. The drug company can say, 'Well, who knew why this guy got cancer. People get cancer all the time, and nobody knows why.' That may make sense to Joe Juror. But if there are multiple plaintiffs who took the drug and developed the same rare cancer, that argument loses its credibility."

"So, it would be best if you filed one suit with both your present client and me, and perhaps others, as plaintiffs?"

"Yes," Garner agreed, but wondered to himself, *Where is he going with this?*

"When I learned I had this condition, my initial reaction was to go to Duke University for treatment. My health plan refused to pay for that. I got a letter from the insurance company's medical director. He said I can get the same treatment here, at less cost, but he authorized my oncologist to consult with the oncologists at Duke. Basically, he said, anybody can administer the chemo. But have your oncologist talk to them and make sure you're getting the best possible cocktail. The plan will pay for the consultation."

That actually makes sense, Garner thought, but decided it best not to say that.

"When your current client –

"Dan Meinhardt."

"Right. When he learned he had this cancer, he wanted to go to The Cleveland Clinic. It turns out he has the same health plan I do. The medical director gave him the same response. You can get whatever treatment you need right here, but we'll pay for your oncologist to consult with the people at The Cleveland Clinic, to make sure you are getting the best treatment plan."

Garner decided he should just listen.

The older man signaled the waiter to bring the check. His lunch was untouched.

"Devin, I've been thinking about that a lot."

"Yes, sir."

"I think you should talk to that medical director and find out how many times he has confronted this situation. He may have a broader perspective than Mr. Meinhardt or I do. I think you should find out just how many people this health insurance company knows of who have taken Hepaticin and gotten this cancer. Do you think you can do that?"

"That's a great idea. I can certainly try. But I don't think he will talk to me. He will be afraid I'm going to sue his company, claiming they should have warned you about the risk."

"Well, I think you should try. And if the health plan won't let you talk to him, maybe we *should* think about suing them."

Garner agreed to reach out to the medical director.

With that, the older man stood, and said, "Please finish your lunch. I am fatigued and need to go home and get some rest."

Garner stood when the older man stood and extended his hand.

The older man shook his hand, asked the young lawyer to send him the necessary papers to sign, and slowly walked toward the door.

The young lawyer sat back down. *Holy fucking shit,* he thought to himself, *I'm actually going to do this.*

WEDNESDAY, MARCH 16 – IT SPIDER UNIT

Maya Naidu learned her mother had taken a turn for the worse and was likely to die very soon. In a flurry of activity, she booked flights to India for herself and her daughter. Her husband was swamped where he worked and would not be able to go. They couldn't afford for both of them to be off work at the same time, anyway.

She got permission from her boss to take her laptop with her to India and to work from there, if her situation permitted. She was moving up her planned trip home by three weeks. If she could work from Hyderabad, she would be able to remain there until Ashika's dance recital. *Besides, who knew how long her mother would linger.*

Naidu called her daughter's school and explained that Ashika would have to miss school, possibly for as long as a month, and made arrangements for her school assignments and tests to be sent to her by email.

Finally, Naidu checked to be sure all of her own projects at work were covered.

On an impulse, she called Dr. Doss to explain that her mother was very ill and that she was about to leave for India.

Doss made the usual expressions of condolences and remembered to ask whether her daughter would miss the dance recital.

Naidu explained she hoped to be able to stay in India long enough for her daughter to participate in the dance pageant. "We'll have to see, but I will be taking my laptop, so that I can be working from there, if I have some down time."

Doss said he wished her all the best and added, "I hope I'm still here when you get back."

"Are you thinking about quitting? You just started!"

Doss explained the possible link between Hepaticin and cancer had leaked. The drug company was upset, and there was a good chance he would be asked to leave to make the drug company happy.

"That is terrible!" Naidu commiserated.

Doss repeated how sorry he was about her mother and wished her a safe trip.

THURSDAY, MARCH 17 – LAW DEPART-MENT

Eileen Wang was not surprised when the subpoena from the Securities and Exchange Commission, or SEC, arrived. Given the story in The Wall Street Journal, it was pretty much a foregone conclusion the SEC would launch an investigation. The story had not revealed the basis for the "rumor" that Galaxy's biggest revenue generating drug had been linked to cancer, but the SEC would begin its investigation by talking with Galaxy. In all likelihood, Galaxy's management would point the finger at the health plan – and possibly at Dr. Doss personally – as the likely source of the rumor.

It was not the first time the company had had to respond to an SEC subpoena, or even the first time she had been responsible for coordinating the response. That work, however, usually fell to the Law Department attorney responsible for the company's SEC compliance and other corporate matters, so Wang sent him a copy and explained why their boss had asked her to lead the work on this one. She sent copies to the company's corporate Secretary, the head of Government Relations, and to the head of public relations – euphemistically called "Communications."

Wang reviewed the subpoena and then opened a dedicated program that she would use to send out "hold notices." That was legal jargon for a notice to those of the company's employees likely to have documents responsive to the subpoena, telling them they needed to preserve their documents: *Under no condition should they discard or destroy anything that might be responsive.* She completed the notice form by describing what documents the subpoena sought.

Wang doubted most of her fellow employees paid much attention to those notices, or remembered fifteen minutes later what they were supposed to keep. But the courts and federal agencies could come down hard on a company for not taking reasonable efforts to preserve documents called for by a subpoena, and the courts universally considered such notices to be an essential first step in compliance.

She could have simply used an email, and in fact, she used to use emails for her hold notices. But the special "hold" program had several advantages. It required each employee who got the notice to acknowledge the notice. And then the system automatically sent reminders every ninety days until the "hold" was lifted. In this case, she expected to comply with the subpoena in much less time than that, but things happen, and so she liked the safeguard of automatic reminder notices.

Aside from some purely routine things, the subpoena demanded the company produce copies of any emails or instant messages from company employees to people outside the company, and from anyone outside the company to company employees, about a possible or actual link between the drug Hepaticin and adrenal cortical carcinoma. For that, Wang was glad the company automatically archived every email the company received, and every email company employees sent from their corporate computers. Unfortunately, company employees sent and received so many emails, it was impossible simply to search the archives for any message containing certain key words like "Hepaticin" or "adrenal cortical carcinoma" or "cancer" – even if the search were narrowed to a relatively short time frame. That could only be done on an employee-by-employee basis or, in IT jargon, on a "custodian" level basis.

Wang would need to develop a list of company employees who might have generated or received or been "cc'd" on any such emails. The company's IT forensic team would pull all of the emails those people had sent or received within whatever time period Wang designated. Someone would then need to review all of those individuals' emails – unless Wang was able to get the SEC to agree that her IT people could scan the emails of the potential custodians using key words. Wang knew from experience it would take some time to negotiate with the SEC attorney how many and which custodians' emails would need to be pulled, and which key word searches to use to identify potentially responsive emails.

In this case, Wang also knew she would be in better shape than usual to manage the production, because she had already asked the IT forensics team to pull what was needed for use in her own investigation. That would pretty much cover what the SEC wanted as well.

Wang called Liz Kolinsky, the head of the IT forensics team, to let her know about the new subpoena. They chatted briefly. Kolinsky agreed that not much additional work would be needed.

Only then would Wang allow herself to think what she had been refusing to allow herself to consider. *I hope*, she thought, *Spencer didn't leak this*.

THURSDAY - FRIDAY, MARCH 17 - 18 – HYDERABAD

After a quick flight to Chicago, followed by a long, overnight flight to Dubai, and a connecting flight to Hyderabad, Maya Naidu and her daughter, Ashika, arrived in Hyderabad, India, completely exhausted.

Her brother, Mannish, picked them up at the airport. After loading their luggage into the trunk, he navigated the crowded and chaotic Hyderabad traffic until they arrived, beyond exhaustion, at his house a short distance outside the giant city. It was late afternoon, local time.

Manish's wife was at home, caring for their mother. "Mother is sleeping now," she said in Telugu, the language the family spoke among themsevles. "She is sleeping most of the time now."

Maya Naidu was relieved her mother had not passed before she was able to see her. She felt guilty enough – the guilt so common among immigrants to America – even though she knew she had kept in contact with her mother more than many of her countrymen who had merely moved to another city within India.

Naidu bathed, changed clothes, and ate, hoping to revive herself.

When she returned to her mother's bedroom, her mother stirred and woke. For the next hour or so, her mother rallied. The old woman, frail and now bed ridden, recognized Maya and Ashika, and asked about Maya's husband, Kanha. She inquired how Ashika was doing in school and about her dancing. And then, just as suddenly as she had revived, the frail woman weakened and said she needed sleep. She closed her eyes, and was soon breathing rhythmically, but shallowly.

Maya herself retired when the nurse, who would tend to their mother during the night, arrived. Maya slept soundly, but the next morning, when her iPhone alarm woke her, she desperately wanted to roll back over and sleep more. She forced herself from bed only by reminding herself that she needed to check on her mother. Besides, she knew she had to adjust to the local time. After her own morning rituals, Maya dismissed the nurse and took up the vigil next to her mother.

Before long, Ashika joined her, and after an hour or so, during which her mother had barely stirred, her brother, Manish, joined the vigil as well.

Shortly after 11:00 a.m., local time, the thread ran out on what little conversation had transpired among the three of them. Maya Naidu sat at the bedside intently watching as her mother breathed in and out, sometimes stopping altogether for a long moment, only to start again with a sharp breath.

As she watched her mother, her thoughts inevitably drifted to special times she had shared with her mother – some pleasant, some bittersweet, some painful. And then – not with a start, but with a gradual awareness – she realized her mother had stopped breathing and had not begun again. She reached over and nudged her mother, then nudged her harder. No sign of breathing. She leaned forward and listened for sounds of breath, then tried to find a pulse.

"She's gone," her brother said quietly.

"I know," Naidu acknowledged. "But I just can't believe it. One moment, she was breathing, and the next she wasn't."

Ashika's eyes were moist with tears. The teenager sobbed quietly at her grandmother's passing.

Manish stood and took charge. He used his cell phone to call the doctor who would complete the death certificate. While waiting for the physician, Mannish placed additional calls to make arrangements for the cremation, which by custom had to take place before sunset. He called relatives who would help move the body.

When the doctor had come and completed his examination, Mannish summoned a neighbor, an ascetic, who repeated ancient Vedic scriptures to revive the body. When the scriptures did not return the body to life, the ascetic told the family the obvious – their mother was truly dead.

Naidu performed the ritual washing of her mother's body, and with help from Ashika, who had never witnessed these rituals, she dressed her mother in a saree.

For Hindus, when the soul and the conscious part of the person leave the body, the body that remains is considered unclean. It is burned to return it to the elements. As the male child, most of those duties fell on Manish. And so, a few hours later, Mannish – with help from several male relatives – took the body to the cremation facility.

When the cremation was completed, the relatives returned to their own homes to perform the ritual washing required by Hindu tradition. Relatives who touched the body are considered unclean until the rituals are completed. No food could be prepared in their homes until they bathed.

Hindu tradition explained these rituals in its own terms, but it occurred to Maya Naidu that these practices had probably served an important role in the past in preserving the health of the community. She performed the ritual washings and collapsed into bed. She slept deeply.

When she woke, her body was soaked in sweat and ached from jet lag. She drank water, ate a piece of fruit, and returned to bed. She would worry about adjusting to the local time in a day or two. For now, she would escape into the emptiness of sleep.

While Maya Naidu slept in, her brother returned to the cremation facility and claimed his mother's ashes. Before returning home, he deposited them in the Krishna River. As the eldest male, this was his duty.

Unlike in the United States, friends and relatives would not visit or bring food. There would, however, be a celebration or remembrance on the thirteenth day after death, and in the days after their mother's death, Maya Naidu set about helping her brother and his wife arrange the small gathering.

MONDAY, MARCH 21 – LAW DEPARTMENT

Eileen Wang opened an email from someone in Network Contracting she knew only vaguely. The email was in response to her inquiry about the contracting status of the six physicians who had attended all three of Galaxy's luxury resort seminars for physicians who prescribed large amounts of Hepaticin.

Each of the physicians she had asked about, the email said, was a network provider – meaning that each had contracted with the health plan to accept the health plan's payment rates. That was what she expected given the number of the health plan's members each physician had treated. Each of the six physicians, the email added, participated in the health plan's Medicare Advantage network under a percentage-of-premium contract. *That*, Wang thought, *was interesting*.

Wang opened each of the contracts. All appeared to be standard contracts. The three Florida physicians had signed their contracts quite some time ago, which was no surprise, because the health plan had used percentage-of-premium contracts for Medicare in Florida for many years. Sylvan Goldbach, the Ohio physician, had switched from a fee-for-service contract to percentage-of-premium shortly after he had attended the first Galaxy luxury seminar. The same was true for the two physicians from Texas, although it had taken them a little longer to get their contracts.

Wang found her reaction to this discovery interesting. On the one hand, it felt good to have her hunch confirmed. *Well, partially confirmed.* But it also felt *icky* – she couldn't think of a better word than that – to find evidence these doctors were gaming the system. And to find the evidence so easily. *People trusted their health to these doctors!*

Of course, she hadn't proven these doctors had hit on a common scheme to bilk Medicare and at the same time win star status with Galaxy. But the fact that three of the physicians asked for percentage-of-premium contracts shortly after attending the same seminar suggested she was on the right track. So did the fact they had suddenly started diagnosing more patients with fatty liver disease and prescribing so much Hepaticin.

None of this had anything to do with whether Hepaticin caused adrenal cancer. Still, she kept turning over in her mind something Boris Bardin had said to Spencer Doss during their disastrous meeting. Bardin had said Galaxy had no reports of this cancer among patients taking Hepaticin *except the ones Doss had told doctors to submit.*

Wang wondered: *How did Bardin know that Doss had encouraged prescribing doctors to report their cases to the FDA?* It was possible, she supposed, that one or more of the prescribing physicians had attached the letter from Doss to the form they submitted to the FDA.

But she had a different theory. Those letters went to – among others – these six doctors and others who had received substantial payments and gifts from Galaxy. Any of those doctors – or all of them – may have picked up the phone and called someone they knew at Galaxy when they got the letter from Doss.

She made a mental note to discuss this with Doss. But first, there was another loose end that had been bothering her. She called a partner at one of the large law firms she worked with frequently.

"I've got a question," she explained after the usual greetings. "Your firm does product liability litigation for drug companies, doesn't it?"

"Yes, quite a bit."

"As I understand things, drug companies have to submit reports to the FDA of any adverse events they learn about. Doctors and even patients can also submit reports directly to the FDA."

"I'm sure that's right," the partner agreed.

"What I'm wondering is – does the FDA make any information about those reports available to the public? I looked at the FDA's MedWatch site, and it explains how to submit a report, but it doesn't give any information about any adverse event reports it has received."

"I'll see what I can find out," the partner promised.

Wang had been careful to keep her question general, so as not to create a conflict with the law firm's drug company clients. For the same reason, the partner had been careful not to ask if Wang was interested in a particular drug, or what had prompted her question.

TUESDAY, MARCH 22 – ACTURIAL DEPART-
MENT

Over the past few weeks, as time permitted, Tam Nguyen Phan had tried several approaches to the Hepaticin data. She had begun by looking at the number of adrenal cortical carcinomas in the over-age-40 population, comparing those known to have taken Hepaticin with those for whom there was no evidence of Hepaticin use in the data. The association was not statistically significant.

Then, she had tried segmenting the data more narrowly by age – looking separately at people in their forties, people in the fifties, and so on. There was a stronger suggestion of an association in the health plan members in their sixties and seventies, but the confidence interval still included the possibility that any association was due to chance.

At Andy Berkowitz's suggestion, she had compared people who were enrolled in Medicare Advantage plans with individuals of the same age group who were enrolled in employer-sponsored health plans – the so-called "working aged." That brought her closer to statistical significance at the 95% confidence level, but not quite there.

She contacted Willow Halfmoon in Pharmacy, and had her translate the Hepaticin NDC's into their dose strengths. With that, she could do a classic dose-response analysis, looking to see if development of the cancer was "dose related" – in other words, if there were more cancers at higher doses than at lower doses. There were, but the association was not sufficiently strong. The confidence interval still included, at the edge, the possibility that the association was due to chance. She looked at how long plan members took the drug, and in particular at those who had taken Hepaticin longer. Same result.

No matter how she sliced and diced the data, there was a strong suggestion that taking Hepaticin increased the risk of developing the cancer, but not at the 95% level of certainty that would be necessary for publication – or would likely be necessary to convince the FDA to act.

She was concerned that the drug might remain on the market, without appropriate warnings, until more-and-more people became ill. More selfishly, she was also concerned that, if she was not able to demonstrate the association existed, this project would not provide an easy-to-understand explanation why she wanted to leave a good job and return to school. But the numbers were what they were.

She called Frank McVeigh, the University of Cincinnati professor who had overseen her Master's thesis. His refrain had always been that a public health disaster was a health problem so obvious even a case-control study could detect it. She asked if she could buy him lunch and discuss a problem she was stuck on. At his suggestion, they agreed to meet at little Vietnamese restaurant in Findley Market, not far from the health plan's offices.

Over lunch, Phan explained the problem and reviewed with him how she had approached it. Aside from a few minor, technical suggestions, he agreed with her approach. As she fully expected, McVeigh repeated his mantra, that insistence on the arbitrary 95% and 99% levels of certainty used by scientific journals and government agencies precluded action on many serious health problems.

Perhaps more importantly, he also agreed with her that there was no way the statistician from Galaxy could have determined that there no statistically significant association with just the information Doss had provided on his PowerPoint.

Knowing that Dr. Doss would need a Ph.D. biostatistician to get any article he might write published, Phan asked McVeigh if he would be interested in collaborating with Dr. Doss. "It's up to Spencer," she cautioned, "but I'm happy to recommend you if you're interested." He was.

Later, Phan briefed Doss on her meeting with her former professor. Doss, of course, said he would very much like to meet the professor, but needed to wait until the company had wrapped up the investigation into whether someone inside the company had leaked his concerns about Hepaticin.

Then, Phan shared the most provocative outcome of her discussion with her mentor: Neither she nor McVeigh believed the Galaxy statistician could have done any serious analysis with just the data Doss had shared with the Galaxy representatives. "He said to you that they were 'blowing smoke up your skirt," she recounted. "Whatever that means."

Phan was interested in his reaction. She could see Doss was doing a slow boil, but he said nothing. Phan concluded Doss intended to bottle up that anger until he could put it to good use.

Not someone to mess with, she decided.

TUESDAY, MARCH 22 – LAW DEPARTMENT

Eileen Wang heard back from the law firm partner, responding to her inquiry about whether the FDA made adverse event data available to the public.

"My partner who does a lot of work for drug companies says the FDA does make a lot of information about adverse reports available. You were just looking in the wrong place.

"She says you need to find," the partner checked his notes, "what the FDA calls 'FAERS.' It stands for FDA Adverse Event Reporting System. It's the system drug manufacturers have to use for their reporting.

"She says the site contains redacted adverse event reports, but the site won't give you any attachments that may have been submitted with the report. If you want those, you have to submit a Freedom of Information Act request."

Wang thanked the partner and told him she would share the information with a medical director who was interested.

"No problem," the partner replied, noting for billing purposes how long the call had taken. "Tell him that my partner says the site is pretty hard to work with."

WEDNESDAY, MARCH 23 – MRA UNIT

From the MRA audit team, Andy Berkowitz received copies of the medical records of a number of the patients the "Luxury Resort Six" physicians had diagnosed as having fatty liver disease. The cover note explained that these records had been pulled in connection with prior years' MRA audits and were not up-to-date. The MRA auditors were still working on the current year audits.

The email stressed that NASH – the progressive form of fatty liver disease that risk adjusted – *was* documented in the medical charts of each of the patients. In other words, the diagnosis had appeared not only in the encounter or claim forms. The physician had written it in the chart as well.

Well, Berkowitz thought, *that didn't answer my question about whether there was evidence in the medical record – like lab results – that actually supported the diagnosis.* He knew, however, that the MRA staff was trained to look to make sure the physician had written the diagnosis in the medical record, and had dated and signed the entry. Under the arcane rules adopted by CMS, only the physician's diagnosis "counted" as adequate support for a diagnosis. An x-ray or CAT scan showing a tumor didn't count. Lab reports – such as those demonstrating diabetes or high cholesterol – didn't count. The results of a cardiac stress test did not count. Only the physician's diagnosis in the chart counted. And so, that's what the MRA team was trained to look for. It would be hard to get the MRA team to look to see if a diagnosis made medical sense.

But with the records in hand, Dr. Doss could figure that out for himself. Berkowitz sent an email to Dr. Doss to let him know to expect the records, and copied Wang, so she would know what was going on. He reminded both that these were records for only some of the patients, and that these records were from prior year audits – the current year audits were not completed.

WEDNESDAY, MARCH 23 – CINCINNATI MARKET OFFICE

The email from Andy Berkowitz reminded Eileen Wang that she needed to let Doss know she had the provider contracts for the doctors Berkowitz referred to as the "Luxury Resort Six" – the six physicians who had attended all three of the luxury resort seminars paid for by Galaxy. She also needed to pass along to him what she had learned about the FDA's adverse event reporting system – FAERS.

It was odd to be both investigating Doss and at the same time helping him with his own investigation, but – at the end of the day – the two investigations were separate things. Doss wanted to know if, as seemed apparent, there was a connection between Hepaticin and adrenal cortical carcinoma. The company wanted to know if Doss or someone else had leaked that concern.

Rather than call Doss, Wang decided to walk down to his office. He was busy as usual, but immediately made time for her. Wang explained that each of the "Luxury Resort Six" physicians were network physicians and each had a percentage-of-premium contract for their Medicare patients. She also explained that three of the physicians had asked for percentage-of-premium contracts shortly after the first of the three "Hepaticin" seminars organized by Galaxy.

That was consistent with her theory that these doctors may have discussed how they could get paid more by over diagnosing fatty liver, how they could avoid detection by prescribing Hepaticin, and how it would be icing on the cake that Galaxy would reward them as well. "Consistent with" her theory, she emphasized, but not even close to proving it.

Fortunately, Doss seemed comfortable discussing these issues – not defensive, as Wang was afraid he might be, given the pressure Galaxy was applying to have him "managed" or fired.

She asked Doss if he recalled what Bardin had said, when he asked Bardin if Galaxy had received reports of adrenal cortical carcinoma in patients taking Hepaticin.

"I do," Doss said. "He said Galaxy had not seen any reports *except the reports I had our network doctors submit.*"

"When you sent the letters to doctors with adrenal cortical carcinoma patients," Wang said, "the first thing some of those doctors did was to call their good friends at Galaxy. That means Galaxy knew about your concerns before Winslow called them. They knew five minutes after Goldbach and the rest of these guys got your letter."

"That's what I think, too," Doss agreed. "But I don't think that's the interesting question."

Wang arched her eyebrows to show he had roused her curiosity.

"What I'd like to know," Doss said, "is if those guys picked up the phone and called their good friends at Galaxy when their second or third patient got adrenal cortical carcinoma."

Wang blinked.

"I had not thought about that," she admitted. "But that ties in with the other thing I've learned. The FDA makes redacted versions of adverse events available on its website."

She explained how to find the information, but cautioned him that she had been told it was not easy to work with.

After checking the site for himself, Doss summoned Nikki Flores Santos, the utilization review nurse on his team who had first two cases of the rare cancer.

"Ready to learn something new?" he asked, before explaining what he wanted her to do.

THURSDAY EVENING, MARCH 24 – MEIN-HARDT HOME

Dan Meinhardt sat in his darkened living room. The only light was the phosphorescent glow from the television set. His chemotherapy sessions were every other week, and this was his chemo week. As a result of chemotherapy, he had lost his hair – not just on top of his head, but from his eyebrows, chest, and even his pubic hair. He had also lost ten pounds and much of his strength. He no longer worked.

On the television, a news program reported the usual daily allotment of terrorist bombings, weather disasters, disease outbreaks, and political grandstanding. Meinhardt did not trust the news media. In fact, since Walter Cronkite had retired in 1981, he had refused to listen to the evening news programs at all. He was certain none of the networks reported anything the government or big companies didn't want people to hear.

Recently, however, he had discovered that one of those cable stations no one listens to rebroadcasts a German newscast at 7:30 each evening. Like many in Cincinnati, Meinhardt believed he was of German extraction. But like most of them, he did not speak a word of German, and so far as he knew, neither had his parents, or grandparents. But still, somehow, he found it comforting to listen to the announcers and reporters pronounce the day's events in German, even if he did not understand what they were saying. It resonated in a way he could not explain.

Before the news program completed its report on the latest developments in the Bundestag, and well before it had given the closing value of the Euro, Dan Meinhardt had fallen asleep in his easy chair. He dreamt he had died and no one came to his funeral except his wife, and even she left the visitation early – to play bingo in the basement of the nearby Catholic high school.

THE BLOCKBUSTER DRUG

FRIDAY EVENING, MARCH 25 – SHANGHAI

Darrin Hightower, CEO of Galaxy China, the British drug company's subsidiary in the People's Republic of China, stepped from his chauffeured Mercedes into the building where Li Ling lived in an apartment he paid for. Hightower's wife, Sarah, refused to raise their two children in China. She insisted they be educated in London and brought them to China only in the summer when school was out. Even then, she preferred to socialize only among the ex-pat community. She refused to learn any of the local language or customs and generally made it clear she did not like being in the Asian country.

Unlike his wife, Darrin Hightower was not averse to adopting local customs, and so, like many successful Chinese officials and businessmen, he had found a Chinese girlfriend to meet his needs for companionship and sex. Li Ling did so, in fact, more enthusiastically and adventuresomely than his wife ever had. In return, Hightower provided an apartment, ample cash, and the vague prospect he might someday leave his wife.

Despite complaints from London that the company's business was not growing fast enough, sales and revenues had been increasing steadily, and the company had been expanding and deepening its inroads. Over the past month, however, disturbing rumors had been reaching his office with increasing frequency and urgency. According to the rumors, the police were taking into custody purchasing agents for hospitals and clinics, and even doctors, and questioning them about payments from drug companies.

Hightower knew – he had been warned frequently enough – that the People's Republic of China had been cracking down on bribery and corruption since Xi Jinping had assumed office as President of the country and General Secretary of the Communist Party in November 2012. Hightower did not believe for a moment Xi or other high party officials actually disapproved of graft. Most of them – and their families – had gotten extravagantly wealthy from kickbacks and bribes. But Xi had apparently decided public corruption had become so rampant, it was undermining support for the Party's control of the country. Xi was now reining in the most flagrant abuses – especially when those involved were political rivals or were simply not sufficiently well connected.

But today, two Chinese nationals from his own staff had disappeared – presumably into police custody. Hightower decided it was time for an urgent trip to London to brief officials there – and to put himself out of reach of China's formidable security forces. Before he left, however, he wanted to explain to Li that something had come up and that he was likely to be gone for a month or more. He wanted to assure Li he would be back – and to leave her plenty of cash. He needed to move quickly, before the police learned of his departure, and so had decided he would not end up in bed with Li tonight. After giving her the money, he would head straight to the airport. But as he thought about sex with Li, it was not his resolve that was hardening.

Hightower knocked twice on the door to Li's apartment and said "Darrin" in a strong voice, before using his key to open the door. The lights to the apartment were out, which surprised him, because Li was expecting his visit. He flipped on the light switch and immediately realized he was not alone. Several strong-looking men in suits and ties were in the apartment. Before Hightower could react, two of the men grabbed him and pushed him into the room and into a chair. The chair was positioned in front of the flat screen television mounted on the wall of the apartment. He had bought it for Li.

One of the men introduced himself in English as a plainclothes police officer. "What in your country, you call a detective."

"I want an attorney," Hightower said. To himself he added, *Don't panic! Stay calm.*

"You will get to speak to an attorney when I decide you can."

"Then I want to speak to the British Consulate."

"The Consulate can speak with you when you are in jail. Do you want to go to jail?"

"What's this about?" Hightower demanded.

"You want a lawyer. You want to speak to the Consulate," the detective sneered. "And I thought you would be worried about your lover. I thought you would at least ask where she was."

"Where is she?"

"She's not here. She is safe. Don't worry about your girlfriend."

"You didn't answer my question," Hightower said.

"You miss your girlfriend," the officer taunted the businessman. "She cannot be here right now, but we don't want you to miss her." With that, the officer nodded to one of the other men, who picked up the remote and turned on the television.

Hightower watched as a montage of him having sex with Li flashed on the screen. His face was clearly visible in many of the scenes. He could feel his face redden.

"We are not interested in your sexual practices, Mr. Hightower," the detective said.

"Then what do you want?"

"We want you to tell us about the bribes your company pays to officials and businessmen in this country to encourage them to buy your company's drugs."

"I don't know what you are talking about."

"You want me to believe your company pays millions of Euros in bribes each year, and you – the CEO – do not know anything about it? How can that be?"

"My company does not pay bribes. We have a strict corporate policy against that sort of thing."

The detective shook his head. "We know your company pays bribes, Mr. Hightower. We have signed confessions from almost fifty people who have confessed to accepting money from your company."

"You coerce confessions all the time. We both know that."

"The Party would not tolerate that, Mr. Hightower," the detective said with a smirk. "Do you really want to insult the Party as well as my fellow police officers?"

Hightower said nothing.

"Perhaps you would like to go to our headquarters and find out how we obtain confessions?"

"I want to see my attorney. And, I demand to speak with the Consulate."

"Maybe, as you say, you did not know your people were passing out money in this way, Mr. Hightower. Maybe you were so preoccupied with your Chinese girlfriend you did not know what was going on around you."

"My people do not pay bribes. But if they did, I guarantee you, they did it without my knowledge. Li has nothing to do with this."

"What should we do with these videos we have of you and this woman?" the detective asked. "Perhaps we should send them to your CEO and your Board of Directors back in London. And to your wife, of course. Maybe we should let them decide if you have been paying enough attention to work."

Darrin Hightower made up his mind he would rather face public humiliation at home than a decade in a Chinese prison. "If you had anything on me," he said, "you wouldn't be trying to blackmail me."

"Mr. Hightower, our courts are not like yours. When the Public Security Bureau brings criminal charges, our courts convict 99.9% of the time. Did you know that?"

"No."

"You are going to be charged, Mr. Hightower, with directing your people to bribe our hard-working countrymen. We already have confessions from the people your subordinates bribed. We will soon have confessions from your subordinates as well. We have over twenty of them in custody tonight. They will either confess, or face prison terms. What do you think these Chinese citizens will do, Mr. Hightower? Do you think they will go to prison to protect you? Or, do you think they will save their own rice bowls, and let the foreign devil fend for himself?"

Hightower said nothing.

"We showed you this video of your sexual escapades, Mr. Hightower, because we were hoping you would make things easy for us. You *are* going to be convicted. If you give us a complete confession, the sentence will go easy on you. If not, it will go hard.

"For us, these videos are just a way of speeding things along. If you make things easy and work with us, these videos can remain our secret. If we have to spend weeks persuading you of the advantages of confessing your crimes, that is extra work for us. I don't mind a little extra work, Mr. Hightower, but it makes my men irritable."

"I'm not confessing. I didn't do anything."

"Did I mention we have twenty of your subordinates in custody tonight? Our colleagues are also examining your offices for evidence. We have seized your emails. We are transporting your servers, computers and cell phones to our laboratories."

Even though he willed his composure to remain intact, Hightower knew his face and body language would betray the stress he felt.

"Our investigation will start, of course, with the travel agencies. We know that you use certain travel agencies to hide the money you use to pay bribes."

Hightower felt a sinking feeling. Not knowing what else to say, he demanded again to see his attorney.

"We shut those travel agencies down earlier today," the detective said, ignoring the Englishman's demands. "Their employees are being most cooperative. They seem eager to confess your company's crimes."

"I'm not saying anything until I get a lawyer and talk to the Consulate."

"As you wish," the detective said, still speaking in English. "But if that is so, we will send copies of these

DVDs to your family, and to Sir Alec, and to your Board. We are sure they will find them most interesting."

The detective spoke in rapid fire Chinese to his subordinates and left the apartment. One of the remaining policemen removed the DVD from the television controller. Two others jerked Hightower to his feet more roughly than necessary. They pulled his arms behind his back and slid handcuffs around his wrists. The policeman who had put the DVD in his pocket stood in front of the British businessman and snickered, before kneeing him in the groin.

Hightower saw a flash of light before he felt the pain.

"Your dick not so hard now," the policeman said. "Too bad your girlfriend is not here to make it hard again." With that, he kneed Hightower in the groin again.

Two policemen dragged the Brit from the apartment.

SATURDAY, MARCH 26 – CINCINNATI MARKET OFFICE

To have an uninterrupted chance to review the medical records the MRA team had obtained for him, Doss came into the office on Saturday. He carefully reviewed the first few charts, looking to see if there was evidence to support a diagnosis of fatty liver disease in either of its forms – Non-Alcoholic Fatty Liver Disease, acronym NAFLD, or Non-Alcoholic Steatohepatitis, acronym NASH.

He decided he needed to get organized. He created a table to record his notes, so he could record the same data for each case. *What was the patient's height and weight when the doctor diagnosed fatty liver disease? Was there a liver biopsy? Was there an x-ray or other imaging study? Were there labs with abnormal liver function tests? Did the patient have diabetes? Was there some other evidence supporting the diagnosis?*

Most of the patients were overweight, but that described much of the country's population. Only a few were – in medical terms – morbidly obese. Some had solid evidence of NAFLD, but quite a few did not.

In fact, for the first two patients who had come to his attention, the records showed men who were fairly thin and healthy. Both had high triglycerides, but both were taking medications to deal with that. There were no imaging studies evidencing fatty liver disease for either, and no abnormal liver test results. Neither had diabetes. Nothing else suggested fatty liver disease.

None of these charts indicated the patients had adrenal cortical carcinoma, but Doss reminded himself the charts he was looking at were a year or even two years old. MRA was still collecting the current year's charts.

Doss added another column to his chart for adrenal cortical carcinoma. He then checked the report Naidu had run showing which Hepaticin users had been diagnosed with adrenal cortical carcinoma. He put a mark in the new column for each patient who had been diagnosed. He wished he could go back to when these charts had been prepared and warn these patients not to take Hepaticin. *To run for their lives.* But he didn't have a time machine, and life doesn't permit do overs.

Doss reviewed his notes again. He noticed that the patients who went on to develop adrenal cortical carcinoma tended to be the patients for whom there was the least evidence of fatty liver disease. He did not have medical records for enough patients to know if that was important, or if it was just because he had so few records.

He emailed Berkowitz and asked him to have MRA send him the current year's records as they collected them, and not to wait until they had completed their report.

With his work completed, Doss let his mind run in a different direction. Remembering the pain he experienced when his father died, he sent an email to Naidu, asking her how she was doing and telling her she was in his thoughts.

With that, he shut down his computer and left for – he couldn't call it home – his apartment.

SUNDAY MORNING, MARCH 27 – HYDERA-BAD

Maya Naidu was surprised to see an email from Dr. Doss, just asking how she doing. *That was so nice*, she thought. Since she had left for India, none of her other "regular customers" had done that. His email had come while she was sleeping, and now he would certainly be at home, maybe asleep. Not that it mattered. He could read her reply when it was morning in the US.

Naidu typed a lengthy message saying she was doing fine, but missed her mother terribly. She explained she would remain in India for a while longer, until Ashika had participated in the dance festival. It had been a difficult decision. Naidu had wanted to return home – she couldn't afford to lose her job. Ashika had wanted to stay. Ashika had even floated the idea of spending the summer with her uncle and aunt, arguing it would give her a chance to improve her language skills.

In the end, she told Voss, her boss had made the decision easy. In addition to more routine requests, he had been routing her last-minute requests – the kind that show up shortly before 5:00 p.m. and request "ASAP" turn around. Given the nine-and-half-hour time difference, she could work on those requests during the day in Hyderabad, but at night in the US. Because she was operating during off-peak times, she could run the reports immediately and make any corrections that were necessary, and then re-run the reports. She would have the results waiting for her boss when he arrived at work the next morning.

The SPDR unit's customers were thrilled with the quicker turnaround time. Her boss had urged her to continue to work from Hyderabad, taking whatever time she needed to attend to family matters. Of course, he would not be willing for Naidu to continue to work remotely from Hyderabad indefinitely, as he would be concerned she would eventually no longer feel part of the unit. He would be concerned about losing her. But given how hardworking and loyal Naidu was, he had assured her he was not concerned about her working remotely for a few more weeks.

As she finished her email to Dr. Doss, Naidu remembered that – as she was leaving for India – Doss had hinted the drug company wanted the health plan to fire him. She ended her message by asking how he was doing and asking if the drug company still wanted him fired.

MONDAY, MARCH 28 – CINCINNATI MARKET OFFICE

Devin Garner called the health plan and asked to speak with Dr. Spencer Doss. When he got through to the doctor, he introduced himself as an attorney.

"I represent two clients who developed adrenal cortical carcinoma while taking Hepaticin," Garner said. "Both requested authorization to be treated out of network, and you denied both requests. I was wondering if I could speak to you about whether there might be a connection between this drug and their cancer. I'm happy to set up an appointment and come to your office if you want."

"I cannot talk to you about any patient unless the patient has signed something authorizing us to talk to you. We've got a form they need to sign. It's on our website. I can have someone send you the form if you can't find it."

"I anticipated that, Dr. Doss." Garner replied. "Both of my clients have signed your form and if you give me a fax number, I can fax copies to you. I also mailed the originals two days ago. You should have them, or be getting them soon."

"This is going to sound like I'm trying to put roadblocks in your way," Doss said, "but you have to go through our legal counsel. She will decide if I can talk to you. Sorry."

"No need to apologize. I understand. Can you give me her name and phone number?"

Doss gave the attorney Eileen Wang's name and number, thanked the attorney for his understanding, and concluded the call as quickly as he could without being rude. As soon as he hung up, he called Wang, hoping he reached her before the attorney did.

When Wang answered, Doss told her to expect a call from a personal injury lawyer. He volunteered that he did not know this attorney and that the call came out of the blue. Doss stressed that he had gotten off the call as quickly as he could. He did not want anyone to think he was leaking information to personal injury attorneys.

He also wondered if the lawyer was really planning on suing the drug company, or if he might be thinking of suing the health plan. *Had they already sat on this too long?*

MONDAY, MARCH 28 – GARNER LAW OFFICE

Devin Garner punched in the number for the health plan's attorney. The attorney, Eileen Wang, surprised him when she answered his call herself, instead of having her secretary take – or deflect – his call.

Once again, he explained that he represented two clients who had taken Hepaticin and developed a rare cancer and was hoping to be able to interview the medical director who had reviewed their files.

"I want to find out," Garner told the health plan attorney, "if your company has other members, locally or elsewhere, who have developed this cancer while taking Hepaticin." He tried to keep his tone as friendly and non-threatening as he could, while still insisting that he speak with Dr. Doss – or whomever the right person might be.

"Have you filed suit?" Wang asked.

"Not yet, but I'm going to. My clients want to sue the drug company."

"When you do, you can issue a subpoena and take whatever depositions you need. I don't want it to look like we're choosing sides in your lawsuit."

"Ms. Wang, I think it is in your client's interest to help me."

"You're an attorney, Mr. Garner. Your job is to protect your clients' interests," Wang responded evenly. "I'm an attorney, too. My job is to protect my own client's interests. I'm having trouble seeing how letting you interview Dr. Doss helps my client."

"Fair enough," Garner countered. "I think I can help you with that."

"I'm listening."

"Several reasons," Garner began. "First, if we file suit against the drug company and get a recovery, you have subrogation rights. From any recovery my clients get, will they have to repay any medical expenses your company paid. Treating my clients for cancer hasn't been cheap, and I'm sure your company would like to get that money back. But you recover only if your members – including my clients – file suit and win."

The other attorney didn't object, so Garner continued.

"That leads to my next point," he continued. When we sue, the drug company will say, 'Who knows why these two people got this rare cancer? It's just a coincidence.' But if I can show that a lot of people are getting this cancer after taking this drug, that defense loses its appeal. Jurors will use their commonsense.

"And if, when I file suit, I can allege in my complaint, that a number of people have gotten this rare cancer after taking Hepaticin, my suit will be more likely to get attention in the media. That means more of your members will hear about it and file their own suits before the statute of limitations runs on their claims."

Garner paused, allowing Wang to respond.

"Statutes of limitations don't run," Wang said, "until people discover, or reasonably should have discovered, that their cancer was caused by a drug."

"Maybe, but we both know Galaxy will argue that these people were on notice when they discovered they had cancer. I don't agree, but who knows what judges will do?"

Wang said nothing, so Garner continued.

"I think there are additional reasons why you should help me," he said, almost like he was arguing a case in court. "You know how subrogation works. When your insureds settle, you get paid only if they don't hide the settlement from you, and their attorney can't find a way to defeat your reimbursement claim. And even then, when you get paid, you have to cover part of the attorney's fees."

"I'm listening," Wang replied.

"Attorneys used to charge 33% of the recovery, but that's ancient history. In a case like this, most lawyers are going to charge 40%, plus expenses."

"And you're not?"

"One of my clients is a very smart businessman. He convinced me to charge 25%. Not just for him, but for anybody else I include in the suit I intend to bring."

"So, your argument is, if we help you, you may end up representing more of our members, and so, we will recover more, plus your fees are lower?"

"That's one way this can go," Garner agreed. "And actually, that was my first thought as well. But my client, the businessman, had a more interesting idea."

"And that is?" Wang asked.

"What if your company joined in the suit? We could bring a subrogation suit on behalf of all of your members who took Hepaticin and ended up with this cancer."

"And roll the dice on the outcome of one suit?"

"I understand your concern, but think about the impact of being able to let the jury know how many people this affected?"

Wang had not anticipated this. "Let me think about it," she replied. "I need to talk to my General Counsel and some other people and see if my management is interested. To be frank, I will be surprised if they are. I'm not turning you down, but I just want to be clear that I'm only checking with my management. I'm not agreeing to anything."

"Understood," Garner parried. "But there is a door number two. You can decide not to cooperate, and I will make your company a defendant."

"On what theory?"

"On the theory that you knew, or should have known, that Hepaticin was making people sick, and you didn't warn your insureds. You protected your relationship with Galaxy and did nothing to protect your members."

"You don't know that."

"Like you said, I can file suit and take some depositions. Besides, I think you're hiding plenty. One primary care doctor in your network had three patients take Hepaticin and get this cancer. You've got how many primary care doctors in your network? You've got more cases. If you didn't, you'd have no problem with me talking with Dr. Doss."

"Like I said, I will run your proposal up the flag pole."

"Tell your management that your company can be a plaintiff and recover some of the money it spent treating your members for the harm this drug did, or you can be a defendant and risk losing even more. And not just money. Damage to your reputation. Let me know what your management decides."

WEDNESDAY, MARCH 30 – CINCINNATI MARKET OFFICE

Spencer Doss regularly met individually with the utilization review nurses on his team every other week. Although sometimes he had specific things he needed to cover, it was mainly an opportunity for each of the nurses to have scheduled time with him – to discuss their development goals, any problems they might be having, and to update him on special projects they might be working on.

Nikki Flores Santos wanted to use her one-on-one time with him to update Doss on the Hepaticin project he had given her. Her report was brief:

The FDA Adverse Event Reporting System, or FAERS, contained 23 reports of patients developing adrenal cortical carcinoma after taking Hepaticin. The reports were redacted, so as not to reveal any personally identifying information, but since she had copies of the original reports, she was able to tell if the FAERS report was one she or another nurse on his team had prepared. Doing the matching had been time-consuming, but not terribly difficult.

The bottom line, she said, was that *all* of the reports were reports she and the other nurses on his team had prepared; *none* were from physicians who had submitted reports – to the manufacturer or to the FDA – on their own.

Santos gave Doss a table she had prepared, showing for each of the health plan's Hepaticin-ACC patients, whether she had found a report.

Doss thanked her, but expressed frustration that so few of the prescribing doctors had bothered to submit the reports Santos and her colleagues had prepared.

Santos suggested that he send the adverse event reports to the oncologists treating the patients. Doss agreed

"You would think," Santos said, "the FDA would be concerned about reports of a rare cancer in 23 patients taking this drug."

"Their hair should be on fire," Doss agreed.

He called in his administrative assistant – actually, his team's administrative assistant – and asked her to work with Santos to prepare letters to Hepaticin-ACC patients' oncologists, asking them to submit the adverse event reports to the FDA.

FRIDAY, APRIL 1 – HYDERABAD

Home to a population of about seven million, Hyderabad is a vast, modern city, with a diverse, modern economy. Once famous for its pearl trade, it has long since developed extensive banking, manufacturing, and service operations. It is a global hub for information technology – sometimes touting itself as "Cyberabad." Naidu had once imagined she would work in Hyderabad's booming IT businesses.

But if Hyderabad can be said to have a signature industry, it is its pharmaceutical industry. Many Indian – and even global – drug companies have manufacturing and research facilities in the city. Those facilities make many of the drugs sold in India. They also produce large quantities of drugs for export, supplying many drugs used in the United States and Europe – especially less expensive generic versions of brand name drugs that no longer enjoy patent protection.

In her brother's home in Hyderabad, Maya Naidu lingered over breakfast and tea, collecting her thoughts and strength. Yesterday, it had been two weeks since her mother's death, and the purification rituals surrounding her mother's passing were largely over. Last night, she and Manish hosted the usual small gathering for family, friends and neighbors celebrating the end of the unclean period.

During the gathering, Naidu learned that Manish had lost his job at Rama Pharmaceutical Co., one of the many drug companies in Hyderabad. Manish had not mentioned losing his job, but during the gathering, several family members and friends told Manish they were sorry to learn he had been laid off. Manish claimed the job loss was only temporary. He said inspectors from the European Union and the United States had found problems at the drug manufacturing plant where he had worked. The plant had shut down only while the company addressed the problems.

Over the years, Naidu had read many stories about drug companies in India running into trouble with European and US regulators – typically for failure to follow good manufacturing practices. She remembered in particular a news story Manish had forwarded a year or two ago. A reporter asked G N Singh, India's Drug Controller General, about an FDA inspection finding flies – among other things – in products made by one of India's largest drug manufacturers. The reporter wanted to know why, if that company was banned from selling drugs in the U.S., he allowed that company's drugs to be sold in India. After trying to dodge the question, he had finally replied in exasperation that if he had to follow U.S. standards, he would have to shut down all of the drug makers in India! The answer probably didn't come out the way the old fool had intended.

But sometimes the FDA and European regulators had discovered out-and-out fraud – faked results on safety testing and worse. She had always worried her brother would get caught up in those problems. Now, Naidu wondered how serious her brother's situation really was.

She turned on her laptop and searched for stories about Rama Pharmaceuticals, the company where her brother had worked. She found several stories, all rather vague about the exact nature of the problem, but the stories mentioned only failure to follow good manufacturing practices, not fraud. The stories suggested the shutdown would be brief. She was unsure how much of that was public relations by the company and how much was true, but it was a significant company, and so she decided to believe that the plant would likely be back in production – and her brother back at work – soon.

That is, until a more disconcerting thought occurred to her.

"Manish," she asked, "does the company you worked for manufacture drugs for international companies?"

"Yes," Manish said, "most of the drug companies in Hyderabad are doing some of that. When the foreign company is not having enough capacity, or is needing to produce the drug cheaper, they come to us. Of course, our companies are also making their own products."

"Did this company you worked for make any products for Galaxy?"

"First, I am working for Rama still. They told me to report back to work on Monday, so Little Sister can stop worrying about her big brother."

"I am so glad to hear that, Manish," Naidu said, genuinely relieved. "I *was* worried about you."

"Not to worry," Manish assured her. "And to answer the other part of your question, no, Rama is not making products for Galaxy. That is another company. I have a friend who works there."

"What company?"

"Vishnu Life Sciences. It is an even bigger company than Rama."

"Do you know if it makes a drug called Hepaticin?"

"I am not knowing that, but if it is important, I can be calling my friend. I wanted to ask him about what's going on where he works anyway."

Naidu thanked her brother. Relieved, she turned back to her computer and searched to see what she could learn about Vishnu Life Sciences. The company, located in Hyderabad not far from where her brother worked, had a history of frequent, but apparently minor run ins with European and US authorities – minor, that is, until recently, when EU inspectors found numerous safety violations. Vishnu managers had allegedly falsified records to cover up the problems. European Union officials were now refusing to allow several Vishnu's drugs to be sold in European Union countries until the problems were resolved. The company had to shut down two of the plants where it manufactured drugs. None of the affected drugs were Hepaticin.

Her brother interrupted her. He had spoken with his friend, who confirmed what Naidu had learned from the internet. "It is being really bad there," he said. "The company lost its contract with Galaxy. Then, EU inspectors found problems. Definitely bad, definitely. Many people are being laid off, including him. He wanted to know if my company was hiring!"

"Manish, the newspapers say they cannot be selling some of their products in Europe. When that happens, what will a company here in Hyderabad be doing with the drugs it has already made?"

"Well, if they were not made right, they should be destroying them, but this is India. Our companies would probably sell them here, or sell them somewhere else. Most likely, they will be selling them in China."

"Manish, when I return to the United States, how can I tell if the drug I am taking is made by a company like Galaxy in its own plant, or if it was made here in India and sold by the international drug company under its own name?"

"Now, Maya, I am concerned. Are you taking this drug? Are you taking Hepaticin?"

"No, no, no!" Naidu assured him. "I am doing something at work involving this drug, and I was just wondering."

"Well, in the United States, you would need to be knowing the NDC, the National Drug Classification number. In America, if a drug is repackaged, it is supposed to indicate that in the NDC. But how you would be learning the NDC is another question."

"This is helpful, Manish. Thank you."

"How is my niece doing with her dancing?"

"It's all she thinks about. I am having trouble getting her to do her homework. I am afraid she will be too far behind when we go back."

"You will be staying here until the pageant?"

"Yes, but it is crazy. I need to be doing some work to keep my job. I need to be keeping after Ashika to do her homework. And, I need to be helping you sell mother's house."

FRIDAY, APRIL 1 – DATA CENTER

Usually, when the Law Department wanted emails pulled, Liz Kolinsky's team simply put copies of the emails on hard drives and sent them to an "*eDiscovery*" vendor. The vendor would load and host the emails on software developed to assist attorney review of emails.

That approach made sense in a big lawsuit, where the company was required to pull large volumes of email for production to the other side. Before the emails could be produced, lawyers representing the company had to review them for communications that were privileged, that were irrelevant, or that did not need to be produced for other reasons. The Law Department would arrange for an outside law firm – or more commonly, for lower-paid temporary attorneys – to review the email. The outside vendor's software would facilitate that review and keep track of the lawyer's determinations.

But this situation was different. At present, there was no litigation, and the number of emails at issue was manageable. The object was simply to look for evidence that someone inside the company was responsible for leaking the suspicion that Hepaticin caused some people to develop a certain kind of cancer. Kolinsky had her team host the emails on their own review software, which permitted searches for key words. That narrowed the task to a relative handful of emails – at least as these projects went.

Eileen Wang still had to review those emails, but the forensic team's review had turned up nothing that revealed a leak, or even hinted at who might have been have been responsible for the leak – if, in fact, there was a leak.

The whole exercise left Kolinsky with the same feeling she had when the project began – that she was missing something. She reviewed the relevant emails and constructed a rudimentary time line of the key events. She then pulled up the email traffic belonging to Spencer Doss and focused on the key time period, scanning the email headers. She found nothing remotely suggesting he had been in touch with a securities broker, or with a friend or relative outside the company.

Well, there was one exception – an email from his ex, giving him a heads up she was marrying some radiologist. From her work with the HMO, Kolinsky knew radiologists make about three times what a primary care physician – like Doss, when he was in private practice – made. Out of curiosity, she Googled the radiologist and found his picture on his practice's web site. He looked older than Doss, balding and paunchy. On another site, she found the radiologist's home address and checked it out on Google Maps. His house was absolutely huge. *The slut traded up*, Kolinsky chuckled to herself.

Focusing again on the task at hand, Kolinsky waded through another hundred emails. She found nothing that appeared odd or that might suggest he had used code words for "Hepaticin" or "adrenal cortical carcinoma."

She conducted a similar review of the email pulled from Bob Wiseman. *Always interesting*, she told herself, *to see what sort of email traffic one of the company's top officers gets*. But after scanning the headings on his email, and opening a few more or less at random, she came to the same conclusion she had reached after many other such exercises. *On the whole, their emails are just as tedious as my own.*

She turned next to the email of Brett Winslow. As she scanned his emails, one header jumped out at her. It came from outside the company and said, "PERSONAL

AND CONFIDENTIAL." Kolinsky opened it and read the message. The email purported to be from an IT consultant and informed Winslow that an anonymous source had posted disparaging remarks concerning him on a blog, along with information his employer might consider confidential.

"Bingo!" Kolinsky muttered. She grabbed her own laptop and pulled up a report she remembered reading. The report came from Fire Eye, one of the best IT security firms in the business, about the threat from what it called "FIN4." Kolinsky skimmed the report to confirm her recollection. "FIN4" was an individual, or group of individuals, who targeted the health and pharmaceutical industries. They sent emails that were much more sophisticated than the usual phishing emails looking for Social Security numbers. FIN4 targeted high-level corporate officers and people in sensitive positions. It appeared to be looking for the sort of information that would move the company's stock – or the stock of a company with which it contracted.

A typical ploy – according to the report – was an email telling the executive that he or she had been disparaged on a website or that the sender had spotted information that appeared to be proprietary and sensitive, indicating the details were in an attachment. If the executive opened the attachment, it released difficult-to-detect malware that created a window through which FIN4 could review the executive's email at will. The malware was particularly difficult to detect because, unlike some "worms," it did not take over the victim's system and force it to send copies of the recipient's emails out during off hours. It left very few trails.

Kolinsky notified her team, and it immediately began searching the other custodians' emails for similar messages. Finding none, they began work on pulling the email of a dozen or so of the company's most senior officers looking for similar messages. They found only one more, but that executive had nothing to do with Pharmacy.

While that effort was underway, Kolinsky turned her best guy loose on finding the code inserted by the malware. It took him nearly two days, but he was able to find it. He also obtained a program from Fire Eye to remove the malicious code, but touched base with Kolinsky before running it.

"Don't run it yet," Kolinsky ordered. "I need to talk with Legal first."

SATURDAY, APRIL 2 – HYDERABAD

The problem bothered Maya Naidu through the night. On Saturday morning, she pulled up her search on persons who had taken Hepaticin and developed adrenal cortical carcinoma. Her search terms had included all of the NDC numbers for Hepaticin she had obtained from Pharmacy. But she had not bothered to include the NDC number for each prescription in her reports – *the NDC numbers all represented the same drug and would have meant nothing to Dr. Doss.*

She now wondered if that had been a mistake.

She tweaked her earlier program, so that the report would show the NDC number for the specific product the member had taken. Because Hyderabad was nine-and-a-half-hours ahead of Eastern Standard Time, it was off-peak time for the health plan's claims system, and the report ran soon after Naidu submitted her request.

When the report arrived, Naidu reviewed it carefully, and then re-reviewed it twice more. She felt a knot tighten in her stomach. There were fourteen NDCs assigned to Hepaticin, but all of the patients who had taken Hepaticin and went on to develop adrenal cortical carcinoma had taken versions of Hepaticin identified by only two NDCs.

Naidu went back to the internet and searched for "Hepaticin, NDC numbers." She selected a site that identified itself as an "NDC Finder." She searched the site for Hepaticin, and the "Finder" produced the same fourteen NDC numbers she had obtained from Willow Halfmoon in Pharmacy, but with brief explanations for each. She found the two NDCs for the versions the adrenal cancer patients had taken. As she suspected, they were the NDCs assigned to product manufactured by Vishnu Life Sciences in Hyderabad and repackaged by Galaxy.

Naidu sat steering at her screen.

Hepaticin was *not* causing these people to develop this cancer. Something about the versions manufactured by the company here in Hyderabad – most likely a contaminant introduced during the manufacturing process – was at fault. The answer had been in her searches all along. She had just not displayed, or reported, the data – the NDCs – that revealed the answer. Naidu felt both guilty that she had missed this and elated that she had finally coaxed the answer out of the data.

She wanted to call Dr. Doss and tell him what she had discovered, but realized it was the middle of the night in Cincinnati. She logged into her corporate email. She carefully explained what she had done, and what she had found. She asked Dr. Doss to look at the new report, which she was attaching, and to see for himself.

When she hit the "send" key to transmit the message to Dr. Doss, she was certain it was the most important email she had ever sent.

MONDAY MORNING, APRIL 4 – CINCINNATI MARKET OFFICE

On Monday morning, Spencer Doss took a sip of his Starbucks coffee and checked for voice mail while waiting for his computer to load and come alive – his usual morning rituals in the office. After entering his password to access the network, and then entering it again to open his email, he was greeted by a couple dozen emails that had arrived since he had last checked on Saturday afternoon. Two email headers caught his attention – one from Andy Berkowitz, the other from Maya Naidu. Doss assumed Naidu was simply responding to his personal inquiry about how she was doing and opened the email from Berkowitz.

Berkowitz had welcome news. The frontline MRA reviewers had started their audits of the "Luxury Resort Six" physicians – the six physicians who had attended each of the seminars paid for by Galaxy at luxury resorts over the last three years. Berkowitz attached electronic copies of the current-year medical records for their Hepaticin patients collected so far. Doss downloaded the medical records and began his review, using the same checklist he had used for the previous records.

The records fell into much the same pattern as the earlier records. For some patients, there was either a clear basis for the fatty liver disease diagnosis, or at least a plausible basis for thinking the patient might have fatty liver disease. But for many of the others, there was nothing in the chart that evidenced progressive fatty liver disease or even suggested it might be present. There were no liver biopsies, and no imaging studies – CT scans, MRIs, or x-rays – documenting fatty liver disease. The patients were of normal weight – or even thin. The lab results for liver function were normal. These patients had slightly elevated triglycerides, but by itself, that was not a reason to diagnose NAFLD, let alone NASH – although it looked like these physicians were routinely diagnosing NASH in every patient with high triglycerides.

Doss checked to see if any of the patients had been diagnosed with adrenal cortical carcinoma. Only a few had – so far. But as before, the unlucky few who had developed this cancer were patients for whom there was no evidence of fatty liver disease, and thus no apparent reason for them to be taking Hepaticin in the first place.

Doss called Andy Berkowitz and briefed him on what he was seeing in the medical records. "Here's my question," Doss said. "Actually, I've got a lot of questions, but here's one you might be able to answer. If these guys wanted to come up with a fake diagnosis, why NASH – Non-Alcoholic Steatohepatitis? Why not just Non-Alcoholic Fatty Liver Disease? It would be easier to defend a fatty liver disease diagnosis if anybody ever questioned what they were doing. I don't get it."

"Oh, geez! I'm sorry. I should have explained that. Fatty liver doesn't risk adjust. NASH does. In plain English, they don't get paid more for Non-Alcoholic Fatty Liver Disease. Medicare only pays more for Steatohepatitis."

"I get it," Doss said after a long pause, "but that's brazen."

What would it take, he wondered, *to overcome corporate inertia – or to be charitable about it, corporate caution – and get permission to share what he was seeing with the government? And importantly, what would it take to get permission to warn plan members who had taken Hepaticin to be checked – to be monitored for – adrenal cancer, so that new cancers could be caught early?*

His revelry was broken by his Administrative Assistant. "Spencer," she asked, "are you going to join the Medical Directors call?"

It was a gentle reminder that he was late dialing into the monthly call – which he already regarded as largely useless.

"Thanks," replied, "I'm dialing in now."

MONDAY, APRIL 4 – CINCINNATI MARKET OFFICE

Doss had not anticipated how much of his time in his new job would be devoted to meetings and conference calls, and he certainly had not anticipated how much of *that* time would be wasted. He had, however, learned that a telltale sign that a meeting or conference call was going to be useless was an email in advance asking for agenda items. He thought of those as "does anybody know why we're meeting?" emails.

Doss logged onto the call in time to learn that Finance wanted to know why hospitalizations had been up in the first quarter, particularly among Medicare members. The answer was obvious: Flu vaccine manufacturers had guessed wrong about which strains of the flu would be most prevalent, and more people than usual contracted the flu. When that happened, seniors and other vulnerable populations were always hit hard.

The Finance guy had apparently anticipated that response and was ready with a second question: *Why were the medical directors pre-authorizing hospitalizations for old people with the flu anyway? Would it be a big deal if they denied in-patient treatment for the flu? No one dies from the flu, do they?*

One of the medical directors tried to explain that, *yes, people do die from the flu, especially older people and people with compromised immune systems.* Another medical director chimed in with statistics. "In a good year, flu kills over 10,000 people in this country," he said. "In a bad year, it can kill five times that."

Finally, Dr. Ellen More, the medical director who had been around longest, interrupted. "You go tell your boss," she told the young Finance guy, "an across-the-board decision not to admit seniors with the flu would be a conspiracy to commit murder."

When the call ended, Doss thought, *that was half an hour wasted.* He had wanted to discuss the Hepaticin problem during the call, but Wang had asked him not to bring it up until she had responded to the SEC subpoena.

He swallowed his frustration and turned to the email from Naidu, thinking it might be an antidote to the toxic mix he had just swallowed.

Doss read, and then re-read, her email. It wasn't the purely personal exchange he expected. Instead, Naidu carefully explained that she had re-run her report of patients who had taken Hepaticin and developed adrenal cortical carcinoma. This time, she had tweaked the report to show the NDC number for the version of Hepaticin the patient had taken.

All the patients who developed adrenal cortical carcinoma, Naidu continued, had taken drugs identified by only two of the fourteen NDCs assigned to the Hepaticin. Those NDCs, she explained, were the two NDCs assigned to product manufactured for Galaxy by a pharmaceutical company in Hyderabad and repackaged by Galaxy for sale in the United States.

With her usual understatement, Naidu said, "MAYBE you will be thinking that only the Hepaticin made here in India is causing this cancer."

Exactly what I'm thinking, Doss said to himself.

Naidu had more.

She said the Hyderabad drug company was called Vishnu Life Sciences. Galaxy cancelled its contract with Vishnu a couple months ago. Naidu said she had searched for the company on the internet. Doss should read the stories himself, but there were several reports that the European Union had recently inspected the two plants where Vishnu manufactured drugs. The inspectors discovered serious manufacturing problems with those drugs. They had also discovered records that had been altered or invented in an attempt to cover up the problems.

According to media reports, Naidu told Doss, the European Union has banned imports of several products made by Vishnu until it corrects its problems and produces assurances it will no longer falsify test data.

Naidu warned Doss she had not found any reports that mentioned problems with Vishnu's production of Hepaticin. She said she believed Galaxy had terminated its contract with Vishnu *before* the European Union inspection.

Naidu ended her email with a profuse apology for not including the NDC numbers in her earlier report.

Not your fault, Maya, Doss thought. *I didn't ask you to include those in your report.*

Doss opened her new report and reviewed it carefully. Naidu was right. Only two of the fourteen NDCs accounted for *all* of the cases of adrenal cortical carcinoma in Hepaticin users.

Doss searched the internet. *Fierce Pharma* and several other sources reported the European Union actions. Several of the stories mentioned specific drugs banned from import into European Union countries, but none mentioned Hepaticin. He found no mention of Galaxy terminating its contract with the Indian company, but suspected such a story would not be newsworthy outside of

India. *Large multinational companies make and terminate contracts with suppliers all the time,* Doss thought. *So, unless there was some angle to the story that made it interesting, like job losses at a local plant, there would not have been much reason for the media to report the contract termination.*

Doss sent Naidu an email congratulating her on her work. He also apologized for asking her to do more, after all she had done, but he needed her to tweak her report one more time. The report stopped at December 31. Doss asked if she could extend her search into the current year. "Let's see if the number of new cancers we're seeing each month has continued."

Next, he forwarded Naidu's email to Andy Berkowitz and Tam Nguyen Phan, saying simply, "I think you will want to see this. Your thoughts?"

That completed, Doss called Brett Winslow, but got his voice mail. He left a message asking Winslow if he or one of his people could verify that Galaxy had terminated a contract for manufacturing Hepaticin with an Indian company called Vishnu Life Sciences. And if it had, Doss wanted to know *when* that happened. Doss added, "Give me a call, and I'll explain what this is about. I *really* don't think we want to do this in email."

Next, Doss called his boss, Robert Wiseman. He got his administrative assistant. Doss asked her if there was any way she could work him into Wiseman's schedule. "It's important," he emphasized. He left his cell number.

Using his desk phone, Doss called Eileen Wang and told her he was headed down to her office with something important. He printed two copies of Naidu's new report and took them with him.

MONDAY MORNING, APRIL 4 – LAW DE-PARTMENT

Sitting in Wang's office, Doss explained Naidu's discovery. As he did, he could see concern form on her expression. Doss watched as Wang skimmed the report, confirming that it contained only two numbers in the column for NDCs, where there should have been an assortment of fourteen different NDCs.

"It gets worse," Doss added. "Naidu says Galaxy cancelled its contract with this company a couple months ago. I don't know how she knows that, but the contract termination was apparently a bigger deal in Hyderabad – she's still there – than it was here. I guess a lot of people got laid off."

"When?" Wang asked. "When did Galaxy terminate the contract with this company?"

"I'm not sure. Naidu didn't say, but she said that, since then, the European Union found some serious problems when it inspected its plants. On top of that, the company tried to cover up the problems. But Naidu says that only happened very recently. She says Galaxy cancelled its contract with this company *before* that."

Wang stared at Doss intently for a long moment.

"When the people from Galaxy were here," she said finally, "their guy– what was his name – Badenoff?"

"Bardin," Doss reminded her. "Boris Fucking Bardin."

"That's right," Wang said. "Do you remember Bardin saying that a few months from now we wouldn't be seeing any more cases in patients taking Hepaticin, and we'd realize it was all just a coincidence?"

"That's the first thing I thought of when I read Naidu's email. That prick knew the problem was tied to the Hepaticin made by this company in India. He knew Galaxy had terminated its contract with this company. You can bet they stopped shipping that product."

"That's what I'm thinking," Wang agreed. "But we can't prove that."

"We don't have to. That's the FDA's job."

Wang nodded, but appeared unconvinced.

"What we have to do," Doss urged, "is lay out what we know to the FDA. We've already sat on this problem too long."

"Who else have you told about this?"

"I let Berkowitz and Phan know, so they can see how it affects their analysis. I've called Bob Wiseman, and told his administrative assistant I need to talk to him today. And I've placed a call to Brett Winslow. I asked him if his people can find out when Galaxy ended its contract with this company in India."

"Excellent."

"I told Winslow not to put this in email." Doss smiled. "See, I'm learning."

"That reminds me," Wang said. "I have to be at the IT Data Center in Blue Ash tomorrow. I've got to read the emails they pulled before we ship them to the SEC."

"You're still investigating me?" Doss smiled to let Wang know he did not take it personally. He wanted her to know he understood it was her job to make sure the company wasn't sitting on evidence that one of its employees had leaked the information to private investors.

"Having that cloud hanging over our heads complicates things," Wang said. "I agree we should go to the FDA, but with that going on, I'm not sure if my boss is going to see things the same way. It will help if you can convince Wiseman we've got a compelling case."

"I'll let you know as soon as I talk to Bob."

Doss stood and checked his cell phone for messages. "I'm seeing Bob at 3:30," he told Wang. "If I convince him, you *have* to convince your boss."

Before leaving for Wiseman's office, Doss gathered the utilization review nurses on his team and explained what Maya Naidu had found. He asked the nurses to pull up the MedWatch Adverse Event reporting forms they had prepared some time ago. He asked the nurses to add the NDC number, or numbers, for the version of Hepaticin that the patient had taken to each report and to get the reports ready for him sign.

MONDAY AFTERNOON, APRIL 4 – LAW DEPARTMENT

For Eileen Wang, it was a cardinal principal that a good lawyer does not panic when confronted with bad news. She also believed, just as firmly, a good lawyer does not over react to positive developments. With that in mind, she carefully reread the email from Naidu, which Doss had forwarded. Then she re-read the attached report. Naidu's insight had been remarkable.

Wang pulled up the EDGAR data base, which provided public access to SEC filings, and located the securities filings by Galaxy Pharmaceutical Company. She checked the company's annual and quarterly filings over the past year, then worked her way backward through its Form 8K filings, which companies use to disclose certain developments between their quarterly filings.

And there it was!

Galaxy had filed a Form 8K on February 27 in which it disclosed that it had terminated its contract with Vishnu Life Sciences for the manufacture of certain products. She downloaded the document into her file on the Hepaticin problem.

Wang moved to the FDA website again and worked her way to the portion of the website dealing with drug safety and availability issues. She scanned until she found a report of a voluntary recall of certain lots of Hepaticin. The recall had taken place about the same time as Galaxy had terminated its contract with Vishnu Life Sciences. Nothing in the public filing indicated that the lots were lots manufactured by Vishnu, but it wasn't hard to guess who had made them. In fact, the recall notice was unusually vague about the reason for the recall.

Wang picked up her phone and called Jeff Reiner, the manager of the company's mail order pharmacy in Chicago. She got lucky and caught him at his desk. Wang indicated that she had just learned that Galaxy had recalled some lots of Hepaticin. She wanted to know if the company had a process for monitoring for recalls like that. She wondered if any of the recalled product was still around.

Reiner confirmed that the mail order operation did indeed have processes in place to monitor for recalls. If it had any of the lots involved in a recall, he assured her, his people would have returned any product covered by the recall, but promised to confirm that.

Wang called her boss, the company's General Counsel, but he was in a meeting, probably for the rest of the day. Wang left a brief message saying there had been some major developments regarding Hepaticin. *Could she possibly see him tomorrow afternoon?*

With that, Wang went back to the FDA website and located what looked like the best number to call to get someone in the agency's enforcement section. She placed the call, got transferred several times, but eventually reached someone who assured her he was the right person.

Wang introduced herself, making clear she was in-house counsel for the health plan. She then explained that her company was seeing excess cases of a rare cancer in patients taking Hepaticin, but only in product manufactured for Galaxy by an Indian company, Vishnu Life Sciences. Wang indicated she would like to bring the medical director who had discovered the problem to the FDA offices, so that they could explain what the company was seeing in detail.

"We can't come tomorrow, but we can come on Thursday or Friday."

The FDA bureaucrat expressed appreciation, but said he could not set up a meeting *that* quickly.

"We know of at least one personal injury attorney who is about to file suit over this, and we expect his suit will get a lot of attention," Wang warned the official. "We think he is going to allege that a lot of people have developed this cancer after taking Hepaticin. We think he is going to have some other pretty disturbing allegations."

"Is that why you want to meet with us?"

"No," Wang replied, irked. "We want to meet with you because people are getting cancer and dying as a result of this drug. We want to meet with you because we believe Galaxy is trying to cover this up. We want to meet with you because we're trying to be good citizens. We want to meet with you because it's your job to protect the public from dangerous drugs. If it's too much of a bother to meet with us, we can go to *The Washington Post* or The *New York Times* and tell them about the problem – and your lack of interest."

"I'm sorry," the bureaucrat replied. "I didn't mean to suggest we weren't interested."

"I mentioned the fact that this lawyer was about to file suit, because I thought the FDA might like to get ahead of this. If we figured out that this drug was causing this cancer, and if this personal injury lawyer figured it out, then we're probably not the only ones. Maybe you would rather tell the media, when they start calling, why you were too busy to deal with this."

"I don't think that's fair."

"Since when are the media fair?"

"Can't argue with you on that," the bureaucrat conceded. "I'll see what I can do and get back to you."

Wang took a brisk walk around the floor to clear her head. When she felt she had regained her balance, she returned to her office and composed a brief email to her General Counsel summarizing in bullet point fashion the latest developments.

With that, she had no choice but to turn to other matters, some of them urgent, having nothing to do with Hepaticin.

Late in the afternoon, an FDA official – not the one who had taken her initial call – telephoned. The official, who identified herself as Constance Hopkins, an Assistant Deputy Director, wanted to know if she and Dr. Doss could meet with the relevant agency staff on Friday morning at 10:00. Wang promised to touch base with Dr. Doss and get back to her.

When she reached Doss, he was just emerging from his meeting with his own boss, Bob Wiseman. Doss said Wiseman agreed it was time to go the feds.

Wang was relieved to hear that – she had gone out on a limb by talking with the FDA before they had Wiseman or her boss's buy-in.

Doss added that he had also touched base with Winslow. "He has no objections to our going to the FDA. Maybe he just doesn't want to be on the wrong side of this, but I think he's genuinely pissed Galaxy played him."

Wang had her administrative assistant book flights to Washington for Doss and herself.

TUESDAY, APRIL 5 – CINCINNATI MARKET OFFICE

Doss decided to shift his focus away from the "Luxury Resort Six" physicians — the physicians who had attended all three Galaxy-sponsored Hepaticin seminars. Instead, he asked Wang if there were any physicians who attended the first of the Galaxy seminars, but had *not* gone to any more of the seminars. He hoped to find someone who had largely stopped taking money from Galaxy – at least related to Hepaticin. Wang was able to identify seven physicians who met those criteria.

Doss set about trying to reach each of them to see if he could find out if they were aware of any discussion about how physicians could get paid more by Medicare Advantage plans if they diagnosed patients with NASH. He was concerned, however, that if he went right to that question, the physician might be alarmed.

He decided to start by explaining that he was investigating whether drug manufacturers' payments to physicians were actually having the negative impact on health plans everyone assumed they did. He would then explain the physician had been selected because he had attended the Galaxy-sponsored retreat three years ago, but – unlike some of the other physicians who attended – he had not attended subsequent Galaxy-sponsored seminars and had not received any substantial payments from Galaxy since then. Doss thought he would then ask, "Why?"

Doss was unable, however, to get the first physician to take his call. The second physician on the list, it turned out, had passed away a few months after the seminar. The third and fourth physicians also did not return his calls – one, apparently, because she was on vacation. The fifth physician had retired. The sixth physician did not return his call.

Doss was finally able to get the last physician on the list to take his call, but the physician immediately objected that he did not participate in the health plan Doss worked for.

Doss disarmed the physician by saying, "Don't care. Not why I'm calling."

"Then, why are you calling?"

Doss decided to cut to the chase and simply explained he was calling about the Galaxy-sponsored Hepaticin seminar the physician had attended three – actually, almost four – years ago now. Before Doss could explain further, the physician interrupted.

"You want to know what they said about Medicare Risk Adjustment."

"Exactly," Doss replied, surprised.

"I've been wondering when I'd get this call – although I thought it would be from the government."

"Why is that?" Doss asked.

"I'm guessing you already know what happened, but one of the speakers – a physician from Florida, I don't recall his name, but I believe he was Cuban – explained how the government pays Medicare Advantage plans. He talked about risk adjustment and explained how Medicare Advantage plans get paid. And of course, he went on at some length about the fact that CMS didn't pay more for Non-Alcoholic Fatty Liver Disease, but did pay more for Steatohepatitis – for NASH. And then he talked about what CMS looks for when it audits the health plan."

"The point," Doss probed, "was just to explain how this works?"

"No, the point of the presentation was that if we diagnosed patients with NASH, the Medicare plan would get paid more, and if we had the kind of payment arrangement with the plan that primary care physicians in Florida have, the health plan would pass much of that extra payment through to us."

"Interesting," Doss said.

"Not really," the physician shot back. "What was interesting was that this guy explained in some detail how some doctors had been gaming the system by making up diagnoses out of whole cloth. He went on about how Medicare plans now sometimes look not just to see if the physician put the diagnosis in the chart, which is all CMS looks at, but at whether the doctor actually treats what he diagnoses. He said, for example, if you diagnose NASH, but don't treat it, the health plan or the FBI might come along later and wonder if you just made up the diagnosis so you could get paid more. But if you prescribe Hepaticin and tell the patient to lose weight, no one's going to question it."

"I see."

"He didn't come right out and tell us to go back to our offices and diagnose all of our patients with NASH, but he laid out how we could get paid a lot more and get away with it if we did. It was all wink, wink – if you know what I mean."

"Were there any handouts?"

"God, no! The drug companies never give you anything that you can point to later. They're too slippery for that."

"This is very helpful," Doss acknowledged. "Thank you."

"I am guessing you've got a shit load of Medicare patients with NASH," the crusty older physician said with a sardonic chuckle. "He mentioned your plan in particular as one that is willing to pass through most of the extra payment to the primary care physician."

"We do," Doss agreed. "But that's not what prompted my call. Like you say, we have a number of physicians with a lot of patients – mainly Medicare Advantage patients – who have been diagnosed with NASH and have been taking Hepaticin. Unfortunately, a number of them now have adrenal cortical cancer. It was the number of those cancers popping up all of sudden that caught our attention."

"I hadn't heard anything about that."

"Galaxy has kept the lid on it so far. It threatened to sue us if we went public with our concerns, so I hope you will treat this conversation as confidential for the time being. But I think it's just a matter of time until the cancer problem comes out."

The physician said he'd let Doss handle that hot potato and wished him luck.

After the call, the physician did, however, take the precaution of going on line and issuing a sell order on the 2,500 shares of Galaxy stock in his portfolio.

TUESDAY, APRIL 5 – ACTURIAL DEPART-MENT

Tam Nguyen Phan had spent Monday at an all-day, company-sponsored off-site meeting for a couple hundred managers and professional staff. Management used the day to explain – and to win support for – its commitment to the latest industry fad.

As usual, management had explained this latest fad in terms that implied it was management's invention and thus gave the company an advantage over the competition. Of course, since business people can't resist a fad, every other health plan in the country was doing the same thing. From her perspective, the day had been an energy-draining waste of time.

Because of the off-site, it was not until Tuesday morning that Phan read the email from Dr. Doss explaining that the Hepaticin problem was apparently limited to product manufactured for Galaxy by an Indian company. After studying the email from Doss, she immediately pulled up her Hepaticin file. She did separate analyses for each of the NDC numbers, and the results – *finally!* – were satisfying. Two of the NDC's produced statistically significant results, and the rest retreated into insignificance.

She repeated the dose-response analysis, using the two NDC numbers, and the data showed a clear dose-response relationship. The line was a little more ragged than she expected, but it was there.

She went to Berkowitz's office, where he was dealing with some hot MRA-issue and intermittently talking with a veterinarian about his dog, which was dying. He interrupted that to take a call from his girlfriend, about to be ex-girlfriend, who was apparently moving out of his apartment. On the speaker phone – unaware that she was being overheard – the girl friend insisted that no, she was NOT taking his Grateful Dead albums.

When the girl-friend drama ended, Phan briefed Berkowitz on what she had found. He told her he thought some of the doctors may have been making up the NASH diagnoses, but only in their Medicare Advantage patients. He suggested she see if she could do something with that.

When Phan left his office, Berkowitz was talking – at his usual mile-a-minute clip – with his boss about the MRA brouhaha, he had his vet on hold, and he was checking his cell phone for something.

Back at her own office, she analyzed the data, focusing on Medicare Advantage enrollees who had taken Hepaticin with either of the suspect NDCs and had been diagnosed with NASH. The analysis nudged the association into the gold standard for statistical significance – the 99% confidence level.

Phan prepared a tightly-worded summary of her findings, detailing her approaches and findings. She laid it aside and reviewed it again that evening at home, making several wording and proof-reading corrections. She sent her analysis to Berkowitz, for him to review. Separately, she sent her memo to Ingrid Berg to review before she released it to Dr. Doss. At 9:00 p.m., she turned off her laptop.

APRIL 5 - APRIL 6 – CINCINNATI MARKET
OFFICE

As he was about to leave for the day, Spencer Doss noticed an email from Andy Berkowitz with several attachments. Then a second email from Berkowitz with multiple attachments hit his in-box, followed by another, and another. Soon, there were almost a dozen.

Doss opened the first of the emails. In it, Berkowitz apologized for the multiple emails, but explained that the frontline MRA staff had collected almost all of the remaining medical records for the patients for whom the "Luxury Resort Six" physicians had prescribed Hepaticin. There were so many, Berkowitz explained, he was afraid to put them all in a single email.

Doss took off his jacket and sat back down. It was going to be a long evening.

One-by-one, he worked his way through the medical records, using the same checklist as before.

Two hours later, he had gotten a good start, but not more than a start, and he decided to finish at home. He shut down his computer, grabbed his jacket and laptop, and headed out, his laptop slung over his shoulder. At home, after a quick meal, he turned the laptop back on, logged in, and picked up where he left off.

At nine, he was halfway through. At eleven, he threw in the towel, determined to finish in the morning.

In the morning, as soon as he reached the office, he cleared his calendar. With that, he closed his door and picked up his review of the new medical records obtained by MRA. By 11:00 a.m., he had completed his review of the medical charts of the patients for whom the "Luxury Resort Six" physicians had prescribed Hepaticin over the last three years.

He then pulled up the report of patients who had taken Hepaticin and went on to develop adrenal cortical carcinoma. Using that report, he quickly annotated his table to show which of the Luxury Resort Six physicians' patients had developed adrenal cortical carcinoma. Doss studied the table, drawing conclusions carefully.

In an email to Eileen Wang, which he marked "Attorney-Client Communication," Doss summarized his conclusions. As would be expected, many of the patients diagnosed by the "Luxury Resort Six" physicians had at least some evidence of fatty liver disease. But for most of the NASH patients, there was no apparent basis for the diagnosis. Many experts would say the only real basis for diagnosing the condition is a liver biopsy, and almost none of these patients had liver biopsies. Most of the patients diagnosed with NASH *did* have high triglycerides, but that was not nearly enough to diagnose Steatohepatitis.

With that, Doss headed to the cafeteria. He would have liked to discuss what he learned with Wang over lunch, but knew that she was spending the day at the company's Data Center reviewing email and then meeting with her boss.

WEDNESDAY MORNING, APRIL 6 – DATA CENTER

Eileen Wang drove her six-year-old Honda Civic to the company's IT Data Center in a nameless industrial park in Blue Ash, a Cincinnati suburb. The buildings in the industrial park were unremarkable warehouses and light manufacturing plants with company names Wang did not recognize.

The IT Data Center was two blocks down a side street. Except for a high chain link fence, it was – at first glance – as unremarkable as any building in the industrial park's maze of unremarkable buildings. But when Wang tried to confirm she had the right building, she realized there was no name or corporate logo on the building or on the security guard's post. The building was – quite literally – nameless.

Several security cameras perched like mechanical crows on the building's roof, keeping vigil. The building itself appeared to have no windows. Concertina wire atop the fence served as the only exterior decoration – unless one counted as decoration several signs with the message that this was private property and trespassers would be prosecuted.

Wang drove to the gate, which was the only opening in the tall fence, and stopped at the security post. She presented her corporate ID card *and* her driver's license to the guard, who checked her name against the list of people to be admitted. Wang appeared on the list as a guest of Liz Kolinsky. The security guard called Kolinsky and stated that her guest, Eileen Wang, was at the gate. The security guard asked if Ms. Wang should be admitted. Kolinsky confirmed Ms. Wang should be admitted, and the security guard returned Wang's identification and raised the gate.

Wang drove in and parked her car in a visitor space. She walked the short distance to the building on foot, the April wind blowing her skirt as she did. At the nondescript door, she pushed a button, and the door clicked. Wang opened the door and entered a small contained space, cabined by thick, floor-to-ceiling glass. A security guard, unremarkable in his physical presence, opened a small window. Wang passed her corporate ID card and driver's license through the window. The guard checked and returned them. While he was doing that, Kolinsky arrived. The guard hit a buzzer, unlocking the door that led into the rest of the building. Wang opened the door and stepped through.

Kolinsky welcomed her and thanked her for coming to the Data Center. "I know you came out to review the email we collected," Kolinsky said, "but first, there's something we need to discuss."

Oh, Christ, Wang thought. *She's found a leak.*

Kolinsky led Wang down a labyrinth of hallways and into a very large room that looked every bit like something out of a Hollywood movie. The far wall was covered top-to-bottom and end-to-end with large, flat screen television screens. Several were tuned to the major news outlets, including CNN Headline News. Others had charts and diagrams that showed the moment-by-moment status and workloads of the company's various IT systems. Workers were arrayed before the screens in long rows, like workers in the control center for a NASA space launch.

Before Wang could take it all in, Kolinsky signaled for Wang to follow her out of the control room and down another dimly lit hallway to a small office, with Kolinsky's name on a gray, stainless steel plate on the door. Kolinsky unlocked the door using her pass card, and motioned Wang in.

When they were seated, Kolinsky said she had a nearby office set up for Wang to use to review the emails her team had pulled, but that there was something she needed to tell Wang first.

"What's that?" Wang asked.

"First, let me ask you. Is this drug making people get cancer?"

"I think there's a pretty compelling case that it does," Wang said, wondering if Kolinsky was just trying to build suspense. "As soon as you tell me Doss didn't leak this, I want to take him to the FDA and lay out what we have."

"I can't prove that Doss did not leak this. He could have called someone from his home phone, or a neighbor's phone, or met someone on a park bench."

"I get it, Liz. You can't prove a negative."

"But I can tell you I don't think Doss leaked it. I think we were hacked."

"Hacked?"

"Have you ever heard of FIN4?"

"No, what is it?"

"It's the name of somebody, probably a group of people, who have been targeting health care and pharmaceutical companies for several years. That's just name a security consultant, Fire Eye, gave them. But these bad guys are sophisticated. They apparently look for information that will move a company's stock – mergers and acquisitions that haven't been announced, or information that a company is not going to meet its earnings projections, that sort of thing."

"How do they do it?"

"Phishing, but these guys are good. They send an email – with good English – to a corporate executive or attorney, with a message that doesn't sound like the usual phishing stuff. For example, their favorite approach seems to be saying they are a security consultant and they found something on the internet that has some very disparaging information about you. Or, they say they found what appears to be sensitive information someone inside your company has leaked. They say they are attaching a copy."

"And when you open the attachment, its put a virus in your computer?"

"It plants some very sophisticated code deep inside your computer's software. It creates a backdoor that allows them to come in and read your email anytime they want."

"They did this to Spencer?" Wang asked.

"Nope!" Kolinsky said, "Brett Winslow."

"You're sure about this?"

"Completely."

"Good work!" Wang congratulated Kolinsky. "I'll let the SEC know."

"Listen, I've got a question," Kolinsky replied. "I know how FIN4 gets its information. For example, here, they were reading Winslow's email. Doss emailed Winslow about members taking Hepaticin and getting cancer. Doss says he wants to go to the FDA. I get all that. But how does FIN4 make money off that?"

"Liz, you probably know more about this than I do, but according to The Wall Street Journal, some private equity firms sold their stock in Galaxy and then shorted Galaxy. My guess is this hacker group sold what they learned to the private equity firms. People have suspected for years that some of those firms frequently trade on inside information. This is probably just one of any number of ways they get inside information."

"That's illegal, right? You get caught doing insider trading and you go to jail?"

"Yes," Wang said, "although recently, some very conservative courts have made it hard to get convictions for insider trader."

"You know I had breast cancer?" Kolinsky asked.

"Yeah, I remember," Wang replied – remembering too that to have a conversation with Liz Kolinsky was to risk whiplash. "How are you doing?"

"I'm doing fine, so far. But it was an awful experience. It really pisses me off that these FIN4 creeps, whoever they are, and these rich guys on Wall Street are making money off other people getting sick."

"I don't like it either, Liz. That's why I want to let the SEC know right away what you found."

"The Feds have been trying to catch FIN4 for several years. I don't think you have to be in a rush."

"I can't think of any good that would come from delaying. I don't think that would sit well with the SEC."

"Hear me out," Kolinsky said.

When Kolinsky finished, Wang said, "I like it, I think. But I don't see the SEC giving us permission to do that."

"So, don't ask for permission. Just hold up telling the SEC about what we found until we get this in place, and then tell them what we did."

WEDNESDAY, APRIL 6 – CINCINNATI MARKET OFFICE

Doss got an email from Eileen Wang. She thanked him for his email concerning his analysis of the rest of the Luxury Resort Six physician's medical records. She had important news as well, but needed to discuss it in person. Unfortunately, she had another meeting she had to attend before she could get with him. She asked him not to leave until she got back.

The message, which sounded more formal than usual, left him wondering what IT had found and if he was about to be fired. He didn't think so, but he wouldn't know what her news was until she arrived.

He decided to use that time to review the stack of MedWatch forms his team had prepared for the patients who had taken Hepaticin and developed adrenal cortical carcinoma. He signed each and put the stack on his administrative assistant's desk, asking her to overnight them to the FDA. He put the address for the FDA on his note – just in case he no longer had his job in the morning.

When he returned to his office, he had a new email – this one from Tam Nguyen Phan, forwarding the memo she had prepared. The email said her boss, Ingrid Berg, had reviewed the memo and had authorized her to forward it to him. She added that Berkowitz had signed off on it as well.

The bottom line, she said, was that there was indeed a statistical association between Hepaticin use and adrenal cortical carcinoma, but only with two NDCs or versions of the drug. After completing her analysis, she had checked with Willow Halfmoon in Pharmacy and confirmed that those NDCs were the NDCs assigned to the product manufactured by Vishnu Life Sciences. For those versions of the drug, she added, there was also a dose-response relationship.

Her email asked if she could share her results with her former professor.

Doss thought about Phan's request. Either IT had found the leak, or it not been able to do so. If IT had found the leak, sharing the results would not be a problem. If IT had *not* been able to find the leak, the company might well decide he was expendable. He replied to Phan, telling her to share the results with her former professor.

He began to study Phan's detailed memo, skipping over the impenetrable paragraphs of technical information about the statistical methodology, when Eileen Wang knocked on his door.

"I've got a lot to tell you," she said, "and I think you're going to like it."

THURSDAY, APRIL 7 – CINCINNATI

The next morning, after his email exchange with Brett Winslow, which he and Wang had carefully scripted so that each statement would be true, but would leave an intruder with the wrong impression, Doss shut down his computer. He slid the photo of his father into his brief case, put his jacket on, and carrying his company laptop and his brief case, stepped from his office. He didn't bother to turn the light off. In two minutes, with no movement, the motion detector would automatically turn the light off.

He stopped by his administrative assistant's cubicle. "Remember what we discussed," he said in a soft voice. "Not a word. If anyone asks, just say you don't know what's going on."

"I promise," she replied. *No problem*, she thought, *because I don't know what's going on.*

"And make sure you ship those MedWatch forms to the FDA."

"They are already in the Fed Ex bin."

"Thanks, Kara," Doss said, turned and left.

***

In his apartment, Doss reviewed and re-reviewed his notes and presentation. He knew he would get only one chance to convince the officials at the FDA that they needed to act, and to do so quickly. He assumed the FDA officials would relay whatever he had to say to Galaxy. His presentation had to withstand the drug company's rebuttal. Lives depended on how successful he was in overcoming bureaucratic inertia and caution within the agency and the inevitable counter arguments from the drug company and its lawyers, lobbyists and captive Congressmen.

THURSDAY MORNING, APRIL 7 – LAW DEPARTMENT

Eileen Wang called Ann Tilley, the SEC attorney responsible for the Hepaticin subpoena. Wang had spoken with Tilley several times before to discuss the scope of the subpoena and to get the usual extension of time – no one can produce emails as quickly as the standard SEC subpoena demands. She had found the SEC attorney friendly and easy to work with.

This call would be different, Wang thought as she keyed in the number.

When the SEC attorney answered, Wang identified herself and the subpoena she was calling about.

"Eileen, how are you doing?" the SEC attorney asked. "Got my documents?"

"Our IT people are going to ship you a hard drive tonight with all of the emails we think are responsive," Wang replied. "But that's not why I'm calling."

"Have you found something?"

"Yes," Wang said. "We discovered we were hacked. Our IT forensics people discovered that someone has hacked the corporate email account of Brett Winslow. He's the VP of Pharmacy here. As you know, one of our medical directors noticed an excess number of cases of this cancer, and most of the members affected were taking Hepaticin. He emailed Winslow the details, and they had some back and forth."

"Your IT people are pretty sure about this?"

"Yes. The head of our IT forensics team believes we were hacked by a group called FIN4. Or at least that's the name a security consultant called Fire Eye has given this hack. I don't know if you have heard of them."

"FIN4?" the SEC attorney said. "Oh yeah, sure have. Listen, would you mind sharing this with someone from the FBI? They have been trying to nail FIN4 for years."

Wang agreed, and the SEC attorney promised to send Wang an email with a call-in number.

A few minutes later, Wang got the email and a request that she dial into the conference call-in ten minutes. When she did, the SEC attorney introduced two FBI Special Agents. Wang repeated what she had told the SEC attorney, and the agents asked a number of questions. Wang answered what she could and volunteered to make her IT expert, Liz Kolinsky, available to answer their technical questions.

"We're going to want to come out and interview her," Special Agent Jim Walden, who seemed to be the lead agent, said. "Has she removed the code?"

"No, she thought you might want to examine it before she did that."

"We do, but you understand that means they can still read your guy's email? His name is Winslow, right?"

"Yes, and that's why we need you to come out and do whatever you need to do sooner rather than later," Wang acknowledged. "But just so you know, we've put the hard drive from his computer on a machine in IT, where it's quarantined – or at least not connected to any of our networks except email. We've given Winslow a secure email account for anything truly sensitive.

"But there's something else," Wang added, "I have to tell you."

The agents waited for Wang to continue. They had conducted enough interviews to know that sometimes it's best just to listen.

"We figured it would take you time to get out here to interview Liz, examine the code, and whatever else you need to do. So, Liz came up with an interesting idea. She suggested we plant something in Winslow's email for these people to read."

"Like what?" Tilley, the SEC attorney, asked. Her voice conveyed apprehension.

"Management told Dr. Doss, the medical director who discovered the association between Hepaticin and this cancer, to review all of his work, to make sure his analysis is solid.

"Liz, our IT person, suggested we have Dr. Doss send Winslow an email saying that he has completed his re-review and that he has to withdraw his analysis. He does not believe the drug made by Galaxy causes this cancer. She suggested Doss say the IT programmer who prepared the initial report with all these members getting this rare cancer missed something."

"I cannot authorize you to do that," the SEC attorney said. The agency she worked for was charged with making sure people did not manipulate the market.

The senior FBI agent worded his concern differently. "I don't think we can *ask* you to do that."

Wang took a deep breath and said, "We've already done it. This morning. About an hour ago."

"Can you send us a copy of the email?" Walden, the senior FBI agent, asked. Wang thought it sounded more like a demand.

"Give me your email address, and I'll send it right away," Wang agreed. "But listen. Liz doesn't think these people, whoever they are, are checking Winslow's email as often as they were. She thinks they backed off after the Journal story. Since then, she says they usually just check on the weekends."

The agents exchanged contact information with Wang and told her, in that commanding way FBI agents have, they would be in touch again soon.

"Oh, one more thing," Wang added. When she said that, she could almost hear the FBI agents snap to attention.

"To make things credible, and in case anyone from inside our organization *is* leaking information, in his email Dr. Doss says he is taking full responsibility for the mistake and has tendered his resignation. We've had IT suspend his email account."

The agents thanked Wang. They could not tell her they had identified FIN4's likely contact point within one of the private equity firms, and so, they could not tell her how helpful the trap she had set might be. They also could not tell her the fire drill they would have to go through to get authorization by the weekend to tap the financial analyst's cell phone.

Over the next hour, Wang pulled up the information she had downloaded on Galaxy's recent settlement with the Department of Justice. She found the civil complaint filed by the Department. She scrolled down to the bottom where the names of counsel appeared. She ignored the lines for the Attorney General, the Deputy Attorney General in charge of the Civil Division, and at least two other tiers of management. She focused instead on the name at the bottom of the list, because that would be the attorney who had actually done the work.

Wang jotted down the name – April Donovan – and the phone number of the attorney. She Googled Donovan and saw that she had gotten her law degree from Harvard, clerked on the U.S. Court of Appeals for the Fifth Circuit, and then in put in three or four years with the prestigious O'Melveny & Myers law firm in Washington, D.C. After her stint at DOJ, she would likely return to O'Melveny or another top D.C. law firm with a burnished resume.

Wang explained to the DOJ attorney that she had information about Galaxy, or at least about some of the physicians who had received gifts and money from Galaxy.

"We settled with Galaxy," the attorney responded. "The papers are on the Department's website."

"I'm familiar with those," Wang replied. "What I've got is new. It pertains to Hepaticin. And people are dying."

"You've got my attention," Donovan, the DOJ attorney, responded.

"I am bringing one of our medical directors to D.C. tomorrow morning to explain what he's found to the FDA. I realize this is extremely short notice, but since we are going to be in town, I was wondering if we could visit with you in the afternoon. I want you to meet Dr. Doss and have him explain it."

"What's the short version?"

"The short version is Galaxy's biggest revenue generator, currently, is a drug called Hepaticin. It's for fatty liver disease."

"I'm familiar with it. And you're right. Our settlement didn't have anything to do with Hepaticin."

"I'd rather do this in person, because our story is complicated. There are several aspects to it, but the gist is, the demand for the drug has been so strong, Galaxy had capacity problems. Galaxy outsourced making some of the product to a company in India. We believe the product made in India, or some of it, was not made correctly. It may have been contaminated. And it's causing some patients to develop a rare cancer, adrenal cortical carcinoma."

"That's why you're going to the FDA."

"Right. We also believe that some of the physicians who have received a lot of money and trips and gifts from Galaxy are prescribing Hepaticin to patients who clearly don't need it. We believe they are diagnosing fatty liver disease in patients that don't have any evidence of fatty liver disease. We believe they are doing that primarily to get paid more by us, and ultimately by Medicare, but also to keep the gravy coming from the drug company."

"I don't follow."

"That's why we need to spend some quality time with you in front of a white board."

"Okay."

"The icing on the cake is, we believe the patients who are most likely to develop this cancer as a result of the defective product are the patients who were healthy to begin with – who didn't have fatty liver disease and didn't need to be taking this drug."

"Two o'clock work for you?"

Wang agreed, and the two attorneys discussed logistics for the meeting.

FRIDAY, APRIL 8 – FDA, WASHINGTON, D.C.

The flight to Reagan National Airport in Washington had been uneventful. Doss and Wang found the Metro station and crowded into a car along with other morning commuters. At Gallery station, they switched to the Metro "Red Line" and took it to the Silver Springs stop. From there, a twenty-minute cab ride brought them to the FDA's White Oak campus. Thirty minutes later, they had negotiated registration and security. Assistant Deputy Director Constance Hopkins led them to a conference room.

Doss plugged his laptop into one of the electrical sockets in the center of the table. There was no internet connection for visitors. Doss reminded himself that didn't matter, because his corporate email account had been suspended. Besides, he had checked his smart phone for personal email, weather, stocks, and everything else he could think of in the airport in Cincinnati, and again at Reagan waiting for the plane to clear, and again in the cab, and then in the lobby downstairs. Not that he was tense.

Wang, he noticed, was not fidgeting. She appeared to be the picture of composure. His suit pants and white shirt were already wrinkled from the morning's travel, but her suit looked as if she had just put it on. *How do women do that?* he wondered.

Four FDA staffers entered the room including Assistant Deputy Director Hopkins, and introduced themselves. They checked to see if an additional, more senior official would be joining them, and determined she was stuck in a budget meeting and would not be able to participate. They inquired whether Wang and her companion had problems with their travel or in finding the FDA campus, and learned from Wang they had not. After further discussion with Wang, they reached consensus that the weather today was really nice for this time of year. And after one of the FDA staffers used his tablet to do some on-the-spot research, they were also able to decide that, *yes, this was the peak time for cherry blossoms*. With those issues settled, Wang re-introduced Dr. Spencer Doss and suggested that he explain what he had found.

Doss began by stating the bottom line. He and his colleagues had found evidence suggesting that the Hepaticin manufactured for Galaxy Pharmaceutical Company by Vishnu Life Sciences, a company located in Hyderabad, India, was associated with a rare cancer, adrenal cortical carcinoma.

He then led the officials through how he had arrived at that conclusion, beginning with two patients with the rare cancer coming to his attention, followed by his attempt to determine if the patients had any obvious medical history in common or were using the same prescription drug. The obvious candidate had been Hepaticin. He shared a chart showing the expected and actual incidence of adrenal cortical cancer among the health plan's members during the previous five years, with data on the total number of health plan members in the background.

Doss explained he had reviewed the data with representatives from Galaxy. The Galaxy representatives had rejected his concerns. Among other things, they suggested that the cancers did not start occurring as early after Hepaticin's market entry as one would expect if Hepaticin caused the cancer and the latency period was what the seemed to show.

Doss recounted that the senior Galaxy representative dismissed what he was seeing as one of those cancer clusters that occur by chance and are alarming, but for which no common cause could be found. He predicted the incidence of Hepaticin would trail off and disappear, despite increasing numbers of people taking Hepaticin. He had urged caution.

Doss explained things might have ended there, but for the fact that the IT person who had done the data mining had travelled to Hyderabad, India, for family reasons. While there, she stumbled on the fact that Galaxy had contracted with Vishnu to manufacture some of the Hepaticin needed to meet demand, but had recently cancelled its contract with Vishnu.

Wang interjected that, to that point, neither Spencer nor she had been aware Galaxy had outsourced production – nor would they have thought anything of it if they had.

Doss explained that the IT data miner played a hunch. She re-ran the data on Hepaticin users who went on to develop adrenal cortical carcinoma – this time showing the NDCs for the product the unlucky patients had taken. Each of the patients who had taken Hepaticin and developed adrenal cortical carcinoma had taken pills manufactured by Vishnu.

Doss was careful to say that he had no direct evidence Galaxy was aware the Vishnu-manufactured product was causing the cancers. But he noted that by the time Galaxy cancelled its contract with Vishnu, several doctors had at least two patients on Hepaticin develop adrenal cortical carcinoma. Those doctors, Doss added, had received substantial payments from Galaxy. They had gone to Galaxy-paid-for seminars, and so on. They would have known whom to call inside Galaxy.

Doss reviewed the statistical analysis Tam Nguyen Phan had performed, focusing on the Vishnu product. Using her calculations, he provided the level of statistical significance and confidence interval. The FDA officials seemed impressed.

One of the FDA officials asked, "Hasn't Vishnu Life Sciences been in the news recently? Didn't the EU find some problems there?"

"Vishnu has had significant problems," Wang responded, "after an EU inspection found manufacturing problems and efforts by Vishnu to cover up the problems – destroyed records, falsified records, the whole nine yards."

"But," Wang added, "Galaxy apparently cancelled its contract with the Indian company *before* the EU inspection. *Shortly* before, but before."

Wang passed around copies of the Galaxy SEC filing indicating that it had terminated its contract with Vishnu. She then removed a paper clip from a second set of papers and passed around the voluntary recall initiated by Galaxy of certain lots of Hepaticin.

"I don't know," Wang said, "if this recall covered product manufactured in India, but I think you might want to check your records."

The FDA officials looked at the recall notice and exchanged knowing glances.

Doss concluded by explaining that he and Wang had taken a close look at six physicians who had attended seminars sponsored and paid for by Galaxy over the last three years, each at luxury resorts. Health plan staff had pulled the medical records for the members those physicians had diagnosed with NASH. While most the patients had at least some evidence of the liver disease, the remainder – maybe 40% – did not. Doss explained that among this sample of patients – admittedly not a large sample – those who did not appear to have fatty liver were at greater risk of developing the cancer.

"Before we open things to questions," Doss said, "I just want to focus on the fact that we have over 100 cases of adrenal cortical carcinoma. About 80 are excess cases – more than expected for our enrollment. Nearly all of those excess cases are Medicare Advantage enrollees. Our company has about one in ten of all Medicare Advantage patients. In other words, if our experience is typical, there could be ten times that many people who got this cancer while taking Hepaticin – maybe 800 cases, give or take – just in the Medicare Advantage population.

"About 30% of all Medicare beneficiaries are enrolled in Medicare Advantage. All told, we could be talking about maybe 2,600, maybe 2,700, Medicare beneficiaries who have developed this cancer. We don't know how many more will develop this cancer, or already have tumors that have not been detected. Toss in non-Medicare beneficiaries, and this situation may go well higher than that. If adrenal cortical carcinoma is not caught in time, it can be a death sentence."

"Have you checked with any other Medicare Advantage plans?" one of the FDA staff asked.

"No," Doss answered. "We assumed you would want to do that."

"Have you spoken with anyone except Galaxy about this?" asked another of the FDA staff.

"No, but I have written this up and expect to submit it for publication."

Wang spoke up. "We are meeting with some Department of Justice attorneys this afternoon."

Doss thought he saw the FDA staffers sit up a little straighter in their chairs. Evidently, he thought, they just decided they would have to move more quickly if others were involved or knew what they are sitting on. He made a snap decision.

"Of course," he said, "we are going to have to start notifying our members who got the Vishnu-made pills that they need to be monitored closely for adrenal cortical carcinoma. We also need to notify our primary care physicians to monitor their patients who may have taken the Vishnu product. And, we have to let our oncologists know what the concern is."

"Can you give us a couple days before you do anything to alert the public?" the most senior FDA staffer asked.

Doss looked at Wang.

"We can hold up for a few days, but that's it," Wang said. "I would like to see our communications go out the door by the middle of next week."

Nice bluff, Doss thought.

"We have to be concerned," Wang continued, "that patients will sue us saying we should have warned them – saying we sat on this information. We know of at least one lawyer who is about to file suit against Galaxy, and based on our discussions with him, we expect his lawsuit will get a lot of media attention."

"When is he going to file?"

"I don't know, but he made it sound like he was going to file any day. That's why we wanted to come in right away. We didn't think you would want to be caught flat-footed when he filed."

The staffers thanked Doss and Wang and promised to be in touch. One of the staffers volunteered to show them out and to make sure someone called a cab.

FRIDAY, APRIL 8 – DEPARTMENT OF JUSTICE

After a taxi ride to the Metro station, and a subway trip to Metro Center, Doss and Wang grabbed lunch. From the sandwich place, they walked the short distance to the address the Department of Justice attorney had given Wang. It took less than fifteen minutes to negotiate the sign in process and to pass through security at the DOJ office. April Donovan, the DOJ attorney, greeted the pair and led them briskly through a series of hallways to a conference room.

The conference room, Wang thought as she took her seat, could have been a conference room in any federal office building anywhere in the country. It looked a bit worn and beaten up – an impression reinforced by a broken chair in one corner of the room. It had none of the panache of the conference rooms in the law firms she visited, with their original artwork and expensive furniture. Instead, it had cheap reproductions of photos of the President and the Attorney General. But it served its purpose.

Altogether three DOJ attorneys and a paralegal participated in the meeting. After brief introductions, April Donovan, the DOJ attorney Wang had contacted, spoke. She told Wang that she and her colleagues were interested to learn what Wang had to share, but could not make any promises they could do anything – especially if the issues had been resolved the recent settlement with Galaxy.

Wang began by thanking the DOJ attorneys for agreeing to meet with Dr. Doss and herself on such short notice. "This morning," Wang told the DOJ attorneys, "Dr. Doss was able to present to the FDA compelling evidence that the drug Hepaticin causes a rare cancer. He gave them a present, all wrapped up with a bow on top. I'm not going to be able to do that."

Wang saw that the paralegal was taking detailed notes on what she was saying.

"But I think what we have will interest you."

Wang asked Doss to repeat the story he shared with the FDA.

Doss recounted how he had discovered the excess cases of adrenal cortical carcinoma, a rare cancer, in patients taking Hepaticin. He also described his meeting with the representatives from Galaxy, and the subsequent discovery that only patients taking Hepaticin capsules made by an Indian company were developing the cancer.

The DOJ attorneys seemed interested, but appeared to Wang to be withholding their questions until she and Doss had finished their presentation.

"The Indian company is Vishnu Life Sciences in Hyderabad, India," Wang said, picking up where Doss had left off.

"Galaxy has terminated its contract with Vishnu." She slid a copy of Galaxy's filing with the SEC disclosing the contract termination. "Note the date on this filing. It was just before the team from Galaxy met with Dr. Doss and me."

"About the same time, Galaxy voluntarily withdrew certain lots of Hepaticin." Wang passed around a copy of the recall notice that she had found on the FDA's website. "I have not been able to confirm that those lots were manufactured by Vishnu, but I imagine the FDA will be checking on that. I am not able to say whether Galaxy misled the FDA about the reason for the recall, but it was obvious the FDA was not aware of a cancer risk with the product made in India. Let's just say – at a minimum – it doesn't look like Galaxy was completely candid with them."

One of the DOJ attorneys asked Wang if that was the substance of what she and Dr. Doss wanted to share.

"No, that's just background," Wang replied. "The reason I reached out to you is a bit more involved."

Wang asked if the DOJ attorneys were familiar with how the government paid Medicare Advantage organizations.

"CMS just pays you a flat amount for each beneficiary, right?" one of the DOJ attorneys responded.

"It's more complicated than that," Wang said. "CMS does pay us a fixed amount each month for each person who enrolls in one of our Medicare Advantage plans, but the amount is determined separately for each enrollee."

Wang hesitated for a moment, thinking how best to simplify what she had to explain.

"Each year, CMS determines a base line payment for a hypothetical 'typical' Medicare beneficiary in good health. Then, for each Medicare Advantage enrollee, it adjusts that amount to take into account how old the enrollee is, the enrollee's gender, and several other things. CMS calls those demographic adjustments. The idea is to pay the MA plan approximately what CMS would expect to pay in medical expense for an individual with similar characteristics who elected Original Medicare."

Wang asked the paralegal if he was able to follow what she was saying. The paralegal thanked Wang, and said he was able to follow her.

"CMS also adjusts the payment it makes to the MA – Medicare Advantage – plan to take into account the health status of the enrollee. CMS calls that 'Medicare risk adjustment' or 'MRA.' It is really complicated, so I'm going to try to do this at a very high level. I'm probably going to oversimplify things.

"Physicians and hospitals and other providers submit bills to MA plans. We call those 'claims.' The physician or hospital is supposed to provide certain information on the claim form, including the diagnosis. We compile the information we have on each of the conditions doctors have diagnosed for each Medicare Advantage enrollee and submit that to CMS.

"For certain conditions, CMS pays the MA plan additional money each month. For example, if a patient has diabetes, CMS pays X dollars a month more. If the patient has lung cancer, CMS pays Y dollars a month extra. And so on."

Wang asked if everyone was following so far. The DOJ attorneys indicated that they could follow her just fine. The paralegal gave her a "thumbs up" gesture.

"Medicare Advantage plans still pay a lot of doctors on a fee-for-service basis, basically the same way Medicare pays physicians in Original Medicare," Wang continued. "But more so than in the past, Medicare Advantage plans and doctors are adopting different payment arrangements. For example, many Medicare Advantage plans now contract to pass through to the primary care physician a percentage of what CMS pays for the MA enrollee.

"This probably works best with an example. Suppose my mother, who's sixty-six and lives in Colorado, is enrolled in one of our Medicare Advantage plans. We would require her to pick a primary care physician and have that doctor coordinate her care. We might have a contract with the primary care doctor that says we will pay him

80% of what we get from CMS, and the doctor agrees to be financially responsible for all of my mother's medical expenses, up to a certain amount."

Wang again asked if everyone was following.

"We don't actually pay the whole 80% to the doctor each month. We hold back much of that amount and use it to pay claims from hospitals, specialists and so on. We settle up with the doctor after the end of the year."

"The problem that we've run into, and that other plans have run into, is that a few doctors were having their billing staff add certain diagnoses to their claims. I'm going to make up an example. Let's say my mother doesn't have diabetes, but her doctor knows that if he bills us for an office visit and puts the code for diabetes in the bill, CMS will pay us more, and we will pass 80% of that higher monthly payment to him. If he does that with enough patients, he can generate a lot of extra revenue."

One of the DOJ attorneys interrupted. "This is ringing a bell now. I think we've gone after some doctors and health plans for that."

"That's right. You have. Because of that, and for other reasons, we audit a lot of medical records to make sure the diagnoses on the bills are documented in the medical records."

"Unfortunately, doing audits to make sure these diagnoses – the ones that generate extra revenue – were documented in the medical record didn't entirely eliminate the problem. Some doctors, again in South Florida, were smarter. They weren't just putting the diagnoses on the claim or encounter form. They were putting these phony diagnoses in the patient's medical record.

"That is much harder for us to catch. These guys usually pick things that are hard to spot. They don't say the patient has lung cancer, because we'd expect to see treatment for that. So, they pick things like depression or alcoholism. Or they exaggerate the severity of something the patient actually has. Say the patient has diabetes. The doctor might diagnose diabetes with neuropathy – nerve pain."

"We were afraid," Wang continued, "that someone would blame us for not catching that anyway, so we began doing some fairly sophisticated statistical modeling to determine if any of these physicians were statistical outliers. We look at those outliers really hard."

One of the DOJ attorneys looked at his watch and asked, "What does this have to do with the drug?"

Wang smiled. "Sorry for the long explanation. Dr. Doss noticed that a few of our primary care physicians had two or even three patients develop this cancer while taking Hepaticin. Even among patients taking Hepaticin, this cancer is still pretty unusual, so we began wondering just how much of this drug those doctors were prescribing."

Dr. Doss asked if he could say something. Wang nodded.

"I asked one of our MRA guys, the one responsible for a lot of this statistical modeling, to look to see if we had doctors who were outliers in terms of how often they diagnosed fatty liver and prescribed Hepaticin. It turns out that we do have some extreme outliers – what our people call 'suspicious outliers" because they fit a certain profile.

"We sent our people out to get the medical records for their fatty liver patients. When I reviewed those medical records, there was at least a plausible basis for diagnosing fatty liver in some of their patients. But there was no apparent basis for diagnosing fatty liver in others – especially among the patients diagnosed with NASH, the progressive form of the condition. In other words, there were no biopsies, no imaging studies, nothing. The patients weren't diabetic, and sometimes weren't even overweight. It looks like they were diagnosing fatty liver in those patients just to get the extra revenue."

"Did any of those patients get this cancer?" Donovan asked.

"Yes," Doss answered. "That's the thing that is really disturbing about this – at least from my perspective. Some of these patients did develop this cancer. In fact, the patients who do not appear to have fatty liver, and shouldn't have been taking this drug, were the ones more likely to get it."

The DOJ attorney who had been checking his watch stood. "I need a break for a couple minutes. I have some other meetings, but I want to move those, and continue with you, if you can stay a while longer."

The group agreed to take a short break.

When everyone returned, Wang picked up the thread.

"I approached this a little differently than Spencer – Dr. Doss – did. I know that drug companies now have to report gifts and payments they make to doctors."

Wang explained how she had reviewed Galaxy's "open payments" data and noticed that in addition to cash payments, meals and the like, Galaxy held a big seminar each year for doctors who prescribed a lot of Hepaticin.

Galaxy scheduled these seminars at luxury hotels and paid all the expenses of the doctors and their spouses to attend.

"Six doctors have attended all three of these annual seminars. Our statistician calls them the 'Luxury Resort Six.'"

"Let me guess," one of the DOJ attorneys said. "Some or all of these six are outliers?"

"You got it."

The DOJ attorneys nodded appreciatively. Wang had evidently hit a sore spot.

"Those are the facts. We can go into any of this in as much detail as you'd like. But if I can," Wang added, "I'd like to give you my theory."

No one objected, so Wang continued. "There are two parts to this. Either may turn out to be true, or both, or neither."

"First," Wang said, "some of the doctors had two – or even three – patients who were taking Hepaticin develop adrenal cortical carcinoma. I think one of them, or maybe more than one of them, made the connection."

Wang pulled another document from the folder she had brought with her.

"Spencer – Dr. Doss – sent a letter to the prescribing physician for each of our members who took Hepaticin and developed adrenal cortical carcinoma. He asked the physician to file an adverse event report with the FDA." Wang passed a document to one of the DOJ attorneys. "Here's a copy of one of those letters, so you can see what I'm talking about."

The DOJ attorney skimmed the letter, addressed to Sylvan Goldbach, M.D., and passed it to the attorney on his left.

"Maybe the light went on when they got this letter. Maybe one or more of these physicians had already made the connection. I don't know. But in any event, I think that one of them, or maybe more than one, told Galaxy it had a problem. Galaxy must have investigated and traced the problem back to the company in India."

"Secondly, several of the doctors who attended Galaxy's first Hepaticin seminar seem to have all come up with the same bright idea: If they diagnosed NASH in their patients, and then prescribed Hepaticin to treat it, they would get more revenue from MA plans, and we wouldn't suspect or wouldn't be able to prove fraud. Plus, they would keep getting payments and gifts from Galaxy.

"I don't have any direct proof that happened, but three of the doctors – the ones in Florida – already had percent-of-premium contracts before that first seminar. The other three – one in Ohio and two in Texas – asked for percentage-of-premium contracts shortly after that seminar."

She turned to Doss and asked him to relate his conversation with the physician who had attended that seminar and had refused to go back.

Doss explained what the physician had told him about one of the seminar speakers teaching the seminar participants how to commit MRA fraud without being caught.

Donovan, who seemed to be the most junior of the DOJ attorneys, asked the first question. "If these doctors were deliberately diagnosing patients with fatty liver disease, when they knew the patient didn't have that condition, that's fraud. We can go after them for healthcare fraud, or for submitting false claims for payment that ultimately comes from government funds. But I'm having trouble seeing a claim against Galaxy. What's Galaxy's exposure?"

"Like I said at the outset," Wang replied. "I can't hand you a box with a fully developed case in it, all wrapped up in wrapping paper, with a bow on top. But I think you should look hard at whether there was a tacit quid-pro-quo between Galaxy and these doctors. Galaxy would provide these lavish seminars and speaking fees, and these doctors would write lots of prescriptions for Hepaticin. I don't know if you can make that case."

Wang looked at her notes again. "I mentioned that I suspect one or more of the physicians who have gotten a lot of money from Galaxy realized that too many patients taking Hepaticin were getting this rare cancer.

"I think you should look hard at when Galaxy found out that people taking Hepaticin were developing this rare cancer, and what it did after that. If that's why Galaxy ended its contract with this company in India, I think it did the right thing by ending the contract. If that's why it recalled some of the Hepaticin already on the market in this country, I think that was the responsible thing to do.

"But as near as I can tell, Galaxy didn't tell the FDA why it was really doing that recall, or it deliberately explained the recall in such a way as to mislead the FDA about the real issue. And, it didn't tell doctors to monitor their patients for adrenal cortical carcinoma. It didn't tell patients they needed to be monitored for this cancer, so that it could be caught before it metastasized. They didn't tell health plans to make sure that their members who took the product made in India got tested.”

“Do you have any evidence,” one of the other DOJ attorneys asked, “that Galaxy did anything affirmative to cover this up?”

Neither Wang nor Doss responded immediately.

“Maybe they had a duty to disclose this,” the DOJ attorney elaborated. “We’ll have to look into that. But can you point to anything affirmative Galaxy did? I’m trying to ask if Galaxy did anything specific, aside from whatever sins of omission it might or might not be guilty of.”

“Galaxy offered us – the company we work for – a contract for data mining,” Doss interjected. “They were talking about paying us several million dollars. But they said they couldn’t, or wouldn’t, give us that contract if we went public with our concerns about their drug.”

“That explicit?” the DOJ attorney pressed.

“It was very explicit,” Doss answered. “But they were clever about. They said if we went public with our concerns, personal injury attorneys would file suit and call me to testify. They said Galaxy didn’t want to be in the position of trying to argue that we didn’t know what we were doing when we did the data mining that led us to conclude Hepaticin was causing some people to get cancer, while they were paying us to do data mining for their company.”

“I don’t know if I buy that,” the DOJ attorney said, “but their position does make some sense.”

Wang volunteered to have all the documents she and Dr. Doss assembled during their investigation put on a DVD, but suggested that it would be best if the DOJ attorneys served her with a subpoena. She explained that would allow her to produce the medical records without worrying about whether she might be violating privacy laws.

The attorneys thanked Wang and Doss and said they would be in touch.

"You've given us a lot to think about," the more senior of the government attorneys said. "We will need to touch base with the FDA and with the lawyers in our shop who have worked on MRA cases. But whether we can do anything with this or not, we think you did the right thing by coming in and laying this out for us."

The more junior attorney was more succinct. "You kept your promise," she said. "What you found is very interesting."

On the return trip to Cincinnati, Wang told Doss that the health plan now had a new challenge. Medicare had paid, or was currently paying, risk adjustment amounts for the Medicare Advantage enrollees diagnosed by the Luxury Resort Six physicians. The company needed to withdraw the files for any of those patients where the diagnosis was not supportable. It would also have to return any payments it had received based on the fraudulent diagnoses. Ultimately, the health plan would likely need to review the NASH diagnoses of all the physicians who attended the Galaxy Hepaticin seminars, but she wanted Doss to start with Luxury Resort Six physicians – both as a pilot for the larger work and as a necessary first step, given what they knew about those cases.

He was still on the payroll, even though he could not go into the office, so he agreed to do the review – provided he could access his files electronically. Wang emailed Liz Kolinsky and asked her to make sure he still had access to his files other than email.

After some discussion, they also agreed that the company should have a second, independent review, if she could arrange that.

As the terminal at Reagan International airport became more crowded, their conversation shifted from those sensitive matters to more personal matters, including family and their experiences at school.

SATURDAY, APRIL 9 – PUBLIC SECURITY BUREAU

Chinese media were the first to report the arrest of Darrin Hightower, Galaxy China's President, and twenty of the company's employees for participating in widespread bribery of hospitals, clinics and doctors. The story quickly became news around the world, prompting officials in Poland, Bulgaria and several other countries to open preliminary investigations of their own. The Wall Street Journal and The New York Times covered the scandal with lengthy front page stories.

A media spokesperson for Galaxy Pharmaceuticals in London angrily denounced the arrests. In a press conference, he announced that the company had, of course, launched an internal investigation, but asserted that the company presently had no evidence that its China subsidiary paid bribes to Chinese officials, businessmen or doctors.

"They could not have been passing around the millions of Euros being discussed in news reports," he told reporters, "without the company's audit and compliance staff discovering it."

He reminded reporters the company had repeatedly instructed its employees that under no circumstances were they to use illegal payments to increase sales of the company's products.

The statements by the Galaxy public relations flak did not sit well in China. In Shanghai, Qian Jie, the head of the Shanghai Public Security Bureau, appeared on a local television report – an hour-long, prime-time exposé – in which he detailed, with charts and diagrams, how Galaxy's Chinese subsidiary had funneled millions of Euros through travel agencies to the purchasing agents for hospitals and clinics and to physicians. He accused Galaxy China President Darrin Hightower of being the "Godfather" of a huge bribery scheme. The news program featured excerpts from recorded confessions by a number of businessmen and doctors, as well as from several of Galaxy China's own employees.

Galaxy's beleaguered public relations officer dismissed the Shanghai news program as "yellow journalism" – prompting Chinese officials to complain that the charge was racist and harkened back to the 19th century European obsession with the "yellow peril."

In the days that followed, British tabloids ran follow-up stories with lurid accounts of a rumored video of the Chinese subsidiary's president having sex with a Chinese girlfriend. The tabloids reported that DVDs containing the executive's sexual exploits had been sent to Sir Alec, the Galaxy Board of Directors, and Hightower's wife. The company refused to comment on the rumors. Mrs. Hightower also declined comment, according to a statement issued by her divorce attorney.

But Qian was restless. The bribery arrests had captured attention around the world and had played especially well within China. And yet, his boss in Beijing was not satisfied.

His boss was Guo Shengkun, the Minister of Public Security. Not that he dare say so, but from his perspective, making Guo the head of Public Security had been a farce. In November, 2012, when Xi Jinping become President, Xi had launched a much-publicized anti-corruption campaign. Despite the initial skepticism, the campaign had actually had some teeth in it.

Before Xi launched his anti-corruption campaign, Meng Jianzhu had headed up the Ministry of Public Security. Meng was a serious hard liner on corruption. Meng had even gone so far as to criticize the practice of party bosses passing notes to judges during trials. Meng argued that this widespread practice left the unfortunate impression that the judge's decision might not be based on the law and evidence. That speech had attracted a good deal of favorable comment, especially from foreign sources, but apparently went too far for some party bosses.

In December 2012, shortly after Xi became President and General Secretary, the Party booted the hard line Meng up to a policy-making position and installed Guo Shengkun as the Minister of Public Security. Guo had no experience with law enforcement or the police. *His whole career had been in making aluminum,* Qian believed. *The guy knew nothing about police work!*

Since becoming Minister, Guo had been preoccupied with the large fines the government in the United States extracted from large multinational companies. As a former company CEO, he was also overly concerned – in Qian's view – with protecting Chinese companies, especially government-owned companies, from foreign competition. *That wasn't police work. That was politics.*

Guo had complained repeatedly that the Shanghai Bureau's investigation had not turned up evidence to support the rumored connection between Hepaticin and cancer. Qian didn't think the Minister actually cared whether there was evidence to support the allegation. He just wanted to collect a big fine and a big headline – like the government in the United States did.

Qian prepared his report carefully. The Shanghai Public Security Bureau had contacted every hospital and oncologist in Shanghai province and in several nearby provinces, but had found no cases of adrenal cortical carcinoma in patients taking Hepaticin. They had also found no mention of the problem in Galaxy's external emails, including those between Galaxy China officials in Shanghai and the company's parent company in London.

On top of that, China's own FDA – "CFDA" – had concluded that the reports in the United States of a connection between Hepaticin and adrenal cortical carcinoma were part of a scheme by unscrupulous market speculators to manipulate the US stock market.

Qian did not know what else Minister Guo could expect, but he was not going to let the party hack's obsession sideline his own career. He qualified his report by noting he did not believe CFDA had conducted a thorough investigation. He used his report to suggest that if Public Security Ministry officials in Beijing remained concerned, they should press the CFDA to conduct a more thorough investigation. They might also direct the Public Security Bureaus elsewhere to check with the hospitals and oncologists in their provinces.

SUNDAY, APRIL 10 – DATA CENTER

It was 3:48 a.m. Sunday morning when the call came. It took Liz Kolinsky several rings before her head cleared enough to realize it was the phone. The IT Data Center wanted her to know that it had detected an intrusion. Someone – in her mind, it could only be the FIN4 group – had penetrated the email account she had asked the IT Security Center to monitor. She thanked the caller.

Sitting up in bed, she called the number the FBI technical consultant had given her. After several rings, a male voice answered, identifying himself as Jack Carver, Federal Bureau of Investigation. *He has his work phone next to his bed*, Kolinsky thought. *My kind of guy!*

She relayed the message that an intruder had penetrated the email account of Brett Winslow, the company's Pharmacy VP.

Kolinsky slid back under the covers. Before she closed her eyes, the FBI technical consultant had placed a call to the technicians monitoring the cell phone of a certain well-paid analyst with a notoriously rich private equity fund.

The health plan's Data Center did not notice an email purporting to be from a travel agency notifying Spencer Doss that he had won an all-expense-paid trip for two to Bermuda. A system-generated response notified the email sender that the email account of Spencer Doss was suspended. The automated message advised the sender to contact the company's call center during business hours for additional assistance.

A little after one o'clock Sunday afternoon, the FBI team intercepted and recorded a call on the analyst's cell phone. A woman, who did not identify herself, reported that she had some "interesting developments" on Hepaticin and Galaxy. "Turns out," she said, "Hepaticin doesn't cause cancer after all."

The analyst listened, and when the caller finished, he said tersely, "You should have our payment. Did you get our wire?"

"We wouldn't be talking," the woman responded, "if we hadn't."

Total time, one minute, twenty-two seconds.

MONDAY, APRIL 11 – HYDERABAD

A week earlier, Doss had asked Maya Naidu to update her Hepaticin search to see how many new cases of adrenal cortical cancer had been diagnosed so far in the current calendar year. Naidu had delayed doing the update. She had relegated his request to the more usual turnaround time for SPDRs, in part because her boss was keeping her busy with rush jobs and Doss's request was not urgent. But mainly, she had wanted to allow more time for claims to come in from hospitals and physicians' offices, so that the results would not seriously understate the number of new cases in January and February.

Once she set about doing the programing, it took little time or effort to update her search on Hepaticin users who had developed adrenal cortical carcinoma. The report ran without a hitch, and she forwarded it to her boss for approval.

Naidu typed an email to Dr. Doss, letting him know that the new run had identified six new cases in January and five more in February, but cautioned him that it was possible additional cases could still be reported. She reminded him that doctors and hospitals were supposed to submit claims within 90 days, but it often took longer for claims to come in, especially if the individual was insured by two plans.

Naidu attached a copy of the report, but told the doctor he should regard it as preliminary, because her boss had not reviewed it.

She also used the email to say that, *yes, she was doing okay.* She asked how he was doing and if the drug company was still trying to get him fired. She hit the "send" key.

A moment later, she got a system reply saying the email could not be delivered, because the email account had been suspended. Naidu checked to make sure she had typed the email address correctly. She had. She tried sending her email again, but got back the same message. She tried a third time, typing the email address again from scratch.

She got the same automatic reply message.

For a moment, Naidu was perplexed. Then, she realized what had happened. *The drug company had won! They are covering up their problem, and they got poor Dr. Doss fired.* She felt sad and angry for many reasons, but mostly because she believed that while things like that were all too common in India, such injustices were not supposed to happen in the United States.

Naidu sat at her computer, deep in thought. What Galaxy had done had – she used the American expression to express her outrage – really pissed her off. After ten minutes, during which she had barely moved, she logged back onto her computer and searched for the stories about Galaxy's problems in China. She perused several the stories and gradually an idea began to form.

Fifteen or twenty minutes later, Ashika entered the room. Naidu stood suddenly, as if she had just made a decision, and said she would be gone for several hours. She reminded her daughter to work on her homework.

"I will be expecting real progress when I get back, not excuses."

Naidu checked her wallet to be sure she had plenty of cash and left the house. She slipped into the car she had rented for her stay and drove to a nearby market. She walked purposefully through the outdoor market until she found what she was looking for – a stall that sold lady's garments in the styles worn by Muslim women. She purchased a hijab, the headscarf worn by Muslim women, forgetting to haggle over the price and overpaying.

Naidu drove a short distance to a restaurant, where she ordered chai, and then slipped into the ladies' room. Standing before the sink, she scrubbed the bindi from her forehead. She put on the hijab, which turned out to be easier to do than she expected. She put sunglasses on, walked briskly back to her table and left money to cover the bill for the chai, which arrived while she was in the restroom.

As usual, the traffic in Hyderabad was maddening, but using the GPS on her cell phone Naidu navigated her way through the chaos to a huge pharmaceutical plant with a large sign proclaiming in Urdu, Telugu and English, "Vishnu Life Sciences." Naidu circled the plant, and then circled again in a wider arc until she spotted an internet café. She parked, checked the hijab and sunglasses, making sure her face was largely hidden.

As she stepped into the internet café, she was not surprised to see that the handful of customers were all men, most of them young. Naidu suddenly realized no Moslem woman would enter such a place – and certainly not alone. But none of the men, most of whom seemed to be playing games, paid her any attention. *The disguise was not for their benefit anyway*, Naidu reminded herself. *It was for any security cameras.*

Naidu quietly made arrangements with the café's bored attendant, a thin man in his late twenties with acne scars, paying him extra so he would not require her to show identification or use a credit card.

At the computer, she set up an email account under a phony name and prepared an email to the US Embassy in New Delhi. Writing in Urdu, she explained that until recently, Galaxy Pharmaceutical had contracted with a company here in Hyderabad, Vishnu Life Sciences, to make some of its products. One of those products was the drug Hepaticin. Unfortunately, Vishnu had cut corners and did not make the drug correctly. Galaxy figured this out when some of the people taking capsules made by Vishnu began getting a very specific cancer – adrenal cortical carcinoma. "Galaxy," she wrote, "is trying to keep this problem secret."

She hesitated to think and then added: "Vishnu may have shipped the drugs to your country. This is very bad."

Naidu re-read the email, making small corrections. She decided to add a paragraph, even though she feared it would make the email sound less credible.

"I am not using my real name," she wrote, "because if Vishnu found out that I told you this, I would lose my job, and things would be very bad for me. Please do not try to find me. Please, just protect the people taking this drug."

She checked the email again, made a copy of its message, and hit "send.'"

Naidu opened a new email and typed in "chinaemb_in@mfa.gov.cn," the address of the Chinese embassy in New Delhi. She pasted the message into the email and sent it off as well, followed by essentially identical emails to the embassies of Singapore, Vietnam, Cambodia and Laos.

Reluctantly, she sent a slightly revised version to India's drug regulator – the Central Drugs Standard Control Organization, which was part of the Ministry of Health and Family Welfare. As she did, she sighed. It was possible all of her messages would be ignored, or dismissed after consultations with Galaxy's lobbyists and lawyers. But it was a foregone conclusion, she believed, that her message to India's drug regulator would be ignored.

MONDAY, APRIL 11 – GARNER LAW OFFICE

On Monday, about ninety minutes after the New York Stock Exchange opened, a private equity fund began buying shares in Galaxy Pharmaceuticals, accumulating a sizable position. About the same time, a second private equity firm began buying Galaxy shares as well, forcing up the price by a small, but appreciable amount.

By then, Spencer Doss and Eileen Wang were meeting with Devin Garner, the attorney who wanted to sue Galaxy. Doss wasn't sure it was necessary for him to sit in on the meeting. He suspected Wang was trying to avoid his feeling isolated, while they waited to see if the FBI made progress trying to catch the FIN4 hackers.

The lawyer's office was small and spare. The lawyer appeared to be fairly young, but according to Wang, had tried a number of cases and had a reputation as pretty good in the courtroom. "He was the one," she told Doss on the way to lawyer's office, "who won the Medawar case – the doctor accused of killing his wife."

As they assembled around the conference table in the lawyer's office, Doss was conscious that this was Wang's environment. He resolved to sit back and let her do her thing.

Wang began by saying she had discussed Garner's offer with her company's General Counsel. She was authorized to retain him to represent the company in a suit against Galaxy, provided certain issues were resolved.

First, she said she needed to reserve the right to bring in other counsel to backstop Garner at any time, if she felt that would be helpful. Garner appeared about to object, but Wang headed him off. "At our expense, of course. Your fee would not be affected." Garner said he would welcome any help he could get, as long as he got to try the case, if it went to trial. Wang agreed.

Second, Wang said she needed assurance that there would not be a conflict of interest between the health plan's interests and his other clients' interests. Garner assured her that his clients had agreed the health plan would be reimbursed first, as long the health plan agreed to reduce their repayment obligation by its pro rata share of his fee and expenses.

Finally, Wang said she needed Garner to agree not to file suit until she gave the go ahead. Wang said she expected to need only a few days, but she had to give the FDA a little time to react. Garner pushed back at that. He wanted to be sure he filed *before* the FDA acted, because he feared once that happened, the big-name firms, and the feeder firms that advertised on television, would sign up everyone else injured by the drug. After some back-and-forth, Wang and Garner worked out an agreement on how to finesse that issue.

Garner had his own issue. He would need the health plan to advance the costs of the litigation to recover the medical payments the health plan had paid on behalf of its members, with repayment contingent on a recovery. Wang had assumed that would be the case and agreed.

With those issues resolved, Wang asked Doss to relay how he had found the excess cancers, and how he had narrowed the problem to the Hepaticin made for Galaxy by the Indian company. Doss repeated the account he had provided the FDA and DOJ, but without the tension he had felt in D.C.

As he listened to Doss's account, Garner was impressed by the doctor and by the detail he provided. But he was completely floored by the unexpected twist in the case. It had never occurred to him that the capsules his clients had taken might have been made by anyone other than Galaxy.

Wang then walked Garner through the data she had pulled from the government website on the payments Galaxy had made to doctors around the country, including Dr. Goldbach, the doctor who had prescribed Hepaticin for Dan Meinhardt and Sam Carson.

Garner discussed his interview with Raj Patel, the oncologist treating both of his original clients. Garner said Dr. Patel did not believe either of his clients had fatty liver or should have been taking the drug.

Doss surprised Garner again by explaining that among the patients who took the Vishnu Life Sciences version of the drug, the patients who did not have fatty liver disease appeared to be at greater risk of developing adrenal cortical carcinoma.

Garner had lunch delivered so they could continue working.

As the morning progressed, Doss realized that they were no longer Ms. Wang, Dr. Doss, and Mr. Garner. They were now Eileen, Spencer and Devin. Doss also noticed that Galaxy's stock had inched up some, but he couldn't tell if that was just a normal market fluctuation or if it was in response to his stage-managed email exchange with Brett Winslow.

During lunch, Wang took a call from Jeff Reiner, the manager of the company's mail order business. He wanted Wang to know that his people had set aside a case of Hepaticin when they got the recall notice, but someone had forgotten to return it. "We'll return it to the wholesaler today," Reiner promised.

"No, don't," Wang protested. "Hang onto it. Make sure it's safe. We're probably going to want to have it tested. Even if we don't, we don't want to be accused of destroying evidence."

Garner agreed to find a first-class lab to test the drug.

Much of the afternoon's discussion involved the legal theories to include in the lawsuit and other issues on which Doss had no input. Perhaps the most important of those issues was whether to name Dr. Goldbach as a defendant. The issue was important to Garner, because the physician had prescribed Hepaticin for both of his patients, although neither needed it. Wang was less concerned about naming Goldbach because she had almost a hundred members who had taken the drug and developed cancer. From her perspective, Goldbach had prescribed the drug for only two --- even if those two were Garner's clients. *Besides, she had other plans for Goldbach's money.*

After some discussion, the two attorneys agreed that while it would be emotionally satisfying to name the physician as a defendant, it would not be worth the potential consequences. If they named Dr. Goldbach as a defendant, Galaxy would try to convince the jury to assign a big percentage of any damages due the individual plaintiffs to the doctor. That could be a problem, given the limits malpractice reform laws put on the damages that could be collected from a physician in a malpractice suit.

That problem would be compounded if Dr. Goldbach's malpractice insurer denied coverage, claiming that Goldbach had committed fraud. Every liability insurance policy has exclusions for fraud, criminal activity, and other intentional acts. It was better to focus on the giant company, than to risk a big, but uncollectable award against the crotchety old physician.

At first, Doss enjoyed watching the two lawyers sizing up the legal issues and planning the legal strategies they would pursue against the big drug company, but it soon got tedious – like watching other people play chess. He decided to work on the letters the health plan needed to send to affected members and their physicians.

By the end of the afternoon, Garner seemed satisfied he had enough information to prepare a first draft of a complaint for Wang to review. Wang reminded Garner again that he should not file until she had signed off on the complaint and gave him the green light. Garner agreed.

By then, Doss had found more than enough time to review and polish the letters he had drafted over the weekend. The first letter was intended for the health plan's members who had taken Hepaticin made by Vishnu Life Sciences. The letter, which would be personalized for each affected member, advised the member to be checked for adrenal cortical carcinoma – a cancer affecting a small, but significant portion of patients who had taken Hepaticin. The letter stressed that only people who had taken Hepaticin manufactured by the Indian company were at risk of developing the cancer. The letter also explained that the Indian version of the drug had been withdrawn from the market, so there was no reason to discontinue taking the drug unless instructed by their physician.

The second letter was intended for the members' primary care physicians. It urged them to make sure their affected patients – listed separately for each physician – were checked for adrenal cancer.

The third would go to the oncologists in the health plan's network, explaining that the health plan's data suggested patients, including Medicare beneficiaries, who had taken Hepaticin made in India appeared to be at greater risk of adrenal cortical carcinoma.

Wang would take the letters back to the company and with Bob Wiseman's help try to push them through the company's member and physician communication channels as quickly as possible.

TUESDAY, APRIL 12 – GALAXY HEADQUARTERS, LONDON

The Wall Street Journal and several other media outlets reported that Galaxy's charismatic CEO, Sir Alec Bright, would be traveling to China for a round of meetings with government officials. The media reports speculated he would attempt to resolve the standoff concerning allegations that the company's Chinese subsidiary had paid millions in bribes to hospitals, clinics and physicians. Based on other recent settlements, the reports suggested the Chinese officials would likely insist that Galaxy lower the price of its drugs in China.

Sir Alec reviewed The Wall Street Journal coverage with interest. Unlike the reporters, he knew that his company's lawyers had negotiated the main points of a deal with the Chinese government. Galaxy would apologize for the conduct of its China subsidiary. The company would announce that, to show its sincerity, it would reduce the prices at which it sold its drugs in China, effective immediately. The company would also agree to have its China subsidiary plead guilty to bribery charges and pay a fine. Sir Alec would negotiate the final figure for the fine, but a general range had been agreed upon.

Darrin Hightower, the president of the China subsidiary, would be convicted and sentenced to a year in prison. Hightower, however, would not be required to serve his sentence, but instead would be expelled from the country – provided Galaxy agreed to fire Hightower. The Chinese national employees would receive sentences ranging from three to nine months and would also be fired. The company's attorneys were putting the final touches on the statement he would read when he had negotiated the final amount of the fine. Sir Alec expected the fine to be as much a hundred million Euros, but his company could easily handle that.

Privately, Sir Alec had agreed to pay Darrin Hightower a hefty severance package, provided Hightower did not discuss any aspect of the whole incident in public. Hightower would have to deal with his wife on his own. Although not part of the deal with Chinese officials, Sir Alec had also decided to fire the public relations officer who had so angered officials in China.

The stock market hates uncertainty. With the prospect of a deal that would allow Galaxy to continue to do business in China, shares of Galaxy Pharmaceuticals Company had risen in recent trading. In fact, two private equity firms – with reputations for an uncanny knack at timing their purchases – had increased their holdings.

WEDNESDAY, APRIL 13 – CHINESE EMBASSY, NEW DELHI

Along with the usual volume of ordinary matters, the Chinese Embassy in New Delhi receives an astonishing number of exotic communications each week, including a bewildering number of anonymous complaints and warnings. These communications may arrive in any of the Indian subcontinent's chaotic jumble of languages. Embassy staff must first translate these communications, before responding or forwarding them to the relevant government agency.

In every embassy in every country, anonymous complaints and warnings are greeted with a special level of skepticism and wariness. Nonetheless, an effort must be made to separate the plausible from the cranky, the misinformed, and the delusional. This work generally falls to the most junior embassy staff, or sometimes, to a well-connected, past-his-prime staffer, biding his time until retirement.

Given the troubled history of pharmaceutical plants in India, a complaint that a specific pharmaceutical company in Hyderabad, the country's pharmaceutical center, was shipping contaminated capsules of a well-known drug, Hepaticin, to China, would not – on its face – fall on the wrong side of the line between plausible and implausible. A quick check would verify there was in fact a company with that name in Hyderabad – and indeed that the European Union had recently criticized the company for sloppy manufacturing practices and fraudulent record keeping.

Only a little more effort would be required to confirm that until recently, the company had a contract to manufacture Hepaticin and other drugs for the giant British drug company, Galaxy Pharmaceutical. That would be enough to push the communication into the category of the concerning – and potentially important. Of course, it was still quite possible – maybe even likely – that a disgruntled employee had written the note out of spite.

The Chinese Embassy in New Delhi had received just such a communication on Monday. After determining the email was not on its face ridiculous, the Embassy routed the anonymous communication to China's Food and Drug Administration, or CFDA, with a copy to the Ministry of Public Security.

At the CFDA in Beijing, the communication and the Embassy's report landed in a Deputy Director's in-box. The Deputy Director realized the anonymous email was the same nonsense he had dealt with earlier, in response to the inquiries from the Public Security Bureau in Shanghai.

The official could not ignore the message, but he also did not want to stir things up further with the police, who should be out nabbing pickpockets, not concerning themselves with possible drug side effects. After some thought, he decided to send inquiries to the EU drug regulators, who seemed to be on top of the problems of the Indian drug manufacturer. He would also send an inquiry to the US FDA, which usually had its head up its ass, but couldn't be ignored, and to several other drug regulators. He also sent inquiries to several the country's leading teaching hospitals, asking if they had seen cases of the cancer in people taking the drug. He did not mark his inquiries as urgent.

It would take time for the foreign drug regulators and the hospitals to respond. Until then, the matter could remain in his in-box – and with any luck, by the time they responded, the whole thing would be forgotten.

FRIDAY, APRIL 15 – PUBLIC SECURITY BU-REAU, SHANGHAI

It was not until Friday that the staff in the Ministry of Public Security in Beijing completed vetting the Embassy report of the anonymous email message, apparently from an employee of Vishnu Life Sciences. It seemed like a matter for the CFDA to handle, but given the Minister's obsession with the issue, the Ministry staff in Beijing forwarded the Embassy letter and anonymous email to Qian Jie, the head of the Shanghai Municipal Public Security Bureau.

When Qian saw the date on the email, he shouted an obscenity, then another. He picked up the cup and saucer on the corner of his desk and threw them across his office, crashing them into the far wall. Alarmed, his secretary came running into the office. He commanded the secretary to summon his deputies, "Immediately!"

When his deputies assembled, Qian instructed one to find out if Customs had any records of shipments from the Indian company – and specifically if the company had shipped Hepaticin into China. He ordered him to insist on no delays in responding by the Customs bureau.

Uncertain if Customs could provide that information, he directed another deputy to follow up with the Embassy in New Delhi for additional information. *Could the ass wipes in the Embassy find out if the Indian company shipped product to China? If so, who were its customers? And could they find out anything about any problems with this drug?* Finally, he directed his top deputy to interrogate Darrin Hightower, the British executive, who remained in solitary confinement.

"Tell him," the Public Security Bureau Chief snapped, "that he confesses *now!* You hear me? *Now!*"

The deputy nodded and turned to leave, but stopped when he heard Qian call his name. When he turned, Qian added a final instruction. "Tell him, if he doesn't tell us everything he knows now, and we learn later that this drug has harmed anyone in this country, he will face the death penalty."

The deputy nodded, turned briskly, and left.

Qian composed himself, returned to his desk, and picked up the phone. It was time to call his boss in Beijing and tell him that new information had come to light about the rumored connection between Hepaticin and cancer. He would ask his boss to intervene with the Director of the China Food and Drug Administration.

TUESDAY, APRIL 19 – CFDA, BEIJING

The China Food and Drug Administration – or "CFDA" as English speakers know it – occupies offices at 26 Xuanwumen Xidajie in Beijing. Formerly known as the State Food and Drug Administration, or SFDA, the agency has a very troubled past.

To begin with, there was scandal involving Zheng Xiaoyu, the former head of SFDA. Once a leading reformer, he was convicted of taking bribes in return for approving substandard drugs – including drugs that killed ten, left more disabled, and made thousands ill. In a remarkable confession, Zheng conceded accepting gifts and bribes from eight drug companies in exchange for special favors. In addition to cash payments, he admitted to gifts of a car, a villa, furniture, and corporate stock. All together, he and his family accepted gifts valued at more than $850,000. At the time, the average worker in China earned less than $2,000 a year. Beijing No.1 Intermediate Court sentenced Zheng to death on May 29, 2007. He was executed on July 10, 2007.

The following year, 2008, a new scandal erupted. Tainted heparin – the familiar "blood thinner" or anticoagulant – killed over 80 people and sickened hundreds.

Even more sensationally, there was the tainted milk scare. To make their watered-down infant formula and powdered milk products appear to contain more protein than they actually did, several producers had spiked their products with melamine, an industrial chemical used to make plastics and fertilizers.

The contaminated infant formula made more than 300,000 infants ill. In a country with a strict one-child policy and a growing middle class in which families famously treasured their little princelings and princesses, the scandal rocked confidence in the government. The government responded by convicting and executing two businessmen and dismissing a number of local officials.

The Chinese public, however, clearly believed the response was inadequate and attributed the feeble response to the government's reluctance to admit the fiasco had been possible only because many government and party officials had been on the take – or had looked the other way, so as not to offend senior officials who were.

Finally, in May, 2013, as part of a larger anti-corruption campaign, the government revamped the SFDA and re-named it the China Food and Administration or CFDA.

The Chinese public – and foreign observers – were never sure to what extent these periodic anti-corruption campaigns were sincere responses to public discontent over rampant corruption, or were simply efforts to placate the public, with officials selecting rivals and out-of-favor officials for punishment. Most believed these periodic campaigns were ultimately intended to preserve the larger structure that had made so many senior Chinese party and government officials very wealthy.

The reason was obvious. Except in extreme cases, the punishments for public courruption were typically lenient, making bribe-taking quite profitable – even for those who were caught and had to spend a year or two in detention. But the execution of the former head of SFDA was a reminder that prosecutions were unpredictable, as were the punishments.

It was against this background that the CFDA Deputy Director Liu Xiang had sent his routine inquiry to the

Chinese agency's counterparts in several other countries, asking if they had received reports of cases of adrenal cortical carcinoma associated with use of Hepaticin.

The official was now surprised to see that someone from the US FDA official had already responded to his inquiry – in an email that arrived overnight. The US FDA official, Constance Hopkins, replied that the US agency had recently received a credible report – still under investigation – that a number of cases of adrenal cortical carcinoma had occurred in the United States in patients taking Hepaticin. The cases, she said, appeared to be limited to persons who had taken Hepaticin capsules manufactured for Galaxy by an Indian pharmaceutical company, Vishnu Life Sciences.

Deputy Director Hopkins cautioned that the US FDA agency had just begun its investigation and could not independently confirm the report it had received. The email ended by asking if the CFDA had new information.

As he read the email, the Liu felt enormous pressure forming in the center of his chest. He had personally approved the Indian company's application to sell Hepaticin in China at discounted prices, well below what Galaxy charged. He had, of course, suspected the product might be defective. To protect himself, he had insisted, and the Indian company had agreed, to sell the drug only to hospitals and pharmacies in the Xinjiang Uyghur Autonomous Region. *No one*, he thought, *will care if the drug kills some fucking Uyghurs on their prayer rugs.* But now he wondered if someone willing to sell a drug that causes cancer could be trusted to keep their word on a promise like that.

Ignoring the mounting discomfort in his chest, Liu scrolled through the emails in his in-box for the email with the letter from the Embassy in New Delhi. He found and re-read it. He printed the report from New Delhi, along with its copy of the anonymous email and the Embassy's translation of the email. He printed the new email from the US FDA official. He pulled the copies from his printer and walked unsteadily to the director's office.

The Director could not be disturbed, the Director's secretary insisted. "The Director," she said, "is meeting with Guo Shengkun, the Minister of Public Security. I cannot disturb him."

Liu realized with annoyance that his right arm was numb. And then, the pain in his chest became unbearable, and he collapsed, still clutching the reports.

WEDNESDAY, APRIL 20 – LAW DEPART-
MENT

Eileen Wang called Constance Hopkins, the most senior of the FDA officials she and Doss had met in Washington. Wang advised Hopkins that the personal injury attorney was likely to file his suit in a day or two.

"He wants to allege that the FDA is aware of the problem, but is sitting on its hands," Wang urged. "Can you give me something to convince him not to do that?"

The FDA official refused to disclose the agency's timeline, but assured Wang the FDA had expedited its investigation and that it appeared likely the FDA would do "something" soon.

"That doesn't give me much to work with. This guy's complaint is going to get a lot of attention. You're going to look bad."

"We can't take action just because some lawyer is going to file a lawsuit. We have to conduct our own investigation. We have our own stakeholders who have to be satisfied."

Wang wondered if those "stakeholders" included the Congressmen and Senators who protected Galaxy's interests – rather than their constituents' – on Capitol Hill.

"Is there any additional information I can provide you?" Wang asked.

"No, you have been very helpful. What you were able to put together was really very impressive."

"About Galaxy's voluntary recall," Wang probed. "Were the lots it recalled made by Vishnu Life Sciences?"

After a long pause, Deputy Director Hopkins said, "Yes, I can confirm that."

Wang thanked the official and was about to hang up, when the official stopped her.

"Eileen, are you still on the line?"

"Yes."

"You have to keep this under your hat. Please don't share it with the lawyer you're talking with. But this is interesting. We've received emails from China's FDA on this topic."

"Have they found cases?"

"They don't say. They don't do much sharing. It's usually all one way, unless they need our help. But they seem very interested. They want all the information we can give them."

Well, that is interesting, Wang thought. *Small world.*

After ending the call, Wang turned back to the document on her desk. It was the final draft of the complaint – the pleading that initiates a lawsuit. She read it one more time. *It's ready*, Wang concluded.

She placed a call to Nancy Allerton, the Galaxy lawyer who had been part of the team from Galaxy. After polite, but terse pleasantries, Wang got to the point. "We are going to file suit against Galaxy to recoup the medical expenses we paid for our members who took Hepaticin and developed adrenal cortical carcinoma. I wanted to give you a heads up. I wanted to see if your company had any interest in trying to resolve this without our filing suit, and without all the publicity a lawsuit would generate."

"You're bringing a subrogation suit?"

"Yes, among other theories."

"Eileen, you know we're not going to settle with you just because you file a lawsuit."

"It might be cheaper if you did. I know what blue chip law firms charge."

"If we settled just to avoid litigation costs, we would get all kinds of crazy lawsuits. Every personal injury in the country would sue. You know that."

"Well, I wasn't thinking just about attorney fees," Wang said. "You *would* save money by settling with us instead of paying your outside counsel the fortune you are going to spend. But we would be suing to recoup the medicals – the medical expenses we paid. That actually helps you."

"I'm not following you. If we settle with you, it just tells the plaintiff's bar we think we're vulnerable and we're willing to settle. We'll get all kinds of marginal suits."

"Here's what I'm thinking. Medicals are usually a big part of the settlement of any personal injury suit – maybe a quarter, maybe a third. Personal injury lawyers usually sue for what the doctor charges, not for what a health plan pays for the expenses. Due to our discounts, providers usually charge about three times what we pay. That inflates the settlement value quite a bit."

"Your discounts are that large?"

"I've seen cases where providers have charged five times what we pay, so yeah."

"I didn't realize your discounts were that large."

"Actually, it's not that our discounts are big. We pretty much pay what Medicare pays. It's the billed charges that are hyper-inflated."

"Interesting."

"Suppose you settle the medical expense with us at our discounted rates, without having to pay a couple million dollars in defense costs. Suppose you were to pick up the phone and call United, Aetna, Humana, and Anthem and offer them the same deal. All of a sudden, a personal injury lawyer thinking about taking one of these cases has to realize that a lot of the potential settlement value of the case has gone away. If he can't recover the medical expense, let alone the hyper-inflated billed charges, because you've already settled that part of the case, he doesn't stand to get as big a fee. A lot of lawyers will think twice about taking that case."

"Eileen, that's a really interesting idea. I'll give you points for creativity. But if you file suit, you're going to have to show that Hepaticin causes this cancer. When we were with you, it was pretty clear you wouldn't be able to do that. Has anything changed?"

"Nancy, we think our position is stronger than you give us credit for. First, in a cancer case, the deck is usually stacked in your favor. The plaintiff argues that because he took your drug, he had a three times greater chance of getting whatever cancer. Or twice the risk or ten times the risk, whatever the studies show."

"Except you don't have any studies."

"And your lawyers respond that no one knows why any one individual patient gets cancer. Even if your drug may have increased the plaintiff's chances of getting a specific cancer, the plaintiff can't prove he got his cancer because he took the drug. Your lawyers will say, 'maybe he was one of the background cancers that occur naturally.'"

"My point exactly."

"When there is just one plaintiff," Wang conceded, "that's a reasonable argument, and a lot of jurors may be convinced. But if we sue saying these ninety or a hundred people, or whatever our final number is, took this drug and got cancer, you've got a problem. You can argue maybe it's just coincidence, but no jury is going to buy that when we have that many people who took your drug and got some rare cancer that is almost never seen in their age group."

"You're good," the drug company lawyer laughed. "Like I said, you are very creative, but you don't get to the jury unless you can show that Hepaticin causes this cancer."

Wang decided it was time to show her cards.

"Nancy, we're not going to have to show that Hepaticin causes this cancer."

"You don't think you're going to have to prove causation?"

"Not what I said. I said we're not going to have to prove that Hepaticin causes this cancer. What we are going to have to show is that the Hepaticin capsules manufactured for you by Vishnu Life Sciences in Hyderabad cause this rare cancer. We will point to the fact that after you learned about these cancers, you figured out where the problem was coming from and tore up your contract with Vishnu. And then you recalled as much of the Vishnu product in this country as you could without attracting attention."

"Eileen, where are you coming up with all this? I've never heard any of it. You can't just make stuff up."

"Go talk with your people. Make them level with you, because I don't think Boris Badenoff is telling you everything he should."

"Bardin."

"Huh?"

"His name is Bardin, not Badenoff."

"Sorry, I don't know why I keep calling him that. I didn't mean to be disrespectful, but I don't think he's telling you everything you need to know to make a good decision. Go talk to him. Or better still, talk to someone who will level with you."

"When are you going to file suit?"

"Our outside counsel wants to file tomorrow."

"I need more time than that."

"Talk to your people, and get back to me," Wang insisted. "Let me know if they are interested in at least talking settlement. Otherwise, we will file Monday, absolute latest."

Wang told Doss she thought Galaxy would agree to settle, but on Friday afternoon, the drug company's attorney called to say that she had not been able to get a decision on whether the company would consider negotiating a settlement. She explained that much of the company's senior management team was focused on the CEO's trip to China.

"You've probably read about our problems there," Nancy Allerton, the Galaxy lawyer, volunteered.

"I understand, but I think you're missing an opportunity. We'll still be here when you're ready to talk settlement, but we won't be able to take back whatever publicity our little suit might generate."

"I hear you. But if Boris had been straight with me to begin with, we might not be in this situation. I only represent the company. I can't make it not do dumb things."

"Thanks, Nancy. Call me when you're ready to talk settlement."

Wang stood up and walked down the hall, following its rectangular path around the floor. *Have I thought this through?* she asked herself. After two trips around the floor, she decided she was as ready as she would ever be.

She returned to her office, called Devin Garner and told him to file the suit. She asked him to send her a copy of the complaint as soon as he filed it. Garner told her he could file the suit electronically and would get her a copy of the "filed" complaint shortly.

Wang turned to the press release on her desk. It was still fine, just as it had been the last three times she had reviewed it. She called Justin Bland, her contact in Communications – corporate-speak for public relations – and let him know that the company was filing its suit as they spoke and that the press release was good to go. She promised to send Bland the filed complaint in thirty minutes or less.

Wang called Constance Hopkins at the FDA, but got her voice mail. She left a message that the company would be filing suit against Galaxy that afternoon.

Ten minutes later, she got an email from Garner with the heading "Filed!" The email's sole attachment was a copy of the complaint as filed with the court.

Wang forwarded the email to her General Counsel. She sent another copy to Communications, urging Bland to get the suit as much publicity as he could, saying publicity would help get Galaxy's attention.

Finally, she forwarded the email to Spencer Doss, Maya Naidu, Andy Berkowitz, Ingrid Berg, Tam Nguyen Phan, Liz Kolinsky, and to the alternative email account set up temporarily for sensitive communications to Brett Winslow. An automated message reminded Wang that Doss still did not have access to his corporate email box IT would restore access over the weekend. She forwarded the complaint to Doss at his personal email address. *It will be nice,* she thought, *to have him back in the office.*

A minute later, her phone rang. It was Doss. "Congrats on the suit!" he greeted her. "Can I take you out to dinner tonight to celebrate?"

"Sorry, Spence. I can't. I have another commitment."

"Okay," Doss said, "we'll celebrate some other time."

Although he did his best to downplay it, Doss was embarrassed and disappointed. Obviously, Eileen was dating someone else. He had misread the situation.

SATURDAY, APRIL 23 – HYDERABAD

Maya Naidu felt a mother's pride and anxiety as her daughter, Ashika, took the stage. She prayed for everything to be perfect.

Ashika danced Bharatanatyam, a traditional dance form that originated in the ancient temples of Shiva in South India. In Hindu mythology, the universe is the dance of Nataraja, the Supreme Dancer. Nataraja, however, was but another name or manifestation of Lord Shiva, the divine destroyer of ignorance and evil. Temple dancers known as devadasis preserved and evolved the dance form through the ages, until recently, when others revived and formalized it.

Ashika wore a beautiful costume, which covered most of her body, but fit loosely enough to permit graceful movements. Around her neck, she wore jewelry in the style of the ancient temple jewelry of the devadasis, and on her ankles, she wore leather anklets, with rows of copper bells on each anklet. She had eight segments to perform.

As Ashika danced, a woman sang the praises of Lord Shiva, and in the background, carnatic music played. The instruments were traditional South Indian instruments – the mridangam or drum; the nagaswaram, a long pipe horn made from black wood; and the veena, a special kind of stringed instrument. The music was rhythmic, and Ashika had to coordinate her movements with the music. Ashika was accustomed to dancing to recorded music. She had never danced to live music. Her mother hoped Ashika would be able to adjust.

Through the movements of her dance, and through her hand gestures, Ashika expressed the immortal themes of love found and love lost, of life and death and rebirth, of courage and compassion, and the triumph of life's energy over ignorance and evil.

When Ashika finished her performance, Maya Naidu thought her daughter had done very well. The chief judge praised Ashika's performance. Ashika's teacher, who sat in a position of honor on the stage near the musicians, beamed with pride.

Maya Naidu could hardly contain her pride – although a bit of sadness shadowed her happiness. She regretted that her own mother, Ashika's grandmother, had not been able to witness the performance. She would have been so proud of her granddaughter!

Maya Naidu was happy, however, that her husband had been able to watch their daughter dance through a remote connection, but she would have been happier if he could have been there in person.

SATURDAY, APRIL 23 – CINCINNATI MAR-KET OFFICE

On Saturday morning, Spencer Doss returned to his office. It was good to be back in the office, he thought, even though it was a Saturday and a beautiful spring day. Other medical directors had handled much of his workload, but he was still behind. Nothing terribly urgent or exciting, however.

His first priority was the report Eileen Wang wanted, identifying the apparently fraudulent NASH diagnoses the Luxury Resort Six physicians had submitted, along with the criteria he used to identify the cases. He had to think hard about what criteria to use, but once he decided on the criteria, he was able to use the table he had already constructed to identify the cases.

Wang would arrange for another reviewer to review the charts as well, and he and the other reviewer could resolve any differences between themselves. MRA would use that report to determine the amounts CMS had paid the health plan as a result of the phony diagnoses. The health plan would then need to withdraw the diagnoses and refund the payments.

Wang had told him that she was already working on letters to the Luxury Resort Six physicians terminating their contracts with the health plan and advising them that the health plan would be seeking repayment of the money they had been paid based on the phony diagnoses. That would no doubt prompt a nasty fight with the doctors.

Two hours later, Doss felt the presence of the security guard before he heard the young man clear his throat. It was the usual, rail-thin guy who haunted the halls on weekends. Sean Higgins, his name tag said.

"Dr. Doss, can I bother you a minute?" the young man asked. "I can come back later if I caught you in the middle of something."

"You're fine," Doss responded, happy for the diversion. "What's up?"

"You see the story on the news last night about that drug?" the young man asked. "You know. Hepaticin."

"I saw the coverage," Doss responded. The report had garnered a mention late in the local news. Doss had recorded it and watched it over-and-over again.

"Do you think I should stop taking it?"

"You're taking Hepaticin?" Doss asked, surprised.

"Yeah, you know, for fatty liver."

"Do you drink?"

"No," the young man answered. "I run. I'm a runner."

"Who's your doctor?"

"Dr. Goldbach. Do you know him?"

"I've heard of him," Doss said. "But I don't know him."

"Is it alright for me to be asking you about this?"

"Yes, Sean, it's fine. I can't treat you, but here's what I want you to do. I'm going to give you the name of another doctor. He's an oncologist. I want you to call his office first thing on Monday and ask for an appointment. Tell his office that I told you to call."

Doss scribbled down a name on a notepad. He looked up the name, Raj Patel, on the company's list of network physicians, and wrote out his address and phone number. Handing the note to the young man, Doss said,

"You're probably fine, but I want you to see this doctor. He's up by U.C. Tell him you want to be checked out to make sure you don't have the cancer associated with this drug."

"Thank you, Dr. Doss."

"And Sean, stop taking Hepaticin. Dr. Patel will tell you if you need to take it."

"Thank you. I sure will."

"One more thing," Doss said. "Get a different primary care physician."

As the young security guard left, Eileen Wang knocked on Doss's door jamb.

Doss smiled.

"It's too nice to be in here today," Wang said. "What do you say we go to the zoo?"

"Great idea!" Doss clicked off his computer.

"Sorry we couldn't go to dinner to celebrate last night," Wang said as they walked toward the exit.

"You don't owe me any explanation," Doss replied.

"*Oh my gosh*, you think I had a date," Wang said. "I was afraid of that."

Doss felt relieved, but said nothing.

"When I can, on Friday nights, I work at the homeless shelter downtown. It's just a few hours, but it's something I like to do."

"You're amazing!"

"I don't like to mention it, because I don't want people to think I'm bragging about it. Like I said, it's only a few hours, and I don't want people to think I'm doing it to get credit."

"It's still nice," Doss said. "What attracted you to helping out there?"

"I'm on the shelter's board. When my parents came to this country, they had it hard. They were homeless themselves. Just for a short time. A church congregation helped them, and of course, the Chinese community."

"Your parents are still alive?"

"Yes, thank goodness. They're doing well. But you can't meet them."

"Why not?"

"Well, for one thing, because they live in Colorado."

"That's where I'm from!"

"You still can't meet them," Wang said, hesitantly.

"Oh."

"My mother keeps telling me that I should marry some nice Chinese boy. But if I introduced her to an American doctor – oh, geez! I can hear it already. 'Why he not your boyfriend yet? Try your best to marry him. He make more money than you!'"

"It's not just Chinese mothers," Doss replied. "A lot of American mothers are the same way."

"It's not that I don't want you to meet my family. It's just that I don't want that pressure. When I get married, I want it to be for the right reason – not because the guy is a doctor, or because he's got money, or whatever."

"Eileen, I don't think I'll ever really know what went wrong between my ex and me, but in retrospect, I think she felt pressured by her mother and her girlfriends to marry me for all the reasons you mentioned. Maybe if she had focused more on whether I was the person she wanted to be with, and less on whether I would be a good financial bet, she never would have married me."

"Spencer, I'm sorry." Wang said. "I really am. I didn't mean to bring up bad memories."

APRIL 24 - 25 – INTERNATIONAL TRAVEL

On Sunday evening, at 8:15 p.m. Hyderabad time, Maya and Ashika Naidu watched the flight attendants close and lock the door to the crowded jetliner. Ten minutes later, the plane accelerated down the runway and took off.

Several hours later, the pair tumbled out of the jetliner, already musty with sweat and the other smells of travel. They were in Abu Dhabi International Airport, where it was a little after 11:00 p.m., local time, Sunday night – they had lost an hour-and-a-half due to time changes. To avoid customs and a hotel bill, the pair had agreed to spend the night in the airport.

On Monday morning, Dubai time, Maya Naidu and her daughter – sleepless and somewhat the worse from wear – boarded another large jetliner, this one headed to O'Hare Airport in Chicago. The flight left at 9:20 a.m., local time – eight hours ahead of Eastern Standard Time, making it 12:20 a.m. at home. After crossing multiple time zones, the flight would arrive in Chicago at about 3:00 in the afternoon, Central Time, Monday.

Maya looked forward to being reunited with her husband. During the long flight, she found time to wonder why her marriage, an arranged marriage, had worked while so many marriages in her adopted country did not. *Like poor Dr. Doss. He was such a nice man, and yet his marriage had failed.*

She also wondered, at least briefly, whether Dr. Doss had been fired or merely suspended pending some sort of investigation. She hoped he would be reinstated, but he was a doctor – he would find a good job. Whatever became of Dr. Doss, she was sure that he had earned good karma by trying to learn why so many were getting that rare cancer.

MONDAY, APRIL 25 – PUBLIC SECURITY BUREAU

Sir Alec Bright and his entourage arrived precisely on time at the offices of the Public Security Bureau, at 593 Fuxing Road, in Shanghai Municipality. A uniformed policeman promptly ushered Sir Alec and his entourage into a large conference room. Silk curtains, deep red in color, covered the wall at the head of the room, behind a raised dais.

Moments later Qian Jie, the head of the Shanghai Public Security Bureau, arrived, accompanied by his own entourage of deputies, attorneys, and interpreters.

Sir Alec and his retinue stood.

The Public Security Bureau chief snapped something in Chinese. The interpreter said, "Please be seated."

"Which of you is Sir Alec Bright?" The Security Bureau chief demanded through his interpreter.

Sir Alec rose again.

"Mr. Bright, when was your company going to tell us that your drug, Hepaticin, is causing people to get cancer?"

"Hepaticin does not cause cancer," the CEO responded confidently.

The Security Bureau chief nodded to one of his subordinates, who pushed a button. The curtains on the wall behind the Security Bureau chief separated to reveal a huge flat-screen television – as large as any Sir Alec seen. The subordinate picked up a remote and turned the television on. One-by-one, a series of Chinese faces – some male, some female, all clearly past middle age – appeared on the screen. Each appeared briefly and panned into the next.

"These, Mr. Bright, are my fellow countrymen who developed adrenal cortical carcinoma after taking Hepaticin."

Sir Alec watched the faces on the screen, mesmerized. The experience was sobering. So much so, it did not occur to him to wonder if those were the faces of victims of cancer, or if they might be the faces of the parents and aunts and uncles of the Bureau chief's subordinates.

When the images on the screen stopped, one of Sir Alec's aides pulled him aside, and the two men had a hushed exchange. Sir Alec stepped back to the table.

"I believe there has been some confusion," he said. "I understand that an Indian company we contracted with to manufacture some of our product may have produced some contaminated product. We terminated our contract with the company and ordered it to destroy the product. If it sold that product in your country, it did so against our instructions and in violation of your law."

"It is still your product. Did you issue a warning to the public? Did you warn the China Food and Drug Administration?"

Sir Alec conferred again with his advisers.

"As I said, our contract did not allow this company to sell in your country. And so far as we are aware, the CFDA never authorized this Indian company to sell Hepaticin in China. We had no reason to warn the CFDA."

The security chief nodded, and his subordinate pushed another button on the remote. Darrin Hightower, the President of Galaxy China, appeared on the screen.

"Of course, we knew Vishnu was dumping product in the western provinces, because we were losing sales," the Darrin Hightower on the screen explained. "We're not stupid."

The video jumped to a different clip. "Yes, we knew about the problem with Hepaticin and cancer, but we couldn't very well say anything about it now, could we?"

"Can we see Darrin in person?" Sir Alec asked.

"He will remain in solitary confinement until the court decides his guilt."

"I was under the impression," Sir Alec harrumphed, "that all this had been worked out. We were prepared to pay $100 million Euros."

"That," the Security Bureau chief stated with icy chilliness, "was before this latest outrage came to our attention."

He glared at Sir Alec Bright.

"We propose," he said finally, "to ask the court to order the death penalty for Mr. Hightower and several other of your executives who have admitted that your company knew the Hepaticin produced in India caused cancer. We will also ask the court to ban your company from doing business in our country for twenty years."

Sir Alec felt a sudden wave of nausea and wondered momentarily if he was going to pass out.

"But we are willing to listen," the Security Bureau chief continued, "to what you think might be a just outcome. If you will excuse me, I have urgent business, but my deputies and our attorneys will be happy to listen to your proposal."

Five-and-a-half hours later, the Security Bureau chief returned to the room. "I understand," he announced, "that we have an understanding."

"I believe we do," Sir Alec agreed.

"If you will sign the agreement."

Sir Alec Bright turned to his counsel, who nodded. With that, the CEO of Galaxy Pharmaceutical Company put his signature on two documents, one in Chinese and the other in English. One of the Bureau functionaries carried the agreements to the Security Bureau chief, who signed them as well.

"Shall we step outside?" the Security Bureau chief asked. "The media are anxious to hear what we have agreed to."

Fifteen minutes later, Sir Alec stepped to the microphone. He read a brief statement in English, and a translator echoed his statements in Mandarin. In his statement, he confessed that employees of Galaxy China had violated Chinese law by paying bribes to physicians and others, in the form of dinners, trips, prostitutes and cash payments. He also acknowledged that Hepaticin manufactured by another company for Galaxy had been contaminated and had been associated with a rare cancer in a number of patients.

Sir Alec apologized to the Chinese people and to the Chinese government, and stated that, as a gesture of his company's sincerity, Galaxy would lower the prices of its drugs in China for the next five years. Galaxy had also agreed to a fine of one billion US dollars and to pay the medical expenses of the Chinese citizens sickened by the defective medicine.

Finally, Sir Alec announced that his company had agreed to enter into a joint venture with a Chinese company for the manufacture of Galaxy's drugs, to assure that there would be no repeat of the unfortunate incident involving the product manufactured in India. Sir Alec did not say – and may not even have been fully aware – that relatives of several members of the State Council owned interests in the Chinese company.

It was 4:09 in the afternoon in Shanghai when Sir Alec finished reading his statement to the assembled reporters. It was 4:09 in the very early morning in New York – still more than five hours before the New York Stock Exchange would open.

Well before the opening bell, CNN and various news programs around the world reported the settlement, many showing clips with Sir Alec reading portions of his statement. From the reports, it was obvious to even the casual observer that the Chinese had made the big drug company swallow some bitter medicine.

MONDAY, APRIL 25 – PRIVATE EQUITY FIRM, NEW YORK

For one analyst at a ritzy private equity firm in Manhattan, Monday morning was not turning out anything like he expected. He had assured the firm's CEO that Galaxy Pharmaceutical Company did not have a cancer problem with its blockbuster drug, Hepaticin, and was about to put its China problem behind it at a very manageable cost. As a result, the private equity firm was sitting on large holdings of Galaxy shares when, early that morning, things began unraveling.

To start with, several media outlets reported a new product liability lawsuit by a major health plan and a couple of individual plaintiffs. The suit – filed late Friday, but first reported in the national media Monday morning – alleged that Galaxy's biggest revenue-generating product, Hepaticin, had caused almost a hundred of the health plan's members to develop a rare cancer – or rather, that versions of the product manufactured for Galaxy by an Indian company had caused the cancers.

The bad news got worse. Before the market opened, the U.S. Food and Drug Administration announced it was asking the Department of Justice to bring criminal charges against Galaxy for hiding the fact that versions of Hepaticin manufactured in India were linked to the rare cancer.

But even that wasn't the worst of it.

Those stories were packaged with dramatic footage of Galaxy's CEO apologizing to the Chinese people and government for his company's crimes. Sir Alec had all but admitted that Hepaticin manufactured in a plant in India had caused the rare cancer. He said Galaxy had agreed to lower the price of Galaxy's drugs in China and pay a billion dollar fine.

Galaxy shares immediately fell over 15% on stock exchanges in several countries, including the United States.

His boss was demanding to see him at once. The analyst knew with certainty what the outcome of that meeting would be – he would be fired and escorted from the building by security. But strangely, the receptionist – on his speakerphone – was insisting he remain where he was. He was about to ignore the receptionist and head to his boss's office, when two FBI special agents intercepted him, and placed him under arrest.

The agents led him through a "perp walk" across the trading room floor. As they did, he guessed, correctly, that television camera crews would be waiting at the entrance to the building when he exited.

Instinctively, the analyst knew that without a job and with a prison sentence hanging over his head, his beautiful, sexy girlfriend would leave him, his apartment in Manhattan would have to be sold to pay legal bills, and his sports car would be repossessed. He would never work in the financial industry again. People he thought of as friends would not return his calls.

MONDAY MORNING, APRIL 25 – GARNER LAW OFFICE

In his office exceptionally early, Devin Garner watched the rebroadcast of snippets of Sir Alec's statement, including Sir Alec's comments on the Hepaticin product made in India. He'd seen it all on the previous night's news, but he still couldn't believe his luck.

He picked up the phone and called Sam Carson. Since their first meeting, Carson had become a very special client. He was classy, smart, and always willing to give advice, but only when asked.

When the older man answered, Garner asked – with no preliminaries – if Carson had seen the news.

"About Galaxy?" the older man asked. "I was just watching it. Will that help our case?"

"From an evidentiary standpoint? Not sure, but probably. But litigation is all about psychology – about how confident parties and attorneys are in their case, and how willing they are to work. This will destroy Galaxy's confidence. They aren't going to want to have people like me depose their CEO. They aren't going to want discovery into what they knew while the Department of Justice is deciding whether to prosecute their company – and maybe some of its execs."

The older man did not respond immediately, to be sure the young attorney had finished his thought, before he spoke. "I have some news too," he said. "I saw the oncologist on Friday. He had what I suppose in his practice passes for good news. He says my body seems to have responded well to the chemotherapy. He wants to do radiation therapy next, but he thinks I may be cancer free for the moment."

"That's terrific, Sam," Garner gushed. "Really wonderful."

"Well, not cancer free, exactly. I imagine there are cancer cells still alive in my body, biding their time. Someday, they will attack again and kill me. My five-year survival rate is worse than my golf game, but we are now probably talking about years instead of months."

Relieved, Garner congratulated Carson again, and rang off.

And then, the phone calls started coming in – some from reporters, wanting a comment to add to their stories, others from people who had taken Hepaticin wanting to be added to the suit he had filed. New emails were also hitting his in-box at a rate he had never imagined possible. Eventually, he did something he had never done before. He called a friend and asked if she could come to the office and help him respond to the calls pouring in.

By late morning, he began to get calls from attorneys he'd never heard of, wanting to know if his subrogation suit included their potential clients. They wanted to know before they agreed to take their cases. *Email me their names, and I'll get back to you, but later, today was too hectic.* The lawyers made it clear they were more than a little angry that Garner was pursuing the subrogation claim. They viewed that as an attempt by Garner to steal a recovery – and the fees that went with it – that rightfully belonged to them.

He also got calls from attorneys he *had* heard of – big name guys, with big egos – who called to offer to take over his cases. Would he accept 20% of the fees they collected from cases he sent them? *No, but thanks for the offer.*

Subrogation managers from two health plans asked if their health plans could be added to his suit. *Yes. His contingency fee was 25%. Yes, he would send contracts.*

A television crew wanted to know if it could come to his office and get him on camera. *Of course.* A newspaper reporter wanted to know if the Sam Carson in the lawsuit was the fellow who had been a senior vice president of a major bank. *Yes, that was him.*

A widow called and said her husband had taken Hepaticin and had died from adrenal cortical carcinoma. She wanted to know if her claim for her late husband's death was automatically included in the suit. *No, she would have to hire him if she wanted to have her claim included. When could they meet?*

A man called from the local jail and said he heard that Garner handled drug cases and wanted to know if Garner could represent him in a drug possession case. *Not that kind of drug case. Not anymore.*

Two people from nearby called wanting to know if he would represent them in cases against drug companies, not involving Hepaticin. *He would need to know more before he could commit, but scheduled appointments to learn about their situations.*

A law student called and asked if he needed an intern. *Could she start today?*

By noon, six people who had taken Hepaticin and had developed cancer wanted to hire him. He would send each a questionnaire to fill out and a contract to sign.

A local man telephoned from a nearby senior citizen center and warned Garner that God hated lawyers, and that God, the judge of all, would cast him into hell for all eternity. *Uh, thanks for the heads up.*

Three eDiscovery vendors called. Garner took the phone number from the first, thanked the second, and hung up on the third.

His mother called. *Yes, he was the one who filed that case. Thanks, he hoped he knew what he was doing too.*

MONDAY, APRIL 25 – O'HARE AIRPORT, CHICAGO

When – after a flight that seemed to go on without end – the plane finally landed at O'Hare International Airport, Maya and Ashika Naidu wearily struggled out of the door of the jetliner and into the terminal. Groggy from jet lag and too little sleep, they lugged their baggage between terminals, waited in line to clear customs, re-checked their luggage, and waited for the flight home – the last leg of the tiring trip.

During the four-hour lay over in O'Hare, Maya Naidu caught the news from a television mounted in the waiting area, tuned – permanently, it seemed – to CNN Headline News. During the segment devoted to financial news, the announcer led with a report that the giant British drug company, Galaxy Pharmaceuticals, had agreed to plead guilty to criminal charges and pay the Chinese government a billion dollar fine. The Chinese government had charged the company with paying millions of dollars in bribes to doctors and hospital administrators.

The charges, the announcer said, also included failing to disclose safety risks associated with the blockbuster drug Hepaticin – specifically, that Hepaticin manufactured for Galaxy by an Indian company had been linked to a rare cancer. The Chinese government claimed that, after learning of the problem, Galaxy's Indian contractor had bribed a Chinese official to obtain permission to sell the contaminated product in China. Galaxy was aware of the sales to Chinese citizens and of the cancer problem, but had not informed authorities or the public.

The broadcast featured a news clip of Darrin Hightower, president of Galaxy's China subsidiary, confessing to the Chinese police that his company knew that people were getting cancer after taking Hepaticin.

Ashika nudged her mother. "I can't believe you're watching that," the teenager complained. "It's so boring!"

FRIDAY, APRIL 29 – LAW DEPARTMENT

On Friday morning, as Eileen Wang went through the largely mechanical motions of turning on her computer, logging in, and bringing up her email, she noticed a message flagging a new result on her now standing alert for articles about Galaxy Pharmaceuticals. She clicked through to the story.

Despite the record-setting settlement with the U.S. Department of Justice, the subsequent debacle in China, and the spate of recently filed product liability litigation involving Hepaticin, Galaxy's Board of Directors had raised the total compensation package for its CEO. For the year, Sir Alex would receive total compensation of $16.5 million.

Wang was still shaking her head at the story when her phone rang. It was Nancy Allerton, the attorney for Galaxy.

"We're ready to talk," the drug company lawyer greeted Wang. "Tell us what you want. Within reason, of course. We're not giving you a billion dollars. That money's spent."

Wang laughed pleasantly. "Our demand is pretty straightforward. We paid the medical expense to treat people for adrenal cancer who were on Hepaticin. We want to be reimbursed for that expense, plus the medical expenses required to treat any other of our members who took Hepaticin and develop this cancer, let's say in the next two years."

"You have a number?"

"No, but I'll get that for you. Our people have been working on compiling that for me, and I should have it in a couple hours."

"Big number?"

"I don't know what a drug company considers a big number, but if each case cost us – on average – $100,000, and if we have 100 cases associated with your product, we would be talking about roughly $10 million. Maybe more, if I'm guessing wrong about how much it costs to treat someone for this cancer."

"So about $10 million, maybe a little more?"

"I'll send you all the details in couple hours, and then we won't be guessing."

"Eileen, we get initial demands from plaintiff lawyers bigger than that for a single case. We don't pay that much, of course, but I'm just saying. So, what else do you want?"

"Well, there's the two individual plaintiffs. Maybe more than that by now. You should talk to Devin about them. I don't represent them."

"But for the health plan, you're just looking for the medicals?"

"I should be asking for punitive damages, or treble damages or something, the way your company jerked us around."

"But?"

"But here's what I'm thinking. Your company dangled a contract for data mining in front of us."

"And you want us to put that back on the table?"

"The way things stand," Wang said, "it looks like you were offering that as a bribe to get us, to get Spencer, to keep quiet. It's not in your interest to leave things like that."

"Meaning what?"

"Meaning suppose you were to get a subpoena from the government? Or from the plaintiff lawyers who will be knocking down your doors? It's not going to look good."

"But if we were to go through with the proposal, it wouldn't look so much like we were trying to buy your silence?"

"That's what I'm thinking."

"So, you're doing us a favor, taking our money?"

"No, I'm just saying it works out for both of us."

"I'll see what I can do, but I don't think that will be a problem."

"You can't make it a condition that we don't use Dr. Doss," Wang added. "In fact, I want you to ask that the company have him oversee the work."

"Did he take some heat?"

"You have no idea."

"Sorry about that."

"Oh, Nancy," Wang said.

"Yeah, what else?"

"Nothing else," Wang promised. "You have to call Devin Garner, the lawyer who filed this suit. Unless he says otherwise, we can't settle unless you settle with his two individual clients. I think he's got a bunch more clients now, but we're only a package deal with the first two."

"I'll call him."

"Thanks."

"And Eileen," Allerton added, "If I'm able to wrap things up with you, I'm thinking about taking your suggestion and calling the other major plans. I discussed your idea with management, and we think it's worth a try to see if that will make these cases less attractive to plaintiff lawyers. We are also going to have a generous program for patients who are not represented by contingent fee lawyers."

"I bet you are going to save a lot money on litigation costs."

"It's obvious what we've been doing isn't working for us – just for the lawyers who bring these suits and the lawyers who defend them."

"If you do, it will be interesting to see who screams more – the plaintiff lawyers or your own outside counsel."

"I know. Don't you love it?"

Wang couldn't resist one last question. "What's Boris up to?"

"Boris has taken a position with another drug company. He's going to be in Geneva, I believe."

"That will make it harder," Wang observed, "for personal injury lawyers in this country to take his deposition."

"Yeah, well," Allerton laughed, "I can live with that."

MONDAY, MAY 2 – IT SPIDER UNIT

On her first day back in the office, Maya Naidu began her morning, as usual, by logging into her computer and then into her email. Even though she had dealt with many emails while in India, there were still quite a few messages to be attended to. As she scrolled though the headers, she saw one from Dr. Doss. Happy to see that he was still with the company, she opened it first.

In his email, Doss said nothing was official, but he was going to be asked to head up a new unit that would do data mining – some for customers, mainly drug companies, but some devoted to looking for problems like the one they discovered with Hepaticin. He would need a good programmer. Would she be interested?

At last, Naidu thought, *I will really get to use my programming skills.*

Naidu looked to see if she had any other out-of-the-ordinary emails and noticed that she actually had another email from Doss, which had arrived while she was on her way back from India. Somehow, she had missed it.

The earlier email was more personal. It inquired how things went with her daughter's dance recital. Did Ashika do well? Was she happy with her performance?

The man actually cares about other people, Naidu thought. *Good karma. Good karma.*

She sent the medical director a digital clip of her daughter's performance at the dance festival in Hyderabad – the organization that sponsored the festival provided each dancer a digital recording of her performance.

Later, when Spencer Doss watched the video of the dance, it occurred to him that the dance and accompanying music did not celebrate time spent in purposeless meetings or in tweaking the format of PowerPoint presentations. Dance and music and poetry would never celebrate corporate profits and losses, or earnings-per-share that outpaced analysts' projections.

Dance and music and poetry, he thought, *would always celebrate love lost and love found, courage and compassion, and the triumph of wisdom over ignorance, of good over evil.*

EPILOGUE

The oncologist strode briskly into the office. The patient and his wife were already there, waiting. The patient was thinner than at his last visit. His hair was gone, but that was usual after chemo. It would grow back.

"Mr. Meinhardt, how are you doing today?" Dr. Raj Patel asked.

"That's what I am here to find out."

The physician looked at the lab results and the imaging reports in the patient's chart. He was familiar with them, but always reviewed them again before giving a patient bad news.

"Mr. Meinhardt, I'm afraid I don't have good news. It doesn't look like your cancer responded to the chemotherapy the way we hoped."

"Goddam!"

"Our next weapon is radiation therapy."

"Is that going to be as bad as the chemo?"

"No, not at all. Your skin may be affected. You may have some redness, like sunburn. But most patients don't have much problem with it."

"Then, why didn't you do that first?"

"We hoped the chemo would destroy your cancer. In other words, we hoped the chemo would cure you, or at least put you into remission. But with radiation, we're only trying to reduce the size of the cancer. We're trying to buy you some time, and maybe reduce pain."

"You're saying I'm not going to beat this goddam thing?"

"I'm going to continue to keep my eye out for experimental protocols and for new developments, but for now, we are going to be concentrating on prolonging your life and managing any pain you might experience. We want to maintain the quality of your life, for as long as we can."

Tears welled up in Norma Meinhardt's eyes. She wiped them furtively with a ready tissue.

"So how long do I have?"

"It's hard to say."

"How long? Best guess?" the patient persisted, as the oncologist knew he would.

"Well, as you know, the cancer has already spread to your liver. By now, you may have metastases elsewhere that we haven't detected. Best guess, I'd have to say about six months, give or take. But bear in mind that's just an educated guess."

Dan Meinhardt processed what the doctor said. After a long moment, he muttered, more to himself than to the physician, "So that goddam drug company is going to outlive me."

AUTHOR'S NOTE

Readers who insist on technical accuracy will be disappointed to learn of several instances of literary license.

Unfortunately, there is presently no drug to treat fatty liver disease. This novel invented such a drug to avoid confusion with any real drug. Several drug companies –including some in clinical trials – are racing to win approval for drugs to treat fatty liver.

Secondly, the Centers for Medicare and Medicaid Services ("CMS") has not established a Hierarchical Condition Category ("HCC") for Non-Alcoholic Steatohepatitis ("NASH"). Thus, NASH does not "risk adjust" or result in additional payment by CMS.

Third, it is unlikely any cancer would develop and metastasize so quickly in response to a drug or contaminate.

India's pharmaceutical industry supplies 40 percent of over-the-counter and generic prescription drugs consumed in the United States. The story referenced in the novel appeared in India's Business Standard, *"If I follow US standards, I will have to shut almost all drug facilities": G N Singh, Interview with Drug Controller General of India, by Sushmi Dey* (January 30, 2014).

At this writing, the Indian government is considering requiring the country's drug companies to conform to international good manufacturing practices. The Indian government apparently believes its drug industry will be able to increase exports if it complies with international standards. Indian drug companies are pushing back, arguing that if they have to adopt good manufacturing practices, they will no longer be able to produce drugs significantly cheaper than non-Indian companies.

Fire Eye is a real company. Its report on FIN4 is available on line. Barry Vengerik, Kristen Dennesen, Jordan Berry, and Jonathan Wrolstad, *Hacking the Street*, (Fire Eye, Nov. 30, 2014), rpt-fin4.pdf (last visited 06/11/15).

Certain of the events in this novel were inspired by the widely publicized problems GlaxoSmithKline encountered in the People's Republic of China 2012 – 2014, but the events described in this novel are entirely fictional. This novel does not purport to offer any insights into – let alone portray what "really happened" – in Glaxo's China drama. Importantly, the allegations concerning Glaxo did *not* involve product safety issues, nor did they specifically involve product made in India. Glaxo in any event has taken remedial measures and at this point considers the bribery allegations in China a legacy or historical issue.

Two final disclaimers: The entirely fictional Galaxy Pharmaceutical Company in this novel does not represent and is not based on GlaxoSmithKline. The entirely fictitious officers of Galaxy in this novel are not representations of or based on any past or present GlaxoSmithKline officer or employee.

ABOUT THE AUTHOR

Gary Reed had an exciting legal career before retiring and taking up writing. He managed litigation around the country, including high-stakes product liability and managed care cases.

More recently, he managed litigation nationwide for a major health insurer, directed investigations into corrupt providers in South Florida and elsewhere, and managed eDiscovery. Mr. Reed wrote and spoke frequently on professional issues during his career.

He is the author of two novels, *The Blockbuster Drug* and *A Fatal Cell Phone Video*.

For more information and updates, check out his author page. www.GaryReed.com